Trapped in the caves of the dead

Ignoring the howling ghostvoices, Jeneba frowned at the reddish glow from the caves below. "There's no fire in the underworld," she said. "Each level is darker than the last."

"In your Dasan underworld, yes, mortal—but now you hunt Kurasi dead."

Jeneba whirled. Behind them stood a great head, as tall as a man, with arms coming out his ears and legs protruding where his neck should be. Scars spiralled on the broad copper cheeks; black and bright red beads decorated thin braids dangling down his forehead.

"Inyabe," Ourassi breathed. Whooping, he ran for the red tunnel.

But the Kurasi messenger of death leaped over their heads to come down blocking the way.

"Only the dead may enter here," he hissed.

THE LEOPARD'S DAUGHTER

Also by
LEE KILLOUGH

Spider Play

Published by
POPULAR LIBRARY

THE LEOPARD'S DAUGHTER

LEE KILLOUGH

POPULAR LIBRARY

An Imprint of Warner Books, Inc.

A Warner Communications Company

POPULAR LIBRARY EDITION

Popular Library®, the fanciful P design, and Questar® are
registered trademarks of Warner Books, Inc.

Cover illustration by Michael Herring

Popular Library books are published by
Warner Books, Inc.
666 Fifth Avenue
New York, N.Y. 10103

Ⓦ A Warner Communications Company

Printed in the United States of America

First Printing: October, 1987

10 9 8 7 6 5 4 3 2 1

For Pat, Carolyn, and Nancy

CHAPTER

ONE

The wind reeked of carrion. Jeneba Karamoke's nose wrinkled in distaste. This wooded lakeshore might provide more water, firewood, and cover for the night than the open grass of the Sahara plains, but how could an experienced warrior and camp scout like Tomo Silla think anyone would be able to eat or sleep in such a stench? Why did he expect his commander and king, Mseluku Karamoke, to do so?

Or did he even notice the smell? she wondered belatedly, uncomfortably. None of her other brother and sister warriors appeared to. Moving through the fading light that emphasized the rich red-brown of their skins, they joked and sang as they hobbled horses and built their fire before night and its dangers closed around them.

Across the clearing Mseluku stared through the trees toward the lake as he chatted with Tomo, but when her uncle pointed, it was only at rounded shapes floating among the grasses sticking out of the water. "Hippos. You haven't scouted out a camp on one of their trails, I hope, Tomo."

Uneasiness flashed across the warrior's face . . . turning to a sheepish grin as Mseluku laughed and Tomo realized that the king had been joking.

And still not a word about carrion.

So Jeneba said nothing, either, just hobbled her horse and leaned her spears and long oval shield against a tree. It would be foolish to remind people of her keener-than-human senses. No one knew what perversity had made her mother, the beautiful Sia Nyiba Karamoke, reject all human suitors to take a leopard-man for a lover, but Jeneba had fought for seventeen years to overcome the curse of her parentage, and had struggled to appear like everyone else. She ran a finger

1

along the raised ridge of the tribal scar stretching from her left nostril halfway across the cheek toward her ear. She strived to make her people forget that though the uba, blood, of the king's sister's daughter was noble and pure Dasa, her father had bestowed upon her the tetena, spirit, of an animal.

Fighting yesterday beside fellow Dasa of Imbu against the Keoru, she had felt closer to success than ever before. With the earth warm beneath her bare feet and the sun heating arms and shoulders bared by the drape of her lion-skin war tsara, she and her fellow Dasa had moved with practiced precision . . . hurling their spears at the Keoru line, raising shields to deflect spears aimed at them while the beads strung on the ropes of their hair clicked together in lively accompaniment to each maneuver. How magnificent everyone had looked . . . tall and lean and dark above the yellow-brown Keoru, and in the evening, dancing in celebration with the spears Joueta Tatauba's warriors threw down on retreat, warriors of both Imbu and Kiba embraced each other, embraced Jeneba, calling her "sister."

For the first time in her life they had seemed to accept her as truly one of them, and not just tolerate her because she was the king's niece and without a brother who might inherit the king's Stool and make her the Queen Mother. No, she would not negate that.

Jeneba joined the party gathering firewood.

The others chattered while they collected dried wood, recalling the battle, too. Jeneba listened in silent pleasure, enjoying just being part of the group, nodding in agreement with their assessment of Nykoro and Mseluku's cleverness. What a masterful insult it had been for Nykoro to ask Joueta to wait while he went for reinforcements, while Mseluku led little more than a handful of warriors.

Behind her, in camp, she could hear Mseluku's bard Kinetu singing. *"Hoooh! Dasa!*

> We are fierce warriors, lords of the Sahara plains.
> The Creator Mala-Lesa smiles down on us,
> Both her moon by night
> And his sun by day.
> Our buffalo totem, powerful, clever, smiles on us.

We fear nothing,
Not men or wizards,
Not demons or ghosts or monsters,
We hunt where we will.
We fatten our cattle on the sweet Sahara grasses.
We march into battle and emerge victorious.
Hoooh! Dasa! Hoooh!

"Hoooh! Dasa!" Jeneba echoed.

A throaty voice spoke from above her. "Greetings, sister."

Startled, Jeneba glanced up before she could stop herself, so quickly that by the time she saw the leopard sprawled along the tree limb overhead, there was no way to ignore the beast. She could only hope that the warriors gathering wood nearby had heard nothing. Jeneba bent to reach for another piece of wood. "I'm not your sister."

"Ah?" the leopard said lazily. Jeneba glanced up to find it regarding her with amusement. Its tawny eyes blinked with cat slowness. "But I smell leopard in you, and see that you have leopard-tawny eyes. You also understand me, which no one fully human can."

Jeneba set her jaw. "I am Dasa and a noble of the city of Kiba, not a leopard's daughter." Turning away, she started back for camp with her wood.

The leopard sighed. "How unfortunate, for if you were my sister, I could warn you about this place."

The smell of carrion seemed suddenly stronger. Jeneba's neck prickled. She whirled back toward the leopard. "What warning?"

But the leopard had gone.

Something else moved in the woods, however. Jeneba heard stealthy steps. Dropping her wood, she raced for the camp . . . for her spears and shield.

Warriors stared in astonishment as she raced past them.

"Spears!" she cried. She had no time to explain further. As her fingers closed around the shaft of a spear, a gust of wind brought a chorus of whoops madder than those of spotted hyena, and a carrion reek of such strength that Jeneba choked while the horses reared screaming, fighting their hobbles.

She whirled to find the woods erupting with men who looked as though they had been split lengthwise. Shorter than the Dasa but thicker, naked except for loincloths and gray paint covering their skin, each hopped on one leg and swung a club in his single hand.

Wachiru! Cold rushed through Jeneba and even as she stared in disbelief—wachiru attacking in a *group*?—she understood why she had seen nothing in the woods. The half-men kept their invisible off-side toward the camp as they approached. All they could not hide was the stench of their man-eating breath.

She answered their cries with a yell of her own, and stabbed at the nearest attacker. He parried the spear with his club, then pivoted away and vanished. Jeneba lunged through the spot where he had stood, but her spear passed without meeting resistance. The wachiru reappeared off to her left, his club already aimed at her head.

Jeneba barely ducked in time, the club catching her hair in passing, clicking off the beads. Fear burst inside her with icy fire. Shifting the spear to her left hand, she snatched her knife from the sheath beneath her tsara with her right and lunged slashing. The copper blade opened the belly of the wachiru the full width of his half-wide body. He doubled screaming, bloody loops of gut ballooning between his hands. Jeneba retreated until she stood with her back against a tree, spear and knife ready for another assault from any side.

Around her wachiru clubbed warriors to the ground. Screaming horses threw themselves or snapped their hobbles and bolted into the woods. Other wachiru dragged unconscious members of the wood-gathering party into camp. Several warriors managed to reach their weapons, however, Mseluku among them, and they stabbed at every wachiru they saw.

Seeing their opponents was the problem.

Jeneba shouted a warning at Mseluku, who had three half-men closing on him off-side first. She sprang away from her tree at them. No monster would eat *her* uncle!

Something moved at the edge of her vision, but before she could dodge the club she sensed coming, pain burst through her. Mala-Lesa recreated the night sky in her skull in a single fiery upheaval and Jeneba fell into a bottomless black hole ... through the earth, through lawariwa, the underworld of recent ancestral shades, through lewarikile, the dimmer kingdom of older shades, and into the lowest depths of luwarilenge, where the oldest shades must finally go, a place without light, warmth, feeling, or even memory.

Or did it have sound after all? Shades gibbered shrilly at each other. Then she saw light, a dancing red glow, and felt a lumpy surface beneath her. Her hand finally convinced her that, astonishingly, she remained alive and on earth. It still grasped her knife.

She opened her eyes painfully to find herself at the base of the tree she had used to guard her back. Although drums pounded in her head and great stones seemed to weight it, she could look up enough to see torches set in the ground and wachiru men, women, and children hopping back and forth across the campsite; children, naked, and women, bare to the waist like their men, chattering excitedly as they bound the legs and arms of warriors. The few they left loose lay with the unmistakable slackness of death. That explained why Jeneba still lived. Dead victims must be eaten quickly. The wachiru wanted some meat for another day, too.

She shuddered at the thought of herself spitted and roasting.

The wachiru had not reached this end of the camp yet, judging by her still-free hands. Was anyone watching her? Jeneba saw no one. Touching her heart four times for luck and praying to Mala-Lesa and to Lubama, Mala-Lesa's youngest son, the evening star she knew must be shining in the west, Jeneba wiggled backward. Drums pounded in her head.

Sota, Sota, great god of thunder, I beg you, still your noise, she prayed. But no one appeared to notice either noise or motion. She kept moving, edging back around the thick tree. Only an arm's length more to go.

A female voice cried in alarm. Jeneba lunged to her feet, but discovered in that sickening moment that she was too dizzy to run. She caught at the tree for support, her mind racing in panic, searching for an escape.

Tree? She looked up. Wachiru could not climb. Perhaps they would not think of her doing so.

Jamming her knife back in its sheath, Jeneba scrambled for the overhead branches.

The buffalo gave her his strength. Her hands found holds that let her drag herself up. And Mala-Lesa smiled. While Jeneba crouched in a fork clutching the buffalo-horn talisman around her neck, her heart thundering like a war drum, the wachiru milled around the bottom of the tree. They sniffed the ground and air, but never looked up. After a fruitless search of the woods floor, the half-men returned to binding their captives. Finishing that, they slung the warriors over their shoulders and started off through the woods.

Teeth gritted in sorrow and anger, Jeneba counted the casualties passing below her. The bard Kinetu hung over a half-woman's shoulder, blood dripping down her back from his smashed skull. Half a dozen other warrior brothers and sisters appeared dead, too. The side of Jeneba's skull throbbed in reminder of how easily she could be among them. Mseluku lived, though. He groaned as his captors bounded past Jeneba's tree.

She bared her teeth. "Buffalo, give me your strength and wiles," she whispered, caressing her talisman. "Kuta, great god of fire, weapons, and war, guide me to vengeance. Grant me the pleasure of introducing these half-men to your brother Ello, death."

The last half-man passed Jeneba's tree. She counted to the sacred number four, four times, then cautiously slid to the ground, never letting her eyes leave the bobbing light of the torches disappearing through the woods.

"Jeneba!"

She spun, snatching at her knife . . . but turned the slash aside to grin in relief at the man behind her. "Tomo!" She hardly knew him but here he seemed like an old friend. "Thank Mala someone else escaped, too. Come on; let's go before they're too far ahead."

Tomo sucked in his breath. His hand clamped around her wrist, holding her back. "Two of us alone can't rescue Mseluku and the others. Find the horses at first light and we'll ride to Imbu for help."

"Leave our people for *two days*?" She stared at him in outrage. "Why aren't two enough? We're Dasa."

"I'm Dasa."

The words pierced like a spear. Jeneba recoiled, snapping her wrist free. "My blood is Dasa, too," she hissed, "and I won't leave my uncle or any of our people for wachiru to eat!"

Tomo shook his head. "The live ones are safe. The wachiru will eat the dead first."

If he thought that, why did she smell the acid reek of fear on him? The beads in her hair rattled as she flung her head. "Then will you face Nykoro with me and assure him that the husband of his sister will still be alive when we return here? If you're really confident, why not ride to Kiba—that adds only two more days—and tell that to my grandmother and mother and aunts?"

He frowned. "Do you really want our people rescued, or the glory of doing so? Heroic effort alone doesn't prove bravery or cause the bards to sing praise-songs to you. Perhaps you can escape the demons and spirits roaming the night, dark being your father's element, but you can't defeat that many wachiru. You'll only become an object lesson in false pride, the warrior who cost her king and brother warriors their lives."

In Jeneba something snarling screamed, telling her to spring on him with her knife. Horrified, she spun and fled, bolting after the distant sparks of the wachiru torches. Shame flooded her. Maybe Tomo was right. Perhaps she was acting in self-interest, and would therefore surely fail. If Tomo Silla, a hero of Kiba who had faced countless Keoru and Burdamu in single combat, was afraid, there must be good reason. Thinking of the host of demons and spirits who owned the night, the skin on her spine ran with fire and cold.

The fear blunted her anger and hurt. Her mind steadied as nerves pulled taut, stretching awareness into the night around her . . . to the shafts of moonlight pouring through the trees that turned the woods into a great palace hall supported by slanting pale pillars, to buffalo and zebra and eland drinking at the lakeshore, to night birds calling from the trees and lions roaring and hyenas whooping out in the plains. The carrion odor carried back from the wachiru ahead.

She sucked in her cheeks. A warrior must fight with honor. It meant more than victory itself. But what about Mseluku's life? Surely saving a maternal uncle served duty and honor most of all.

Footsteps ran behind her. Jeneba's heart caught. Was it a nogama, ready to slash her with its clawed palms . . . a ghost demanding food offerings to sustain its existence? Heart drumming against her ribs, she risked a glance backward . . . and let out her breath in relief. Tomo Silla again.

Anger replaced fear. "Have you lost your way to Imbu?"

The whites of his eyes glinted in the moonlight slanting through the trees. "Sister, do not speak with such disrespect to a hero who has contemplated your words and concluded that you're right; being Dasa, we *can* rescue our people without an army."

In the warmth flooding her, she regretted her anger. *Sister. Our people.* "Please forgive my words, Tomo." Despite his fear, he would still run through the night with her and face the wachiru? That was heroism indeed. "I spoke in haste and ignorance."

He grunted acceptance and they fell silent as they ran together behind the wachiru party, watching both the torches and shadows around them for anything not plant or animal.

What did Tomo see? To her the night had always stretched in shades of gray, mottled with the shimmer of countless little bursts of light in what her mother called total darkness . . . not that she had that problem now. The moonlight turned the woods into colorless twilight.

Jeneba could have wished for less carrion smell, the better to detect approaching demons. Still, without that stench, she, too, might be among the dead or captives. Somewhere in the woods a leopard screamed and the sound brought an unbidden thought: if she had only a human nose, she might never have noticed the carrion smell until too late. Mere human hearing would not have detected the wachiru footsteps, either, nor could human sight, so night-blind, let her find her way and search the shadows for demons. Irritably, she hunted for something else to think about.

"Tomo, why do you think the wachiru attacked this way? It's always been one man meeting one half-man in the forest and being challenged to wrestle. I've never heard of them attacking in a group."

Tomo hesitated. "Things . . . change. The seers tell us that many things are changing, that the plains are drying up, dying, that the grass will vanish and the buffalo and wild sheep and our cattle disappear with it. They say that sand will swallow the great cities like Kiba, Imbu, and Kouddoun. The wachiru must be changing, too."

Cold slid down Jeneba's spine.

Ahead, the line of half-men broke. Jeneba caught her breath. Their village! Slipping from shadow to shadow, she and Tomo worked their way to the edge of the huts and climbed a tree to study the village.

It consisted of a circle of low mud huts with conical grass roofs. No walls or dogs protected it. Entering should be easy . . . except that the captives had been taken to the open common in the center and hung by their wrists or ankles from racks there. She and Tomo would have to walk into the very middle of the village to reach them.

"We can keep in the shadows," she whispered, "but how do we tell if a wachiru is watching us with his off-side toward us?"

A leopard screamed off toward open grassland, answered by a howl neither animal nor human. Tomo caught his breath. "This is madness. No one would bother saving you if you hung from a wachiru meat rack."

Jeneba sucked in her cheeks. Maybe not, but . . . "Wasn't it madness when you rode into combat with the Burdamu outlaw chief Utembesaba Akaha, carrying only a hobble rope to show your contempt for him? These are our people; we have a duty to them."

He did not respond for a moment, then said, "We'll wait until the wachiru are asleep, then slip in and cut everyone loose."

She settled back in a tree fork to wait.

It was hard. She had to watch the dead warriors disappear

into wachiru maws, eaten raw after being butchered with their own knives. Only rigorous self-discipline kept her silent while the half-men finished their hideous meal and celebrated with shrill singing and a leaping, whirling dance accompanied by drumming on the rack uprights with the bones of their victims.

Finally the half-men disappeared into their huts and the village fell silent. She and Tomo swung down from their perch to stand at the tree's bottom, flexing stiff, numbed limbs, waiting for feeling and function to return.

"You have the night vision," Tomo whispered. "Go first. I'll guard your back."

Jeneba nodded. Knife in one hand, the other gathering her tsara snugly around her hips to keep it from snagging on something that might betray her to the wachiru, she slid from the deep shadows beneath the tree and across a pool of moonlight into the shadows again beside a wachiru hut.

The stench of carrion nearly overwhelmed her.

Holding her breath, she listened intently for sounds that would indicate some wachiru still remained awake. There were only the noises of the woodland and night. She glanced back toward Tomo.

He stood at the edge of the tree's shadow, waving her on.

Jeneba faced the common. The nearest warrior hung only strides away . . . in open space, with no cover for Jeneba to use, faced by every hut in a village flooded with moonlight.

She sucked in her cheeks. "Mala, Creator, please close your eye. I need darkness."

But Mala ignored the whispered prayer. Her eye remained open, a moon full and bright.

"So be it." Jeneba located Mseluku across the common from her. He must be freed first. Glancing backward toward Tomo one last time, she touched her heart four times and sprinted out through the circle of racks. Her bare feet made no sound in the dust.

"Jeneba!" someone hissed in surprise.

She paused only long enough to press her fingers across her lips before racing on to where Mseluku hung tied, his feet barely touching the ground. Jeneba smelled fresh blood where he had been working his wrists against the bonds holding them to the overhead bar of the rack. His eyes widened at the sight of her, but he made no sound, only strained to give her room to slip her knife between his wrists and the bar.

"When I cut you loose, run for the woods," she breathed in his ear.

He nodded.

She sawed at a strap. The tough, well-tanned leather cut with agonizing reluctance. Human skin from some previous wachiru victim? One wrist came free. She started on the other.

A shout of alarm tore apart the night air.

She sawed frantically and as the strap gave, whirled, bolting for the space between the nearest huts. "Follow me, uncle; we'll come back for the others later."

Wachiru came rolling out through the low doorways, one of them into her path. She kicked him under the chin and jumped his limp body. A second half-man appeared out of invisibility, and a third, who caught her tsara. Slashing their arms, she tore free of them. Then she was between the huts and into the woods.

She looked back for Mseluku, but to her horror, saw him nowhere. A handful of howling wachiru followed her instead, covering the ground in incredibly long hops.

With the blood turned fiery cold in her veins, Jeneba stretched into the long-strided run the warriors practiced every day along with wrestling and spear-throwing, a run that often left her brother and sister warriors behind. Not tonight. Her pursuers gained.

She strained to stretch her stride longer.

Suddenly pain shot up her leg and she crashed forward over a root. Somehow Jeneba kept her wits enough to curl and use her momentum to somersault back onto her feet with almost no break in stride. She forgot to hang on to her knife, however. It sailed out of her hand and off into the brush.

"Mala, give me the buffalo's strength and speed," she shouted. Only that could save her now. The wachiru had gained so much she could hear the rasp of their breathing.

Movement flashed on the edge of her vision. Jeneba dodged away. The wachiru followed her evasion, however, and a thunderous heartbeat later pain ripped through her scalp. The wachiru had caught her by the hair. Shrieking, she found herself jerked backward, off her feet.

The wachiru turned back toward the village without slowing, dragging Jeneba behind him. Brush tore at her arms, stones and roots bruised and scraped her dragging legs. At every leap, her hair felt as though it were being jerked out by the roots. Still screaming, she clawed at the wrist and fingers wound in the long, bead-strung cords, but his skin felt as impervious as bridle leather. He appeared unconscious of her nails. His speed made it impossible to bring her feet under her, either.

Ahead, his brother and sister wachiru whooped and gibbered. Visions of being strung up to await dismemberment, never to see Kiba or her mother again, never even to have the proper burial rites, flooded Jeneba with terror. Perhaps if she pled, begged, he would let go of her, she thought in panic. Was there some bargain she could make? Or some way to break loose from the half-man? There *must* be! If only she could regain her feet!

Feet. The word echoed in her head. Feet. She forced terror aside and thought fast. Gritting her teeth against the agony in her scalp, she twisted to take a sight on the muscular leg moving ahead of her. Reaching out, she locked both hands around the ankle.

He crashed full length to the ground. Before he or any of the others could react, Jeneba tore free from his loosed grip and fled back into the woods. Whoops of triumph changed to furious howls. The entire group bounded after her.

The breath scorched Jeneba's throat, seared her lungs. She ignored it, ignored the yells behind. Her entire attention focused ahead, and on driving her legs faster, faster.

Until a scream stopped her short and jerked her around, an animal scream, answered by cries of dismay. She spun to see a leopard crouched in the path behind her, with fangs bared and tail lashing. The wachiru retreated toward their village.

Jeneba sagged gasping against a tree.

The leopard turned to face her, yawning. "That's twice I've saved you, sister."

"I'm not—" Jeneba stopped. "Twice?"

"The first time when the wachiru attacked."

"You didn't—" But in all fairness, she had to admit that of course he had . . . not giving her specifics of the danger, perhaps, but certainly alerting her to its presence. "I thank you, leopard." She gulped air. "Why did you?"

His tail twitched. "Balance. You risk your life to save those who do not accept you as fully one of them, so Mala-Lesa commands that I intervene for a sister who will not acknowledge her kinship to me."

"Then I thank Mala-Lesa, too." Jeneba slid down the tree to sit on a root. "I hope Tomo escaped."

"If you were my sister," the leopard said, "I could tell you about Tomo Silla."

Sudden cold washed through Jeneba. "What about Tomo?"

The tawny eyes flashed. "You say you aren't my sister."

"I—" She almost choked on the words, but forced them out, reminding herself that she needed his knowledge. "I *am* your sister."

The leopard sniffed. "Words. Very well, though. Tomo Silla was never in danger. He remained by the tree and when he gave the alarm, he escaped into the woods before anyone ever saw him."

"That's a lie!"

The leopard's tail lashed. "As you wish." He turned away.

She scrambled to her feet after him. "Why would Tomo warn the wachiru?"

The leopard peered back over his shoulder. "He couldn't let you free the warriors. They were the price for his life."

The price—Remembering her own panicked thought about trying to bargain with the wachiru to release her, understanding came with the force of a blow in the stomach. "Tomo met a wachiru when he was scouting for the campsite and lost the wrestling match."

"Yes," the leopard said. "But he offered an exchange for his life."

She hissed. Remembering how she felt when the wachiru was dragging her back to the village, she could understand what kind of terror drove him to the bargain, but outrage still boiled up in her. "He gave them *us*!" No wonder she had smelled fear on him when she insisted on going to the rescue. "Where is he now?"

"Waiting in a tree for morning."

Waiting to set out for Kiba and report how everyone but him had been tragically lost, no doubt. She bared her teeth. As soon as they were home, she would challenge him to combat.

Jeneba retraced the path of her previous flight until she found her knife, then headed for the village again.

The leopard followed. "Do you still believe you can rescue your people?"

"I have to try."

At the edge of the village she hesitated, however, sucking in her cheeks in dismay. The half-men now had guards around their captives.

The leopard blinked. "If you were truly my sister, I could tell you how to save them."

She whirled. "How, brother?"

His eyes glowed. "Would you call me that if you didn't need me?"

Guilt spread heat up her face. "Probably not."

The leopard sighed. "You're honest anyway. I give you this much, then. The knife is no use. The warriors must be won as they were lost. You may prevail if you can find that in you which your father gave and use a thing born of Mala-Lesa, who sees wachiru when men cannot."

With a final lash of his tail, he vanished into the darkness, leaving Jeneba staring in dismay. The leopard advised in riddles!

Part of the answer was obvious. Winning the warriors as they had been lost meant by wrestling. She grimaced. Win at wrestling, when Tomo, stronger and more experienced than she, had lost. That in her that her father had given must mean her spirit, but how could she find any more of it? What, too, was this thing born of Mala-Lesa? Since the High God had created the entire world, that could be anything. How could she use it in wrestling anyway?

Shrieks of wachiru glee mixed with human protests jerked her attention back to the village. She instantly forgot the leopard riddles. The half-men had discovered Mseluku's severed bonds and were dragging him toward the place in the center where earlier they had butchered the dead warriors. A wachiru man waited with one of the captured knives.

"Uncle!"

The cry echoed through her head but she was not aware of screaming it, or of moving, until she found herself charging across the common toward the group holding Mseluku. As reason reasserted itself, she stumbled and froze. Around her, shock paralyzed the wachiru, too, but that would not last long. Even now their mouths opened to cry in warning and their hands spread into claws. The half-man with the knife raised it over Mseluku's chest.

The knife was useless, the leopard had said. Jeneba dropped hers, then spoke loudly in Burda, the trade language. "It is the custom for wachiru to challenge men to wrestle. Now a man comes to challenge the wachiru."

"No," Mseluku gasped in their own language, Dase.

Wachiru eyes glittered in the moonlight. "To wrestle?" The speaker's voice rang deep and hollow, as though coming from a cave.

Jeneba locked her knees to keep them from trembling. "Yes . . . but I don't care about the healing herbs and plants you normally show to men who win. This time *they* must be the prize." She gestured at Mseluku and the warriors.

A hiss of surprise, human and wachiru, ran around the common. Wachiru heads shook. The deep-voiced one said, "No."

Jeneba lifted her chin and forced her voice louder, despite a drought-dry mouth. "You have no right to them. Tomo Silla dishonorably exchanged them for his own life after you outwrestled him." She ignored her people's hisses of disbelief to watch the wachiru spokesman. "Pick your best wrestler to answer my challenge."

The spokesman turned away and vanished. She still heard his voice, though, gibbering at the other wachiru. They answered shrilly.

Between his captors, Mseluku said, "Daughter of my sister, this is madness. You can't win. You'll be eaten like the rest of us. Run. Go for help."

Part of her longed to, but she set her jaw and stood firm. She could win, the leopard said. If she answered his riddle. What could the answer *be*!

The spokesman reappeared. "We accept. I will wrestle you."

Jeneba swallowed. "We meet at dawn, then."

His eye gleamed. "We wrestle now."

Now? Her heart lurched. "But I've been traveling all day, and have just run very hard. I'm not rested."

"Now!" the wachiru repeated.

"Animal-spirit fool," a warrior sister spat.

Mseluku said grimly, "Niece, unlike men of noble blood, wachiru aren't compelled by honor to wait until their opponents are prepared before fighting."

She swallowed again. "May I at least speak to my gods first?"

After a moment, the wachiru nodded.

Her mind raced. If she could not answer the leopard's riddle, then she would have to fight another way, which meant, first, keeping away from the wachiru. She still felt the grip on her hair as the other lifted her off her feet. Her toe brushed the knife. She glanced down at it. Perhaps it could be of use after all.

Crouching, she picked it up with one hand and reached for her hair with the other. While the warriors stared aghast, she chopped off the long, oiled, beaded ropes until nothing remained on her scalp but fuzz too short for anyone to grab. Then she untied her tsara at the shoulder and dropped it. Her copper, ivory, and wooden arm bands joined it on the ground. She debated over keeping her talisman but finally decided there must be nothing for the wachiru to use as a handhold. It joined everything else folded up in her tsara. Finally, Jeneba rubbed the shorn ropes of hair all over, covering her skin with the heavy oil dressing.

After cleaning her palms in the dust, she stood. "I'm ready."

The wachiru bared his teeth, showing fangs.

The other half-men backed toward the racks, pulling Mseluku with them and leaving the center clear of all but moonlight, Jeneba, and her opponent.

Crouching, Jeneba warily circled the wachiru, moving toward the side with his arm. He side-hopped a few steps, too, then spun and vanished. Jeneba froze, holding her breath and peering around her. Where had he gone? Her hands felt sweaty and it was an effort not to wipe them on her thighs.

"Behind you," Mseluku called.

An arm closed around her throat. The hours of wrestling practice repaid themselves. Almost without thinking Jeneba tucked her chin into the crook of the elbow and grabbing the wrist with one hand and the elbow with the other, pushed up on the elbow, slipping out under the arm. Rather than release him, however, she held on, moving around him, dragging the arm with her until it twisted behind him. She was reaching to hook his ankle with her foot when the wachiru suddenly leaped high in the air, whirling free and vanishing again.

Jeneba glanced toward Mseluku, but a wachiru beside him brandished a club. "Keep silent."

Her stomach dropped. Without help tracking the half-man, she was lost. If only she could answer the riddle.

Wait. She held her breath, straining to hear over the gibbering of wachiru. Was that breathing and a footfall behind her? She spun toward the sound.

The half-man lunged out of the moonlight. Jeneba met him head-on, locking arms with him, leaning her shoulder into his. They pushed at each other, side-shifting, straining as each tried to push the other off balance. Jeneba shifted her weight suddenly toward his off-side, but as he stumbled, the half-man broke free and pivoted, vanishing yet again.

But she heard the hop of his foot. Could that be the answer, using her hearing to track him? But the leopard seemed to indicate she must find something more than what she had used all her life.

Her ears followed his bounding progress behind her. Turning, she realized, however, that sound still gave her no indication how and when the half-man might move next. She needed more than hearing.

A shadow flickered over her. An upward glance found the

wachiru arcing over her, silhouetted against the moon. For a moment, though he was landing on her, she could only stare, lightning flashing in her head. Shadow! Of course. A thing born of Mala the moon and Lesa the sun, for those bodies of light certainly saw wachiru when men could not!

She flung herself sideways barely in time to avoid being knocked flat.

The half-man snarled at missing her, but he landed like a cat and rebounded straight at her. They went down on the ground together, each straining to find a hold on the other. He hung on like a snake, either sliding away from her or kicking loose with his powerful leg. On the other hand, her oiled skin gave him no grip on her, either.

He tried to flip her. She used the momentum to come up on her feet and bring him with her, up and over, then hard on his back. She slammed down on him, but he rolled, squirming free. And vanished . . . but not entirely. A pool of shadow remained, shortening as he stood. Her hearing traced the thump of his foot and the rasp of his breathing, just audible above her own panting, but she watched the shifting pool where the moonlight did not reach.

He tried circling her, time and again. She pivoted, following each of his bounds, evading the tentative moves toward her.

The wachiru voices went silent.

Her opponent spoke near her. "Running is not winning."

She sidestepped another rush. True. Only pinning won. She might have just one chance at him, though; after that he would be warned. Somehow she saw him. Keeping her distance, Jeneba plotted strategy, then braced herself and watched the shadow, praying silently to Mala.

The shadow moved, broadening subtly in a way that told her the half-man was crouching to spin and spring. She moved as he began the turn, leaping forward and catching him around the neck from his off-side. He turned his chin into her elbow as she had done, but before he could grab her arm, she caught his wrist with her other hand and leaned backward.

His spring, already begun, helped her lift him off his feet. The momentum kept them moving. The wachiru cried out, but Jeneba flung them on until her back arched in a bow with her and the half-man's heads touching the ground behind her.

No sooner had they touched, however, than she rolled, turning him facedown on the ground. Her arm slid free of his neck to join her other hand cranking on his arm. Her knees landed on the nape of his neck and in the middle of his back.

Beyond them, wachiru gibbered again and Dasan voices shrieked in glee. Jeneba barely heard them. Under her, the half-man bucked with a strength that needed all her concentration to fight. She had his arm twisted up behind him, but the muscles in it bulged and rippled until the paint on his skin cracked and flaked, and with agonizing slowness, the wrist started to slip through her grip. She gritted her teeth, hanging on with all her will.

"Mala, Creator, High God," she gasped. "If you would have me save my people, give me the strength of the buffalo."

The wrist writhed, slipping still more, the arm slowly and inexorably straightening despite Jeneba twisting hard with both her hands.

Sister, the voice of the leopard whispered in her head.

She shook it away.

Her grip slipped still more.

You must find in you that which your father gave.

The wachiru writhed under her. Jeneba gritted her teeth as her fingers began to tremble in fatigue. She could hang on, she told herself. She must. She could ... not ... let ... go!

Sister.

All right! She would use anything that could help her right now, even her father. Think, then. What came with the leopard spirit? Night sight, hearing, a keen nose? What else? Strength? Leopards dragged full-grown antelope up trees. She certainly needed some of that power right now.

She dug in her nails. Her chest heaved and sweat streamed down her body, yet the arm continued to slip away from her.

Desperately, she tried to imagine herself as a leopard with a fresh kill. How would it feel inside that spotted skin ...

moving on all fours, muscles sliding smoothly, tasting the warmth of the fur and blood of the throat between her jaws.

And suddenly it was no longer imagination. She *felt* it. Jeneba snarled in exultation as power surged through her. She felt molten in her grace, limitless in strength, sinuous and lithe, body moving in perfect obedience. She rode the writhing back with new and confident balance.

Grinning, she crooked her fingers. Nails feeling like claws dug into the half-man's leathery hide. The slip stopped. Jeneba applied new pressure, twisting the arm, forcing it farther and farther. Until the shoulder joint grated and popped with the strain.

The wachiru screamed, "I yield!"

Jeneba purred in his ear, "Order your people to cut mine loose and return all the weapons you took."

The half-man gibbered. Frowning wachiru moved to obey.

Panting, Jeneba released the half-man and looked around for Mseluku.

He was pushing dazed warriors toward the edge of the village. "On your way, quickly. It's over. Let's go."

Over? Jeneba grimly scooped up her bundled belongings. Not quite over. Not until she dealt with Tomo Silla.

CHAPTER

TWO

They spent the rest of the night in the trees, well away from the wachiru village. In the morning Mseluku led them back to their camp to see what remained.

Lions and hyenas quarreled for possession of it. While the hyenas snarled and whooped, defending the carcasses of three hobbled horses from the lions slouching around them, the pride's male amused himself by shredding the pig-stomach water bags and sacks of busumwo, balls of millet dough, King Nykoro had provided for the warriors to eat on their way home.

The warriors slid back into the woods and left the predators to their dispute.

They buried the dead warriors in the middle of the woods in trench graves dug with spears and knives. Over a few objections.

"Every Dasan hero deserves a burial jar," Kempu Abata complained.

Ayoka Tubeda elbowed him. "Any burial is better than being eaten by the wachiru, or leaving them for the hyenas as Burdamu do."

Jeneba shuddered. How could any tribe leave their dead out? Everyone knew the hyenas brought such corpses back to life with the magic staff Chikura and questioned them about their lives and manner of dying before eating them. It cost many offerings to appease the ghosts' tempers after such torment.

Tears ran down Mseluku's face as he tamped the earth over the bard Kinetu.

"Kinetu," he sang,

Magic voice,
Prodigious memory,
For your artistry, thank you.
For your service, thank you.
Who will make the praise-songs
And keep the Karamoke history
Half so well,
Half so faithfully?

One by one, the party sang praise-songs for each of their
dead brother and sister warriors, those buried here and those
eaten the night before. Afterward, they scattered berries across
the graves to keep the ghosts pacified until their blood-kin
could arrange better offerings, then shouldering spears and
shields, the warrior party started the march for Kiba.

Beyond the woods, the Sahara rolled away before them,
waist-high grass stretching to the horizon. Grazing herds
waded through it in the distance, dark and legless, as though
they floated on the sea of green. The sun shone hot overhead, Lesa's golden eye riding high in the sky. Burying the
bodies had taken most of the morning.

Jeneba's stomach snarled. She had eaten some of the berries they gathered, but those hardly replaced the supper and
breakfast she missed. Or the midday meal about to be
missed. If Ogata, god of the hunt, frowned on them, the
warriors might not kill anything for supper tonight, either.

"We should have hunted for our horses as soon as we
escaped. Maybe we would have found a few," someone
grumbled. "We could be riding home."

"Or Jeneba could have taken two of those horses after the
attack, before the hyenas killed them," Ayoka said, "and
ridden relay to Imbu. She could have been there before dawn
and been back with Nykoro's warriors by sunset. They'd
have rescued us and given us horses *and* food."

Jeneba frowned. "You might not have been alive by the time
I came back." But a thread of uncertainty trickled through her.
Ride all night and be back before sunset. Yes, she might have.

Batu Camara said, "It would have been wiser than challenging the wachiru to wrestle."

The peevish tone struck anger in her. She spun to face him. "I won, didn't I?"

"By Mala's grace only," Kempu Abata said. "Most people lose to wachiru; you know that. The challenge was foolishly irresponsible."

Her gut jerked into knots of protest. "*You've* gone singly against a group of opponents. Many of you have. How was that less foolish?"

Kempu frowned. "We fought against men, not monsters, not creatures without honor."

"Don't judge her too harshly," Nunuwo Nkeba said. "She's young and inexperienced, and you know how things always look more fearsome by night. Everyone imagines greater dangers, and even dangers that aren't there. Remember how she thought Tomo had betrayed us?"

Jeneba stiffened. Why was Mseluku saying nothing? He should be defending her. "I'm not imagining it. When he lost the wrestling match to the wachiru, he told it about the camp we would be making so they could take us instead of him."

Ayoka bared her teeth. "If I thought Tomo could be such a crawling coward, I'd run him through with my spear the moment I next saw him, but—a noble, a Dasa, a hero of Kiba behaving so dishonorably?" She shook her head.

Jeneba's jaw set. "But it's true."

Mseluku asked gently, "Did you see him?"

"No," she had to admit, "but the leopard told me—"

She stopped herself too late. Hair beads cracked together as heads snapped toward her. Mseluku's forehead furrowed unhappily. "A *leopard* told you Tomo betrayed us?"

It was too late now to deny. She nodded.

Kempu hissed. "And you *believed* it? When you know how often wizards take leopard form? How could you be so *stupid*?"

That stung. She snapped back, "Something made those wachiru attack in a group."

"Maybe a wizard told them to," Nunuwo said.

"For what reason?"

Batu Camara shrugged. "Why does a wizard do anything? They're evil. Joueta Tatauba could even have paid for witchcraft to retaliate because we insulted him and defeated his warriors."

Her mind raced desperately. "But the leopard warned me about the attack. A wizard wouldn't have done that. And if Tomo didn't give us to the wachiru, what happened to him when the half-men chased me? Where is he now that you're free?"

"As soon as he saw you being chased, he knew you'd be caught, and I expect he went to Imbu for help. I would have," Batu said.

She appealed to Mseluku. "Uncle?"

But he only put a hand on her shoulder. "I will be forever grateful to you for my life, but . . . the warriors' words have wisdom. Next time, you should think more carefully before acting and not accept a stranger's words so unquestioningly. Nunuwo, Byoko," he called back down the line, "go to Imbu. When you intercept King Nykoro's warriors, tell them we've been rescued and to take my wife's brother my greetings and thanks for his attempt to save us."

Watching the two warriors jog away south, Jeneba reflected angrily that while she was not supposed to believe unquestioningly, *they* could. Unfair! She said nothing aloud, however. Even in anger, she had no right to speak disrespectfully to her uncle and superiors. Beyond that, Mseluku's voice held a note of finality which told her he had passed judgment and considered the discussion ended.

No one else said another word about leopards or Tomo Silla, either. Throughout the day's march, though, and at their night camp on a rocky hill above a spring, Jeneba caught expressions of exasperation, scorn, and pity aimed in her direction. Each glance pierced like a spear.

On watch, squatted on the tumbled stones around the camp, she stared out bitterly across the moon-silvered grasslands. Being a warrior had once looked like the best way to earn honor, since it seemed unlikely any family would permit its son to pay the bride price for her. Many eldest and only daughters of women without sons became ndosoa, "my mother's son," adopting all the ways of a man: profession, dress, mannerisms, even taking a wife. She had not. Ndosoa

inherited from their maternal uncles like any nephew and
people might think she had ambitions for the king's Stool. No
matter what she did, though, she always remained in the
wrong.

Jeneba hugged her knees and brooded over the camp. One
chance still remained. Finding Tomo in Kiba claiming he
had seen all of the warrior party killed by the wachiru would
show everyone that she had been right.

She lifted her face to the moon. "Mala, mother of everything, speed our journey. Let us catch the traitor betraying
himself."

And at midmorning the next day, it seemed the prayer had
been answered. From her place toward the rear of the line,
Jeneba spotted swiftly moving dots on a distant hilltop, dots
that scents on the wind identified as horses carrying riders
she knew...Dasa...other warriors of Kiba, and with
them, Sia Nyiba and her aunt Abara Bari.

Whooping, Jeneba left the line and leaped forward, running to meet them. The power that had come during her
fight with the half-man poured automatically through her
again, carrying her swiftly down the game trail away from
Mseluku and the others.

Her mother and aunt rode at the head of the riders. As
Jeneba neared them, Sia Nyiba called, "What happened?
Where are Mseluku and the other warriors?"

"Behind me." Jeneba gestured back with her spear. "Most
of us survived the wachiru attack, no matter what you've
been told."

"*Wachiru* attack!" some warrior exclaimed.

The horses halted in front of Jeneba. Abara Bari frowned.
"No one told us about wachiru. The Queen Mother sent us to
find what happened to you because your horses came back
riderless."

Cold lumped in Jeneba's gut. "You haven't talked to
Tomo Silla?"

"Tomo?" Sia Nyiba's brows rose. "Isn't he with you?"

Tomo had not gone home to play the heroic only survivor
of the attack. Jeneba's stomach dropped toward her feet.

* * *

Back in Kiba, she exchanged the war tsara for her everyday red-ochre one and tried to resume life as before. Tried. Practicing spear-throwing with the other young warriors, racing with them around the city walls, or wrestling in the afternoons at the end of the common between Mseluku's palace and the market filling the rest of the common, she saw the glances in her direction. She heard the whispers.

The older warriors drinking honey beer on the verandah outside Tegetu Okabo's wineshop did not even bother to whisper. In recounting past heroism of their own they would wrap feet back behind the carved buffalo or elephants rearing from the base to support the rectangular seat of their stools, and say, "But I never believed a leopard or falsely accused a hero."

Jeneba buried her anger beneath doubled efforts to be the swiftest, most agile and accurate warrior in Kiba. But when, with the leopard strength flowing through her, she won her race or wrestling match, the warriors and city elders shook their heads, beads clicking. "Now see how she flaunts her animal spirit. The hero of yesterday is the tyrant of tomorrow."

Without even having been treated as a hero, Jeneba reflected bitterly.

Byoko and Nunuwo came back from Imbu alone. Those in search parties Mseluku sent to every village and city in the area also came back shaking their heads. No one had seen Tomo.

After four months Tomo's mother and sisters tied grief cords around their heads and petitioned Mseluku to declare him dead.

"Grieving indeed," one of his wives complained one morning to other women at the well on the common. "His sisters can't wait to throw us out of his house and claim it for their sons."

"Lubama has had a hand in this," the other said. She stared hard at Jeneba. "The hero is lost fulfilling his duty while others less deserving live."

The women nodded. Mala-Lesa's youngest son, messenger and linguist of the gods, had a well-known history of also being a trickster.

Tight-lipped, Jeneba finished drawing her water and carried the jar back to her grandmother Suwenata's compound.

"You'd think it was dishonorable to have saved everyone's lives," she complained to her mother.

Sia Nyiba looked up from overseeing a servant girl grinding millet and pulled her daughter to the far end of the verandah fronting the compound. "Do you believe you were right?"

When everyone said she was wrong, it became hard to believe in herself with conviction, but Jeneba replied, "Yes."

"Then cool your heart and ignore what other people say. I do."

"But you don't *care* what anyone thinks of you!" Around them the verandah-fronted compounds of the Karamoke clan families made a long, narrow U, facing onto a small common that opened into the larger city common at its western end. Jeneba eyed the women at work on each veranda... grinding grain; mixing flour, water, and fat into doughy balls of busumwo they would serve for lunch and dinner; dressing each other's hair; calling encouragement or reproof to the children on the common playing noisily at being wrestlers and warriors. "You'd give up being Dasa in a moment if it would bring your leopard-man back to you."

Sia Nyiba's head tossed in a click of beads, still the red, yellow, and uncolored woods of an unmarried woman. "Don't presume to know my mind too well, daughter! I'm Dasa and proud of it. I will fight to the death rather than deny my blood. Still, Dasa aren't gods. A world of other people lies beyond us, with different customs and different beliefs, some perhaps wiser than our own."

Jeneba scowled. "How much do you know about them? You've never been outside Dasan territory, except to the villages of the Malekuro, and they aren't different. They used to be Dasa until—"

"Until their founder Silamunga was cheated of his chiefhood by his aunt, who tricked her dying brother into believing that her son Baranu was Silamunga so the chief's Stool would pass to him," Sia Nyiba finished. "I know the history songs, too, daughter. The rest of the world I heard about through stories your father told me."

Jeneba grimaced at the reference to her relationship with the leopard-man. "Believing leopards runs in my blood, then."

Sia Nyiba's voice sharpened. "Spirit speaks to spirit. Be proud of yours! Huso Ntatabe was the most gloriously alive man I have ever known, filled with exultation and a fierce joy in his body and existence. Possessing me, he filled me with it, too. You would do better to emulate him than many of your blood-kin."

She should have known better than to go to her mother for comfort! Jeneba spun away.

Her racing feet carried her into the city common and down its length toward the gate at the far western end, dodging market women setting up their wares under broad parasols . . . piles of melons, citrus fruit, and peppers . . . baskets of millet, guineacorn, and ground nuts . . . tethered goats . . . caged fowl. She leaped sideways to avoid stumbling over a display of gourds and raced on while the village woman who had brought them to sell called angrily after her.

"The girl is as crazy as her mother," she heard someone say.

Someone else replied, "The king ought to marry her off. She's almost past good marketing age, but she has enough of her mother's beauty that he should be able to find some man who'll see only that and overlook the spirit."

Jeneba did not stop until she reached the city gate and scrambled up the narrow flight of stairs to the top of the wall. A warrior on guard above the gate eyed her but said nothing as she paced the sun-warmed mud bricks.

Could Tomo really be dead? She scowled out at the rolling plains. Deep down, she refused to believe it. He haunted her dreams, images of him hiding in villages beyond Dasan territory and laughing at how he had evaded retribution.

He could be anywhere from the camps of the nomad Burdamu north to the cities of the Keoru and Sullo in the south, or the villages of the Malekuro and Nbaba west and east, or beyond, with tribes she had never heard of, swallowed by the immensity of the Sahara. Jeneba turned, peering at the distant horizon in despair. He would never be found.

She stopped turning to squint at a thin veil of dust rising northeast of the city beyond the grain fields and the distant grazing forms of Kiba's cattle. A moment of study found the source, a line of lumpy shapes strung along the road from Chizomwe. Jeneba's breath caught. She knew those shapes. Perhaps Mala-Lesa had given her a way to find Tomo after all. She scrambled down the steps from the wall, breathing thanks to the High God.

"Where are you going?" the guard called as she dashed out through the gate.

"To meet Knife-nose," she shouted, and stretched into a hard run up the north road.

For the first time since that night in the wachiru village, delight in her body burst through her. She found joy in running, in the leopard grace and strength driving her. Driving her toward the caravan of Knife-nose, the Abedda trader. His name was actually Quada Malam, but everyone called him Knife-nose or No lips for his facial features so different from a Dasa's. And sometimes they called him Lubama, because like the god, there seemed to be nowhere he had not been, no tribe or news he did not know.

As she passed the fields of millet and guineacorn, the lumpy shapes became distinguishably donkeys, wiry little animals trudging along under loads nearly as large as themselves, packs that would be spread open in Kiba's market to reveal a richness of cloth, spices, salt, ivory, copper, exotic woods and stones, kola nuts. Trailing them came goats and cattle—red and white, black and white, brindled, with horns like a huge V—and horses, sleek, fiery creatures from Quada's homeland somewhere east beyond the Tarasi Mountains and the vast inland sea of the Uchaga water.

"Welcome!" she shouted in Burda to the man in a long, loose robe riding at the head of the caravan on a gray mare. "Kiba welcomes the trader Quada Malam. The king of Kiba greets you. The nobles and the people of the court greet you. The warriors and women of Kiba greet you, the priests and artisans, the workers of the field and herdsmen greet you."

Quada's horse snorted and shied from the scent of her, as almost all horses did until they became used to her. The Abedda held the beast, however, and grinned beneath the headdress he wore against the sun. "The trader Quada Malam thanks Kiba. I have never been met so far from the city before, nor by such a small but enthusiastic reception party. I hardly recognize you except for your eyes. What's happened to your hair, Jeneba Karamoke? King Mseluku has not died, I hope, nor the Queen Mother, and not the beautiful Sia Nyiba your mother, surely?"

Grimacing, Jeneba ran her hand through her fuzz, growing but still too short to string with beads. "You'll hear the story soon enough. Tell me, does anyone but you wander so far? Do you ever see any of my cousin Dasa in the foreign cities you visit?"

Looking down at her, a gleam jumped in Quada's dark eyes. "An interesting question. Is the answer important to you?"

That question had been a mistake, she realized, remembering another reason her people called the trader Lubama. But did the gleam mean he knew something, or only that he smelled profit, and did she dare try bargaining with him to find out? "Of course not," she said. "I'm only making idle talk. Have you brought us anything unusual this year?"

The interest died out of his eyes. "Wait and see."

She stood aside and let the caravan pass her, greeting his sons and wives shepherding the donkeys along on foot. Several replied. The women were not the same as those last year.

A final son rode at the rear, keeping close watch on the cattle and horses . . . Namid, who had come with his father every year that Jeneba could remember, and who would probably inherit the trade route, Sia Nyiba said, as it had been passed down to Quada from his father and father's fathers for generations.

She fell into step at Namid's knee and reached out to stroke the shoulder of his mount, a copper-red mare. "Your horse is beautiful."

The mare danced sideways, blowing. Namid jerked the reins. "She's a superb animal. Note her large, intelligent eyes, and the depth of her chest, and how clean and straight her legs are. She's one of my favorites, but if you're interested in her, your uncle the king may be able to talk my father into trading her."

Jeneba grinned inside. There could be no doubt who Namid's spirit came from . . . preparing already for long, hard bargaining over the mare. She peered up at him. "I wanted to buy a gelding the same color from Tomo Silla a

few months ago, but it went lame." Her heart leaped at a
flicker in his eyes. Knife-nose and now Namid. But the son
could not be questioned any more directly than the father.
"Did you know the horse?"

"No, but it's interesting you mention Tomo Silla. We saw
someone up north last month who looked enough like him to
be his twin."

Jeneba feigned a thoughtful frown. "If you mean in the
Burdamu camps, he was there with an uncle trading cattle."

Namid shook his head. "This was in Yagana, and it
couldn't have been your warrior; he had the shaved head and
tribal scarring of a Malekuro."

Praise Mala! She dropped her eyes back to the horse to
hide the leap of her heart that might show in them. "No, it
couldn't have been Tomo. May I ride the mare?"

He grinned. "If she'll let you. I'll ask my father after
we've reached Kiba."

Jogging off around the caravan, she raced to reach the city
ahead of them. With every long stride her mind churned
faster. She had information, but what could she do with it?
Tell Mseluku that Quada Malam had seen someone who
might be Tomo Silla with his head shaved and a new scar
added across his right cheek to match the one on the left and
make him look a Malekuro. And that this possibly-Tomo had
been seen in Yagana? Everyone knew it existed; it lay at the
western foot of the Bumala Mountains and traders brought
stories and songs and trade items from it, but from the de-
scriptions the city always seemed more fantasy than real. *I
have been to Yagana,* people said to mean they had experienced something extraordinary.

She could hear the arguments. Why would Tomo go to
Yagana? Why change his appearance? Anyway, people of a
tribe often resembled each other to foreigners and a Malekuro might well look Dasa, even to someone who knew Malekuro and Dasa as well as the trader did. No, Mseluku
would never send someone to Yagana to look for Tomo. The
only way to find him was to go herself.

CHAPTER
THREE

Jeneba felt like a fugitive. While the population of Kiba milled on the common, examining Quada's wares, she slipped through the crowd and out the gate with her horse, a wiry little bay of nondescript appearance but stubborn endurance. No one noticed. Not even the warrior on guard questioned her.

Only her mother knew. Sia Nyiba had caught her filling a cowhide pouch with busumwo and hot peppers from her grandmother's kitchen. Her mother said nothing, just stood on the open side of the three-walled kitchen, silhouetted against the sunlit center of the compound.

Jeneba lifted her chin defiantly. "I'm going to find Tomo Silla." She slung the pouch over her shoulder.

She could not read her mother's expression against the brightness of the compound, but after a long silence Sia Nyiba said, "Yes."

Jeneba stared. "You won't try to stop me?"

Sia Nyiba sighed. "Dasan women do what must be done. To avenge the murder of her chieftain father and rescue her twin brother, our founding Queen Mother Naruwa lay with the conqueror Korote, remember. She tore out his throat with her teeth because she had to come to him naked and weaponless. She helped Ndabu and the warriors faithful to him escape across the great Unchaga water from the vengeance of Korote's brother. You wouldn't be Naruwa's daughter if you didn't hunt Tomo Silla. Mala protect you."

Only as she moved past her mother did Jeneba see the glisten of tears.

That memory stabbed at her, and with it persisted the thought that her mother might have a change of heart and send someone after her. So a wide circle around the cattle and goat herds avoided any encounters with the boys guarding them. Then she headed north at an easy trot, keeping the humped silhouette of the Mburi hills on her right-hand horizon.

Like a fugitive, she found herself looking backward all afternoon, watching for the dust of pursuit. Fortunately she had said nothing about where she intended to look, but if the trader or his sons mentioned the man in Yagana, Sia Nyiba might guess.

She decided to ride all night. The open offered nowhere safe for a person alone to sleep anyway. A tree might protect her, but not the bay. Nor did she dare ask a village for hospitality. This close to Kiba, they all belonged to Mseluku, and even those Dasa who did not know her by sight had heard of the king's leopard-fathered niece. Her tawny eyes would give her away.

Sunset turned Lesa's eye into a bloated, bloody fireball spreading sideways across the western horizon. Jeneba halted at a spring to let her horse rest. While he drank and grazed, she opened the pouch and swallowed two of the busumwo balls stuffed with peppers, then wrapped up in her kadoru to doze. Her ears, however, remained tuned to the sounds of the hobbled horse tearing the grass in sharp bites, and she kept one hand on her bow.

The roar of a lion somewhere near roused her. Jeneba rolled to her feet and stretched. Lesa's eye had vanished, leaving only a wash of red on the clouds; Mala's was rising, full and orange. Jeneba shivered. Twilight . . . the onset of night, of darkness. She took a deep breath and shook off the kadoru. Time to go on.

Folding the long length of blue cloth from a cloak into a riding pad, she tied it over the horse's back. The lion roared again and she grimaced wryly. Twilight was also the time of the big cats. Mala grant that movement would protect her from beasts and demons.

She slung her bow across her back and started to vault onto the horse when the lion roared a third time. Another cry answered it . . . not an animal voice. Jeneba stiffened. It sounded like a woman's scream. Above her.

She whirled.

The yellow-brown figure of a slender, naked girl a little younger than Jeneba stumbled down the slope toward her, eyes glistening in terror. At the sight of Jeneba, she reached out, wailing wordlessly.

"What is it?" Jeneba called in Burda. "Lions?"

The girl wailed again.

Jeneba sucked in her breath. The bow pressed into her back but she did not reach for it. Only a very good shot indeed would stop a lion. Instead, she vaulted on the horse and held out a hand to the girl. "We'll outrun them."

The girl sprang up behind her, sobbing in relief. Jeneba dug her heels into the bay's sides. He leaped forward into a gallop that quickly left the spring behind.

When after a bit a glance backward found no lions in pursuit, she pulled down to a trot. "You're safe now. What are you doing out here alone?"

The girl did not reply, only sighed and snuggled into Jeneba's back like a child seeking comfort. The sweet scent of some herb she had chewed or rubbed on her body enveloped Jeneba with such pungent strength that Jeneba grimaced.

What village could she be from? Jeneba wondered. She was not Dasa. A foreign bride, perhaps, though Jeneba had not seen any scarification which would identify her tribe and the short hair had no distinctive styling. The girl wore no jewelry, neither ankle bracelets nor arm bands, no necklaces or collar or earrings, not even a talisman of her clan totem.

"Where's your village? I'll take you to the edge of it."

Still the girl remained silent.

The skin prickled on Jeneba's neck. Slowing the bay to a walk, she turned for a closer look at her passenger.

Suddenly the arms clamped down with bruising strength. Fingers dug through Jeneba's tsara into her ribs, and her passenger's true odor broke through the cloying scent of the herb . . . the stench of a flesh-eater's breath. Teeth sank into the back of Jeneba's neck.

With the pain came understanding, and a fiery blast of fear. Uchami! A beast, for all its human appearance, unable to speak, and worse, virtually invulnerable.

Jeneba threw herself off the horse.

They landed with the uchami underneath. It gasped at the impact, but its bite loosened only momentarily, then the teeth closed again and the uchami wrapped its legs around Jeneba, too. Jeneba groped for her knife . . . to find it impossible to reach with the beast's grip pinning her tsara to her body. Spitting, she clawed at the uchami's arms and smashed her head backward into its face.

A snarl and a hot splash on her shoulders told her she had managed to bloody the beast's nose. The teeth, though, just worked deeper.

Screaming with the pain, she rolled, letting the uchami on top of her in order to drive it under her again. And she writhed. With all the leopard strength she could summon she bucked and twisted and pried at the crushing circle of arms and legs.

The uchami remained indifferent to her weight mashing it down, to elbows driving backward into its ribs, to the flaying whip of the long grass as they rolled through. It seemed to feel nothing, either, of the bow and arrows between them that ground into Jeneba's back. Its limbs could be levered loose, but as soon as Jeneba let go of one to work on another, the first whipped back around her as tightly as ever.

Her blood ran hot over her shoulders and down her back. Desperation flooded her. What if she could not work loose?

Fear became a hot flush of humiliation. Die her first night out, a victim of the first danger to come along? Never even come close to finding Tomo Silla?

"*No!*" she screamed. There must be some way to break free, to fight it off!

Like a whisper, a thought slid through the terror and fury: she had fought and failed; what if she stopped fighting? The beast must not be able to kill by breaking her neck or it would have already done so. It must need to reach her throat.

She went limp.

For a lifetime nothing happened. The uchami continued to cling. Then, gradually, the teeth withdrew. One arm loosened and the free hand grabbed Jeneba's hair. Dismay spread through her but Jeneba forced herself to remain motionless.

The legs and other arm peeled away. Keeping a tight grip on
Jeneba's hair, the uchami wiggled from beneath her.

Jeneba hardly dared to breathe. Using the uchami's own
movements to cover her own, she slowly slid her hand inside
her tsara to the knife and drew it.

Through slitted eyes she watched the uchami kneel beside
her. The hand in her hair jerked her head back. Then the
uchami leaned forward, silhouetted against the fading red-
ochre of the sky. The cloying sweetness of the herb filled
Jeneba's nose. The uchami's mouth opened.

Jeneba drove her blade upward into the bloody maw.

Howling, the uchami flung backward.

The moment the grip on her hair loosened, Jeneba rolled
sideways onto her feet and sprinted for her horse. Before her
hands could touch the reins, however, he shied, rearing. At
the same moment Jeneba heard movement behind her. She
spun to find the uchami incredibly spitting out the knife as
though it were no more than a seed from the middle of some
fruit. The beautiful girl's face smiled at her, so human but
for the bloody lips, then the beast charged.

Jeneba dodged aside. Dashing back in the direction the
uchami had come, she swooped up her knife and spun to
brandish it at the beast. The uchami still charged straight for
her.

The blade slid aside as though the creature were made of
stone, not flesh.

Jeneba retreated barely in time. The uchami's nails raked
her forearm.

Shaken, she danced backward out of reach and jammed
the knife back in its sheath. If the knife, too, was useless,
how in Ello's name could she kill the uchami?

Her mind raced. Thought of the knife touched something
in the back of memory . . . no, it had to do with invulnerability to a knife. A song, a tale of a wicked warrior who could
not be harmed by knife or spear or arrow, no weapon of
metal. But one kind of weapon nullified the charm against
metal . . . wood.

Jeneba reached back for an arrow as she dodged another
charge. She fled, putting distance between her and the beast,
then paused to break the arrow over her knee, and with a

piece of arrow in each hand, whirled just in time to meet the uchami's rush. Jeneba rammed the splintered ends of the wooden shaft into each of the beast's wide, so-human-looking eyes.

The uchami reeled backward, screaming in agony.

Without waiting to see if the stroke was fatal, Jeneba fled for her horse. He shied again, but this time she caught the flying reins and his mane and used his momentum to pull her on.

They did not slow down until Jeneba could no longer hear the uchami's shrieks.

She spent the day in a lone tree by a spring with the bay grazing hobbled below. Only after first cutting a branch with her knife, however, and sharpening the wood into an arrow-length stabbing spear, and not before she sawed her hair off to fuzz again. No one would *ever* use her hair in a fight again!

Sleep came hard. Water cleaned the wounds on her neck and draping the kadoru around her kept the flies off, but nothing stopped the pain. Every movement of neck and shoulders sent a searing blast through the muscles. Perhaps she should risk visiting some witch doctor for a healing ointment?

No. She had to avoid all villages and domestic herds. No one must have proof of which direction she had taken, not until she found Tomo Silla.

Wedged into a sun-dappled fork in the still heat of midday, she watched the eland and wildebeest grazing beyond her horse and grimaced. Leopards liked lounging in trees by day, too. Despite herself, she seemed forced into the habits of her father.

In a few days the pain eased. By the time her busumwo and peppers ran out, even the stiffness in her shoulders had faded enough not to interfere with hunting. She found herself copying the big cats there, too . . . creeping hunched through the grass until close enough to bring down an antelope or eland. That she could use only a small portion of the kill bothered her, but the hyenas, jackals, and vultures who converged to scavenge the rest made sure nothing went to waste.

Once, a leopard carried off the carcass. "Thank you, sister," it called after her.

Jeneba hurried away without replying.

When the next village she passed was a cluster of circular compounds—abandoned, judging by the collapsing conical roofs of the woven-grass huts—rather than the west-facing U-shape of Dasan settlements, she knew she had entered the lands claimed by the nomadic Burdamu. The knowledge brought a sharp pang. From now on, anyone she met would be a stranger.

She hand-fished for her meal that afternoon on waking, but only after peering closely to make sure the shapes beneath the surface of the stream were fish, not ghosts or water spirits waiting to pull her under. Rapidly spinning the blunt end of her stabbing spear against another dry, flattened stick provided her with fire and soon the fish roasted over it on a spit made from yet another stick.

Something moaned.

Her horse flung up his head, snorting. Jeneba spun with her knife in one hand and the stabbing spear in the other. But saw nothing.

The bay blew through his nostrils. Carefully, Jeneba followed the direction of his stare. His attention seemed to be fixed on a small grove of trees upstream.

She took a tighter grip on her weapons. "Come out," she called in Burda.

No one answered. Nothing stirred in the grove. Jeneba sniffed the air but detected nothing like the carrion-breath of a wachiru or the decaying-flesh reek of a demon, nor even sweet herbs like those the uchami used to hide the smell of its breath. But there was something. She tested the air again. A human scent, only . . . not quite human.

"Who's in there!"

Only leaves replied, stirred by the breeze.

Jeneba turned back to her fish. All her straining senses remained focused on the grove, though. There! A sound . . . a rattle of branches. She whirled toward the grove, but still saw nothing, and once more smelled only that tantalizing whiff of something not-quite-human.

With nerves stretched taut, she turned away again, and then, as branches rattled again, realized with a chill that a thorny bush at the edge of the grove did not sit in the same position where she first saw it.

She spun to find the bush—now with arms, a head, and feet—charging her. Jeneba scooped a burning brand from her fire and hurled it at the bush-man.

He flung himself sideways. "No, no! Take it away!" The grass where the brand landed began smoldering. The bush-man shrieked, "Put it out! Put it out!"

"Not until you leave." A flame jumped. Jeneba let it burn.

The bush-man fled back to the grove in a rattle of branches.

Jeneba beat out the small fire with her kadoru and triumphantly returned to her fish.

Then she heard the sobbing.

She stiffened. The bush-man? Surely not, unless it was a trick. Trying to ignore the sound, she tested the fish with the point of her knife. Ready. Jeneba picked the spit off the fire and laid the fish aside to cool.

The sobbing continued unabated.

After a while the sound rasped on her nerves. Taking another brand from the fire, she stalked into the grove. The bush-man sat at the bottom of a tree, head bowed and almost hidden among the black-thorned branches growing from his body.

She scowled down at him. "You can stop, bush-man. An uchami has tricked me by pretending to be in distress. Nothing else will."

The bush-man shrank back from the flame. "I wasn't going to hurt you." Free from the shrillness of panic, he had a deep, rich voice. "I only wanted the fish."

She blinked. "The *fish*?"

Tears ran down his cheeks. "It's been so long since I've eaten cooked meat, not since I was a man."

Jeneba blinked again. "A man?"

His chin came up. "Once I was Burdamu. A wizard bewitched me into . . . this." He flicked at a branch.

He did have the elongated head and hands and blue-black skin of a Burdamu, and though his hair was a shaggy mane instead of a horse tail gathered on top of his head, his forehead and cheeks bore the Burdamu's V-patterns of dotted-line scars.

Her suspicion wavered, slowly giving way to pity. "It's a large fish. We can share."

For a moment he stared in disbelief, then his face lighted with joy. Could that be feigned?

Just in case, she kept the campfire between them, but the bush-man never seemed to notice as he gobbled down his portion of the fish.

"How long have you been a bush-man?" she asked.

"I can't remember." He worried at the fish's bones, licking the last scraps of meat from them. "A very long time. I was a handsome man, the most handsome man in the camp. All the women wanted me to be their lover." He looked up and grinned. "I tried."

It was a charming grin. Jeneba found herself smiling back. "Why were you bewitched?"

The grin faded. He licked his fingers. "Among my people adultery is a grave offense. Some of my lovers were married." He grimaced. "I think one must have been the wife of a wizard."

Jeneba frowned. "Couldn't your witch doctor counter the witchcraft?"

He sighed. "Two of my other lovers were the witch doctor's wives."

She clapped her hands over her mouth too late. The whoop of laughter leaked through them. But it died instantly in horror at herself and remorse over his stricken expression. "Please, I'm sorry. It's wrong to laugh at the tragedy of another. I don't know why I did." Or why she still wanted to.

To her astonishment, the bush-man suddenly began laughing, too. He chuckled. He howled. He rolled over helplessly on his side, branches crackling. Jeneba stared.

Finally he sat up, wiping his eyes. "It has been a long time since I've laughed, and almost as long since I've talked to another person." He paused. "I was called Ngmengo."

She smiled. "I am Jeneba."

He peered at her. "And not fully human, either, I think."

She grimaced. "My father was a leopard-man."

He looked pleased. "The leopard is the totem of my clan. How can I repay your kindness, leopard's daughter?"

Must everyone keep referring to her sire? "It isn't necessary. Unless—have you heard of Yagana?"

Ngmengo arched his brows. "Who has not? Cities make captives. Men were meant to be free, to follow their cattle to the good grass and weave their huts where they wish. But if the Burdamu were to choose captivity, it would be Yagana."

"Am I headed toward it?"

"Most assuredly. In a few days you will see mountains rising to the north. Head west of the tallest peak and I am told Yagana lies at its foot."

Now she thought of another question even more important. "Have you seen anyone else passing this way in the last few months? It would be a man, the same height and color as I am, but with his head shaved and face scarred in the Malekuro fashion."

The bush-man shook his head.

She sucked in her cheeks. That meant nothing. Tomo could have gone another route, perhaps the less direct one from Chizomwe. Perhaps not, either. The man in Yagana could really be Malekuro and have been there for years. Her entire journey might be for nothing.

She glanced west. Lesa's eye almost touched the horizon. Pushing to her feet, she tossed dust over the fire. "I must go."

"So soon."

The bush-man's sigh wrenched at her. Mounting and riding away, she felt him staring after her. Impulsively she turned to call back, "I'll come this way again and we'll share another fish."

His nod had the stiffness of someone longing to believe but not daring to.

"On my word as a noble and Dasa!" Just as soon as she found Tomo Silla and took him to face Kiba.

In the fading day the plains stirred to life. Birds called overhead. A buffalo bellowed in the distance, answered by the grunt of a wildebeest. A baboon male keeping watch on the tall spire of a termite mound screamed a warning to the troupe below of some predator. On a nearby slope a pride of lions sprawled on their backs and sides, seemingly oblivious to everything . . . she and her horse, the baboons, the zebra grazing below . . . even the cubs tumbling over them and batting at an occasional twitch of tail. While Jeneba watched, however, one lioness shook off the cub on her and climbed to her feet, stretching languorously. She nudged another lioness, who grunted, but after a moment also stood and pawed another lioness in turn. Soon all of the adult members of the pride were shambling down the slope, all except the male. He snarled at the lioness nudging him and flopped his head back to the ground.

Zebra heads jerked up, ears pricking toward the lions. All but one lioness dropped onto their bellies and began fanning out stealthily sideways . . . alternately creeping and freezing. The other lioness remained on her feet in plain sight, padding through the grass but never crossing that invisible line of safety margin the grazers drew around themselves. And while the zebra watched, waiting for her to cross that line and send them into flight, her sisters circled the herd.

Jeneba watched, too, turning on her horse to keep track of the hunt as she passed. Until a sudden scent of humans and flash of movement at the edge of her vision jerked her attention forward. Four tall, blue-black men leaped from the grass around her, reaching for her horse. Burdamu, but not herders, instinct told her instantly. Outlaws!

The bay reared in a squeal of alarm. Jeneba kicked at one man. Her foot caught him under the chin, knocking him backward. Another outlaw, though, managed to grab the mane with one hand and reach for her arm with the other.

Jeneba hauled the reins sideways. As the bay came down again, she rammed her heels into the animal's sides. He wheeled, bowling over a third man, and bolted into a gallop.

The outlaw still hung on. Jeneba hammered at him to no avail, and he caught her wrist in the bargain. A quick twist freed her, only to have him reach for her arm again.

He grinned. "You're spirited. How sad we have to break you of that before we can sell you to the Djero or Buwa."

She swung for his nose but he ducked. She bared her teeth. What did it take to knock this hyena off?

Then she saw the direction they headed. The snarl became a grin as she grabbed the mane.

Squealing zebra scattered before her, and the lioness poised to launch herself at one of them reared up almost underneath the bay. He leaped straight sideways. Jeneba's hold on the mane was all that kept her astride.

The outlaw lost his hold. Moments later a shriek behind her told Jeneba that the lioness had fallen happily on this prey which Ogata, god of the hunt, laid before her.

Jeneba chuckled in glee. The amusement was short-lived, however. Over the slope behind her came four more outlaws, mounted this time, and the bay tried to wheel toward them, away from the lion scent before him.

Her mind raced. She could force the horse into a path across theirs. Could she outrun them? While she would normally wager the bay's endurance against the speed of any other horse, the outlaws' mounts were almost certain to be better rested. Forget running, then. No matter. Attack was better than going on the defensive anyway, and she remembered a tactic Quada Malam told about his people using.

Praying to Kuta, the spear-headed god of war, weapons, metal, and fire, and guiding the bay with her knees, she whipped the bow off her back. If only she did not fumble the stringing, doing it on a galloping horse.

Kuta smiled. The bow strung on the first attempt. One of the outlaws dropped flat on his mount's neck. The remaining three did not understand until an arrow sank into one's chest.

Her second arrow missed as its target ducked. But he also lost his balance and tumbled into the grass. She aimed for a third outlaw.

The arrow impaled his horse's shoulder. The animal somersaulted over the lamed leg to land flat on its side, and on its rider. Three gone. And she was past them.

Wheeling the bay, she nocked another arrow . . . only to find the outlaw who had ducked first almost on top of her. The bow became a club lashing at his head and reaching hand. He caught it and jerked.

If she hung on to the bow she would be pulled from her

horse. Jeneba released it. But the outlaw also caught her reins, and down the slope she could see the three remaining men afoot racing toward her. When they arrived, a chill instinct whispered, they would spread out to surround her, like the lionesses.

The outlaw saw them, too. His dark face split in a grin. "You belong to us, Dasa."

She fought a wave of panic.

Which died in a grin.

Behind the three, gaining in leaps and bounds, raced a thorn bush. It hurtled at the outlaws. Two went screaming under it.

The outlaw holding Jeneba's horse jerked around. She went for her knife and slashed the outlaw's near leg and his hand holding her reins, then jerking back her bow, she kicked the bay into a run. The outlaw who had fallen from his horse saw her break loose. He nocked an arrow of his own.

"Cousin lions!" she shouted. "I give you your supper."

The outlaw spun in terror toward where the pride tore at the body of the one outlaw. Jeneba ran the bay over the top of him.

Ngmengo the bush-man had thrown himself on the third man now, she saw. He pulled back. All three staggered, moaning, bleeding hands to bleeding faces. The pride looked around, eyeing them.

The deep voice of the male called, "We accept them, and thank you, cousin leopard."

Jeneba urged the bay north, away from the screams and smell of blood.

The bush-man bounded along beside her. She smiled down at him. "*I* thank *you*, Ngmengo. You pay your debts quickly."

He shook his head. "The benefit is still to me. How can you come back to cook me another fish if I let outlaws sell you into slavery?" He paused. "Perhaps you would let me accompany you a bit farther . . . in case there are more of these hyenas? Since I never sleep, I could stand watch while you rest."

She regarded the bush-man thoughtfully, an idea stirring.

"If you're not restricted to a certain territory, how would you like to accompany me all the way to Yagana?"

The whites of his eyes glistened in the fading light. "Do you truly mean that?"

"Two travel more safely than one. I can offer you companionship and cooked meat, and the chance to see Yagana. What I can't offer you is a ride." She smiled. "You'll have to walk."

He grinned. "What's a horse but a witless creature who fears everything and goes lame at every pebble and thorn? Burdamu have followed our cattle on foot for generations upon generations. Daughter of my totem, for someone to talk to and food cooked on a fire, I would walk to the ends of the earth or the underworld of our ancestral ghosts."

CHAPTER

FOUR

The day had the glow of a new-made world. Lesa's eye burned golden above the wooded hills and air crisply clean from rain that had fallen during the night. A gentle breeze carried a hundred animal smells and the sweet fragrances of green growing things. As much as she had begun enjoying the world of night, Jeneba did not regret changing to daylight travel. Leading her horse along the woods trail after Ngmengo, Jeneba breathed deeply and savored the scents. It had to be just such a day that tempted Nbalo and Aminuba, the first man and woman, into leaving Heaven and sliding down the rainbow serpent Binwa to earth. So perhaps they had not truly minded that the Binwa's scales proved too slippery to climb back up, forcing them to remain on earth.

A bird's screech overhead interrupted her reverie. Jeneba quickly sniffed the air again, testing for the source of the bird's alarm . . . animal predators or monsters and demons haunting the forest. She had detected a number of them since entering the hills, but except for one nogama, always soon enough to avoid meeting them. The nogama had come from downwind and, like the uchami back on the plains, looked incredibly manlike as it stepped onto the trail ahead of them. But its tail had betrayed it for a demon. Ngmengo jumped in front of Jeneba just as the nogama sprang, its hands spread to expose the terrible claw growing from each palm. It flung itself aside and fled snarling. Not even demons cared for the bush-man's thorny branches.

But now she smelled nothing dangerous in the air. The bay showed no signs of alarm, either, just picked his way along the trail with foot-weary care. Jeneba sucked in another breath. New scents had joined the others. Welcome ones. "I smell water, Ngmengo."

His eyes glittered. "Lake Kujhata."

Her pulse jumped. That meant . . . Yagana. At last. For four days they had passed valleys with increasingly larger villages and cities inhabited by a magnificent people . . . shorter than she, muscular, narrow-nosed, fine-lipped, skins colored the light bright yellow-red of new copper. Their intricately braided hair shone copper, too. Just when she felt sure she had reached the fabled city, though, someone they asked would laugh and shake his or her head.

"This poor village? You flatter us. Yagana is far bigger and finer than this. But Yagana belongs to us. We are Kurasi, and the Kurasi and Yagana are one."

"What do they mean?" Jeneba asked Ngmengo.

The bush-man replied, "Their legends say that when the first man Jhokete was sent down from heaven by his father Kuma, the sun, he used the mud from Lake Kujhata to make himself a wife. then his sons built Yagana from the same mud. So every Kurasi is kin to the city, and the city is part of every Kurasi."

She smiled. "You sound like a bard."

He glanced back with a rueful sigh. "I could have been. My father was training me to follow him."

"Is that why you know so much about another tribe's legends?"

"No." He grimaced. "That came of loneliness, after I stopped being so angry about my bewitchment that I attacked every man I saw. At night I would creep close to the camps of Burdamu and travelers and sit listening to them talk and sing. I—look!"

They had reached the top of the hill. Below, the trees thinned and the slope flattened into a huge valley, where orchard groves alternated with broad fields of grain and green pastures dotted by cattle, sheep, and horses. Across the valley the land rose toward the peaks of the Bumala Mountains. West, the waters of Lake Kujhata stretched to the horizon, shallow, marshy, with the shadows of hippos and crocodiles sliding beneath its surface.

And in the center of the valley, surrounded by open

meadows that no enemy could steal across undetected, sat a city. Though city seemed an inadequate word. Jeneba stared in awe. Kiba shrank to a village by comparison. Yagana sprawled out and out, thick walls the color of copper swallowing the valley floor. Instead of one gate it had four, facing north, south, east, and west, and a long common stretching inward from each to meet in the center.

Jeneba breathed deeply. Four, the number of power, repeated four times: four gates, four quarters, four commons . . . and most potent of all, a meeting of four ways within. The gods must rule here.

Markets filled all but the western common. The figures of people swarmed through those markets like inhabitants of a termite mound. In the quarters of the city between the commons, the roofs made an almost unbroken surface. Only a few twisting passages showed here and there to divide one building from another.

"It's even more than I thought from the stories," she breathed.

Ngmengo sighed. "Yes. Yet one day it must be abandoned. I hear that each year less rain falls, and see, the lake is drying up." He pointed toward the band of barren red mud around the water's edge.

"No!" she protested.

His branches shifted in a rustling shrug. "Kuma wills, as the Kurasi say. But for now the city thrives. Half the world must live here. How will you ever find your traitor?"

The question had just occurred to her, but . . . she had not come all this way to turn back because of a little difficulty. "I'll look hard. Will you come in with me?"

"Into a city? No. I—" He broke off, biting his lip, staring down at Yagana. "Well, maybe this once, just to see it."

The city grew more awesome with every step. The thickness of the walls made its southern gate a tunnel which at its mouth towered above them in a massive, sheer red cliff that made Jeneba feel like an ant.

The view from the hilltop and outside had only suggested the true grandeur of Yagana. Inside the sandy-red building walls rose six or seven times the height of a man, carved with the images of great animals: lions, elephants, buffalo, giraffe, rhinos. Sound assaulted her, horses neighing, pigs squealing, dogs' barking, and voice upon human voice chattering in Burda and dozens of other languages and dialects. Smell overwhelmed her with a profusion of scents from plants, animals, and humans, dizzying, tantalizing. What did that spicy odor come from? Or that musky one?

And who were all these people? She recognized a few of the tribes—Burdamu, child-sized Ifute from the southern forests, Buwa, Abedda traders—but most she had never seen before. Around her in suffocating numbers swarmed people of all heights, all colors from light yellow-brown to blue-black, faces with broad flattened noses, faces with long narrow noses, shaved heads, heads with hair braided in all manners, heads shaved but for a sagital crest braided or dressed with oil and ochre powder into a tall, stiff red crest, bodies scarred in all manners, bodies painted white or red, lighter bodies tattooed with geometric designs or the images of birds and snakes and lizards. Metal coils supported impossibly long necks. Ears drooped to the shoulders, laden with rings. Wooden plugs stretched lips to astonishing size. And the tribesmen wore everything from a hip cord with leaves draped front and back to cloth draping the entire body with holes cut for the head and arms. Jewelry rattled on ankles, encircled arms, hung on ears, piled layer on layer around necks.

She wondered if she and the horse could have forced their way through but for the bush-man. Everyone gave him room.

Tears ran down his face. "What a cursed creature I am! Look at the women. Have you ever seen so many exquisite creatures? It is a feast; I cannot even nibble!"

It was a feast, yes . . . for the eyes and ears and nose. The market left Jeneba agog. More goods than she had ever imagined lay displayed beneath not mere parasols but vast lines of open-sided tents made of colorful cloth or from woven grass mats. As in Kiba, women tended most of the displays, calling out the virtues of their wares to the people streaming by . . . fruit and grains and vegetables of dizzying variety, cloth and spices, leather goods, pottery, jewelry, musical instruments. Nothing as individual as a drum sat on

display, of course, but Jeneba saw a woman representing a
drum-maker, and another offering the services of a smith
who could make knives which, according to her, never lost
their edge, and spears that never missed a target. Several
women had large displays of stools, drum-shaped for the
most part. That astonished Jeneba until she remembered that
some tribes regarded a stool as just a place to sit, not a
personalized item indicative of rank and family position.

Male traders offered animals for sale, not only livestock
but exotic creatures: monkeys, screaming as they lunged
around their cages, cheetah cubs, and smaller cats like cara-
cals and servals.

Jeneba sucked in her cheeks in awe and dismay. How
would she find Tomo in such a mass of people? Back in Kiba
she had imagined herself asking the first person she met
where to find the Malekuro of Tomo's description. But then,
she had also expected to find a city not much larger than
Kiba. Now . . . she had better plan on spending days searching, which meant also finding a way to eat, and somewhere
to sleep. It also occurred to her, as it somehow had not
before, to wonder: if she found the man, and he *was* Tomo,
what could she do if he refused to return with her?

She forgot the question momentarily in the pain of running into the thorns of Ngmengo's rear branches. The bush-
man had stopped short at musical instruments displayed on a
bright red ground cloth. While the Kurasi woman gaped at
him from her stool behind it, he leaned down to pick up a
bone flute carved with a vine design. The marketwoman had
the same pattern, worked in delicate dotted scarring that
wound from her cheeks and neck across bare shoulders and
down around her arms.

Ngmengo blew a few sweet, clear notes.

The marketwoman recovered her composure. "That is a
fine instrument. Made of antelope bone so the music will
always dance lightly."

The instrument maker had used animals in his harps, too,
Jeneba noticed, the boss and horns of cattle and larger antelope for three-stringed ones, ribs for the one-stringed bow-
harps, polished to the gloss of ivory. Carved snakes wrapped
the ribs in long coils.

The marketwoman followed her gaze. "Very fine bow-harps, too. They sing as beautifully as Bisiri's original."

Whose original?

"Who was Bisiri?" the bush-man asked the marketwoman.

Jeneba fought the urge to dive out of sight around the far side of her horse. Why did he say that and make them sound ignorant?

And indeed the marketwoman's tone implied they must have been living in the far bush all their lives as she replied. "The prince whose pride lost Yagana, of course."

Ngmengo's eyes brightened. "I've never heard the story. Can you point me to a bard who—"

"By Kuma, what's come to Yagana now?" a voice exclaimed.

The mocking tone jabbed Jeneba. She swung around in irritation.

Two men stood on the other side of her horse, staring at Ngmengo . . . bright-skinned Kurasi dressed identically in garments made of loosely woven, indigo-and-saffron striped cloth hanging straight from the shoulders to the knees with the sides closed between arm and waistline. A sweet-oil scent drifted to her from them.

One with hair braided in precise rows from the hairline up to a topknot had dotted line scars circling the outside of both eyes and wavy lines of scarring down the outsides of his legs. He grinned at his companion. "The seers are wrong about the sand coming for Yagana. Obvious it's to be forest."

No scars interrupted the smooth sheen of the companion's skin. A fringe of short pigtails around his hairline bounced as he nodded. "Which might be useful, not a curse. If we train them to stand shoulder to shoulder, they'll make an ideal fence for our cattle."

Irritation flared to anger. Jeneba ducked under the bay's neck. "Is this the hospitality of Yagana, ridiculing its visitors!"

They stared at her. The unscarred one drew himself up, as though trying to reach her eye level. "Who are you? His wife?"

She crossed her arms. "I am Jeneba Karamoke, Dasa, noble, and a warrior of Kiba."

"Warrior?" They snickered. "A *woman* warrior?"

For a moment she blinked in bewilderment at what they found so amusing, then her anger blazed. Not even her most critical fellow Dasa had ever scoffed at her ability as a warrior. Her hand itched to pull her knife, but an honorable warrior used bladed weapons in single combat only with an equal. She reached for the strap tying her kadoru on the bay's back.

Thorns blocked the way. "Soften your belly," Ngmengo muttered.

The Burdamu way of saying: cool her heart. Probably wise advice. If she made trouble, she might be thrown out of the city and never find Tomo. Still, this insult could not be allowed to go unanswered.

Jeneba bared her teeth. "You're amused by my friend and me. Do contests also entertain you?"

They stopped laughing to eye her. "Contests?"

"Footracing and wrestling. I'll race and wrestle either of you for a prize of my arm bands." She held out her arms to show off the copper and ivory.

The unscarred one snorted. Both turned away.

"What?" she called after them. "Are Yagana's men so timid?"

The scarred one spun back. "Yagana's warriors are too honorable to steal a pretty woman's trinkets."

"Ah?" She smiled thinly. "How can you be warriors when you're afraid to test yourselves against me?"

That stung, she saw. Muscles twitched along their jaws.

Jeneba kept prodding. "Or perhaps you don't feel the prize is worth the possible loss of face. So. I'll be the prize. Whoever of you bests me in a footrace or wrestling can spend tonight demonstrating his spearwork."

They looked her over with new appraisal, eyes flaring, and Jeneba watched with satisfaction. Good. Adding lust to anger trapped them.

"Meet us on the heroes' terrace at the head of the west common," the scarred one said, and the two marched away.

"What about finding Tomo Silla?" Ngmengo asked.

She stared after the Kurasi warriors. "Personal honor comes even before Tomo Silla."

"You're a foolish girl," the marketwoman behind the musical instruments said. "Ododo Yanka and Chomba Lijhuma are among the best warriors in the king's army."

Jeneba frowned. "All the more reason to teach them not to ridicule visitors."

The building on the southwest corner where the four commons met had been constructed with its outer wall on the diagonal, leaving a large, triangular platform ankle-high and shaded by a canopy of scarlet-and-black striped cloth. As Jeneba and Ngmengo approached, the two warriors and other Kurasi men also wearing saffron and indigo rose from drum-shaped stools to come to the platform edge. The others stared.

Someone whispered in the Kurasi language. Several other men smothered laughter.

Tight-lipped, Jeneba tossed the bay's reins to Ngmengo. "Who is my opponent?"

"Neither," replied a man standing to one side of the warriors. His hair had been braided in a spiral that started at the top of his head and ended with a copper-beaded pigtail hanging down his left temple. Spiral scars decorated both cheeks, his forearms, and the outsides of his thighs. His eyes swept her. "I am Duaffa Luze, a commander in the army of his majesty King Biratha and Yagana, and I can't permit this contest. It's unfair to you."

Jeneba flung up her head, hissing. "Unfair! When I'm answering an insult? Or don't you believe I'm a warrior, either?"

"I believe," Duaffa said. "I've heard of the Dasan warrior women. But you're still a woman. Ododo and Chomba are heavier and stronger. How can you win?"

"Do you fight a battle only when you're assured of victory?"

He regarded her in silence a moment, then sighed. "Very well. No magic is allowed, though, no charms to help you run faster, no ointment to make you impossible to hold in wrestling."

"No magic." She lifted her chin. "On my honor as a Dasa and noble and a warrior, I bring nothing but my blood and spirit."

"Then we'll throw bones to determine your opponent."

"Give them both a chance," she said. "Let one run the race and the other wrestle."

Duaffa scowled. "That *is* unfair. The second one will be fresh when you aren't."

She set her jaw. "The choice is mine."

He shrugged and shook his head. The two warriors grinned. Mentally licking their lips in anticipation of victory, no doubt, Jeneba thought acidly.

In the babble of warriors all speaking their own language, Jeneba caught Chomba's name several times. The unscarred warrior hopped down to the common and strutted across it, grinning.

Duaffa stepped off the terrace, too. He used his knife to scratch a line in the grass in the middle of the common. "Chomba races. Start at my signal, run to the gate and back. Prepare."

Jeneba handed her bow and arrows to Ngmengo. As she lined up beside Chomba, the Kurasi smirked at her.

"My spear is long and sharp, as I'll be pleased to show you."

"Take care not to wound yourself on it in the race first," she snapped.

"Go!"

They leaped forward.

Chomba ran well, she gave him that. He could have beaten most of the warriors in Kiba. She adjusted her stride to stay beside him. Halfway to the gate he glanced sideways and frowned. Annoyed to find her keeping pace? He speeded up. So did she.

Turning at the gate, he tightened his jaw and leaped forward in a greater burst of speed. Jeneba pushed to keep beside him. This time the frown that accompanied his side glance carried angry disbelief, and perhaps concern. He leaned into his stride, stretching himself, straining until he must be running harder than he ever had in his life. His breath rasped like that of a wind-broken horse. Staying with him came harder than she had expected, but she matched him stride for stride, and reveled in the strength driving her legs and in the liquid flow of her muscles. Then as they reached the heroes' terrace, she imagined herself as a leopard springing for a fleeing antelope. The effort carried her over the line a body-length ahead of the Kurasi warrior.

Amid a chorus of hoots and cheers from warriors on the terrace and a crowd of curious citizens who had gathered at the head of the common, Ododo called out. Jeneba looked back to see a brighter red tone in Chomba's skin.

The warrior saw her looking at him and smiled thinly. "My friend Ododo says it's kind of me to let you win so that he may have you for himself tonight."

"Perhaps he'll be surprised."

Duaffa snapped something that stopped the hooting. Turning to Jeneba, he asked, "Do you need to rest?"

"No." While she breathed deeply, willing her breath and heart to slow down, she untied her tsara at the shoulder and dropped it.

Duaffa eyed her. "You have no loincloth?"

"I didn't expect to be wrestling here."

He called to the watching warriors. Someone produced a loincloth for her. Duaffa nodded approval as she tied it on. "Both shoulders must touch the ground for a fall. Three falls wins."

Jeneba crouched across the line from the scar-decorated Ododo. For a moment, though, her attention wandered past him to the gathered crowd, studying them. None looked immediately familiar, not among the crowd from the markets nor the warriors on the heroes' terrace, nor among the Kurasi gathering on the wall of the building on the northwest corner of this city center. Warriors in saffron and indigo guarded its tall, broad gate. More appeared on the wall. The king's palace. What else would stand at this crossing of the four commons, except perhaps a god-house?

A Kurasi woman came out of the gate and crossed the common behind Jeneba to the heroes' terrace. Each step opened the sides of her ankle-length saffron garment to bare a long, sleek leg and hip. Her hair hung to her waist in long strings of braid, past strings of beads around her neck, and past arm bands of some metal too brightly yellow to be copper coiling like snakes around each upper arm. A beautiful woman, and an important one to judge by the heads bowing and the space being cleared for her on the terrace. She stared at Jeneba with an intensity Jeneba felt like a physical touch.

"Are you ready?" Duaffa said.

Jeneba jerked her attention back to Ododo. He stood crouched, grinning in anticipation. She crouched, too.

"Wrestle."

Ododo grabbed for her arm and pulled it across him, obviously expecting to take the first fall quickly by using his weight to drag her down and pin her. Before he could squat to reach for her leg, however, she locked onto his arm and dropped. The pull and his own movement forward sent him belly-down in the grass. A quick change of her grip to the back of his neck and a leg, a lift on the leg . . . and he somersaulted over to land flat on his back. Jeneba threw herself across him.

"Fall to the Dasa," Duaffa said.

The warriors hooted. Chomba called something in a questioning voice.

When they crouched for the second fall, Ododo wore no grin.

This time he engaged more cautiously, head to head, his hands on her upper arms. They pushed against each other, testing . . . engaged tighter, his head against her shoulder, hers against his, hands shifting their grip, exploring for weaknesses. Then he abruptly rolled his right arm, breaking her hold on his elbow, grabbed her arm with both hands, and stepped forward, hooking his right leg behind hers.

Just another variation of his move in the first round. She locked on his arm and let him trip her, but dragged him down with her and reached for the back of his thigh. As they hit the grass, she rolled him over. That should have put her on top of him, but his hand grabbed the hip string of her loincloth and pulled. The roll continued one more half turn . . . and he lay on top.

"Fall to Ododo," Duaffa said.

The warrior's grin returned.

Jeneba clenched her jaw. So. He could think and react quickly. She would remember that.

The third round she made the first move, breaking from the head-to-head tie-up hold to drop to her knees and tackle him. That caught him just enough by surprise that she had him down on the ground under her, but far from under control. He rolled and reached backward to grab her arm and break her hold. She found another. He broke it, flipped, landed on her. She broke free and came up on top of him again. But this time she locked her legs around him and set her fingers like claws. When she flipped him onto his head and the back of his shoulders, he could not move.

"Fall to the Dasa."

Ododo's fellow warriors called shrilly at him and leaned back, whooping in laughter. He crouched for the fourth round with lips set in a grim line.

Jeneba glanced toward the Kurasi woman. She was saying nothing. She appeared not even to have moved on her stool, only sat staring unwaveringly at Jeneba.

"Wrestle," Duaffa said.

The white rims of Ododo's eyes told her he longed to hurl himself at her, to overcome her with brute force and tie the contest. But he did not. He engaged head-to-head, moved on to a tie-up, then tried a classical trip. It failed. She ducked under his arm to grab him from behind for a takedown. He countered with a hip lock which she escaped only because of her agility and strength. Then from a tie-up she reached one of his legs, and they were on the grass again, rolling, flipping, each applying holds, each countering. He wrestled well. He had a defense for every offense, and a way to turn each of her defensive moves against his opponent. But so did she, plus the agility, speed, and strength of her father's spirit. The moment came when he could not break her hold and could not counter her move.

"Fall to the Dasa; match to the Dasa," Duaffa said.

Jeneba offered him a hand to help him to his feet. He slapped it away, snarling.

Chomba stepped out of the warriors surrounding them to catch his friend's arm. "We might as well admit it . . . she's very good," he said in Burda, and grinned at Jeneba. "I think I'm glad we don't have to fight you Dasa and your warrior women. I'm ashamed that I ever laughed at you or your thorny friend. I beg you to forgive me."

Ododo bit his lip as he eyed the warriors watching him, but managed a smile. "I'm ashamed, too, and I also ask for your pardon."

She smiled back. "Given gladly. You're a fine wrestler and I would rather be your friend than your opponent. I—"

The words choked off in her throat. A head rose behind the coppery ones of the laughing, chattering warriors, a head richly red-brown, familiar despite a shaved head and scars stretching across both cheeks from the nostrils.

Tomo Silla.

All the way from Kiba she had tried to imagine this encounter. In some versions she drew herself up and hissed, "Traitor!" Sometimes she chased a Tomo who fled from her on sight. Sometimes he threw himself at her feet begging forgiveness. Always she had been dignified and cool-hearted, always in control. She had never seen herself standing paralyzed and open-mouthed.

He turned away.

Jeneba's paralysis broke. She plunged after him, frantically elbowing a path for herself through the warriors. But by the time she broke through, his striped tsara, the same cloth the warriors wore, had vanished from sight.

She whirled, looking for the bush-man. "Ngmengo! Tomo's here. Did you see him? Where did he go?"

"The Malekuro who stood on the heroes' terrace during the wrestling match? There." Ngmengo pointed toward the north market. "You're sure he's your traitor?"

"Yes!" Even saying it, though, uncertainty crawled through her. She had seen no fear in his face, not even recognition. But . . . he *must* be Tomo.

She started for the north common.

"Dasa!" Duaffa's voice barked. "Wait!"

If she did, the man would completely vanish in the crowd. And if she did not? This was a Kurasi city and she a foreigner. Reluctantly, she turned.

The commander stood at the edge of the warriors with the Kurasi woman behind him. "Why did you come to Yagana?"

Why did he want to know? She could not lie while standing on this ground, but the Malekuro had stood among the warriors and wore a tsara of the same striped cloth the warriors dressed in, obviously somehow connected to them. Her mind raced, searching for a truthful answer short of *the* truth. "I've heard of Yagana all my life from the Abedda traders. I wanted to see it."

Duaffa strolled toward her. "How long do you plan to stay?"

"I don't know." No need for evasion there.

The woman, still at his shoulder, whispered something. Duaffa asked, "Is your archery and spear-throwing equal to your racing and wrestling?"

Her neck prickled. What? "Yes. Why?"

"Our army includes more than Kurasi. We also invite outstanding visiting foreign warriors to join, so we can learn from them and improve our own fighting abilities. We'd be honored to have you become a guest warrior for as long as you're in Yagana."

Jeneba knew she must be gaping in astonishment, but at least her mind kept working. "Foreigners? Like the Malekuro?"

"Do you know Tshemba Diasi?"

Her pulse jumped. So that was what he called himself now. "He reminds me of someone I once knew. Commander Duaffa, it will be my honor to serve Yagana."

Duaffa and the woman strode away through the palace gate.

Jeneba let out her breath. "Who was the woman?"

A warrior turned to reply. "The princess Jhirazi, daughter of King Biratha and a priestess of Kuma."

"And more the king's adviser than the elders are," another muttered.

"You're really joining their army?" Ngmengo whispered.

She strolled away from the warriors and lowered her voice. "What better way to watch Tomo? Sooner or later he will reveal himself." She smiled grimly. "And I'll be there to claim him."

CHAPTER

FIVE

"Guest warriors and warriors on palace guard duty for the month all live here in the Warriors' Court," Duaffa said.

Jeneba could only nod. This room was small, little more than space enough to hold a drum-shaped stool and a grass-stuffed sleeping mat, but the size of the palace they had passed through to reach it left her wordless . . . a seemingly endless maze of long, narrow courtyards, *two* levels of rooms in each, incredibly, the walkway outside the upper making a verandah roof for the lower. And instead of standing open to the court like Dasan houses, the rooms all had a fourth wall with a doorway and a wooden door. Her gaze slid speculatively toward the sleeping mat. With such privacy, perhaps she would invite Ododo and Chomba to demonstrate their spearwork in a wrestling match neither contestant had to lose.

Then the meaning of Duaffa's statement sank in. All the guest warriors. That meant Tomo, too. She swallowed a grin of triumph. Mala smiled on her! She had wanted Ngmengo to stay in Yagana instead of living up in the woods as he insisted on doing, not only to give her someone familiar to talk to, but to be a second pair of eyes watching Tomo. However, living in the same compound as well as training together in the army, her quarry could do almost nothing without her being aware of it! Her constant presence might even help force him into self-betrayal. She would tell Ngmengo of her good luck when she took some cooked meat up to him tomorrow.

Duaffa strolled back out into the courtyard. "The court has its own kitchen and a servant woman to cook for you.

Tomorrow at spear practice you'll be given your shield and spears."

Jeneba nodded again, but scarcely heard the words. Two warriors were coming into the court through the wooden-barred gate in the long side opposite her and suddenly nothing else existed but the taller of the two. She moved from the shadow of the upper level walkway into the sun. "Greetings, cousin Malekuro."

Did he start? Was that a flicker of dismay across his face? To her irritation, the expression vanished too quickly for identification, wiped away by a nod and polite smile. "Hardly surprising after your victories over Ododo and Chomba. I congratulate you."

She listened intently to the voice. Tomo's? Some of the tonal quality sounded familiar, and yet . . . where was the pride and self-assurance that always rang under Tomo's words? This man spoke quietly, almost deferentially. Would Tomo? Could he?

Jeneba drew a deep beath, testing his scent. But all she smelled was the same sweet-oil odor Duaffa, Ododo, and Chomba gave off.

Her inward snarl stopped abruptly, though. She stared. Scars covered him. Interlocking spirals chained down his arms and parallel diagonal scars striped his thighs. Uncertainty chilled her. Would anyone endure so much pain to hide himself? Different hands had done the work at different times, too. The spirals, worked in the precise dotted lines she had seen on the marketwoman, Duaffa, and Ododo, looked more recent than the unbroken but cruder, often irregular ridges on his thighs.

Did it mean anything? The shorter warrior, a yellow-brown man with a cheetah skin wrapped around his hips and his head shaved to leave only a fuzzy little skullcap and a forelock braided into three thin pigtails, also had relatively new spirals on both arms and calves. Perhaps they were like Ifute, who when Keoru enslaved them, adopted their masters' dress, hairstyle, and scarring. The only new scar of real significance would be the one on Tomo's right cheek . . . and hard as she looked, Jeneba saw no difference between that one and its match on his left cheek. Both looked more prominent than Tomo's single scar had been.

But could a man with his honor as blackened as Tomo's continue to talk to her and show nothing? "I'm Jeneba Karamoke of Kiba," she said. "Daughter and only child of my mother Sia Nyiba, niece of my uncle Mseluku."

She watched for some reaction to indicate he knew the names. Nothing showed in either face or eyes, and he hesitated only a moment before replying. "I am Tshemba Diasi of Ntomutagu, son of my mother Rumayo, brother of my sisters Samaduka and Jajata. I look forward to talking with you later. Perhaps we'll discover mutual relatives."

He walked away with the shorter warrior.

Jeneba stared after him, biting her lip.

She watched him covertly the rest of the afternoon and evening . . . while he and several other warriors bathed in the courtyard, ladling warm water over each other . . . while everyone brought drum stools out to the hard-packed earth of the court and ate a stew of meat and vegetables and dough balls a servant woman cooked in the court's kitchen . . . and while they spent the evening under the flickering oil lamps of the courtyard entertaining themselves with jokes, riddles, and the game whose different name in every tribe translated roughly as "stones-and-cups."

If he noticed the scrutiny and was disturbed by it, he hid his feelings well. The riddling became anecdotes about tricks they had played on other people. Tomo joined with a story of how he and several other boys kept stealing and hiding the house of an ill-tempered woman. More uncertainty crawled through Jeneba as she watched him explain to the puzzled Kurasi that the Malekuro built their dome-shaped grass huts without attachment to the ground, so they could be picked up and carried to a new, clean site. He had told the story so . . . easily, with the effortless detail of something intimately familiar to him.

Tomo made all those cattle-trading trips with his uncle, though. He must know a number of Malekuron villages, some well enough to talk about them as though he lived there.

She ran her fingers through the short fuzz of her hair. Was he Tomo or not? "Mala, help me," she murmured.

"You seem troubled, warrior woman," a voice said.

Jeneba looked around to meet the eyes of the yellow-brown warrior who had come into the court with Tomo, from the Tou tribe she thought she remembered someone saying. All the names had gone by so fast during the introductions at supper. "Not troubled," she lied, "just dazed. I came to visit Yagana, not . . ." She groped for something to complete the thought.

"Defend her?" the Tou finished. "But she has called us and we will fight for her, because what will the world lose if she dies?"

Something in his tone sent a chill up her spine. She eyed him. "You sound like there's a threat."

"Perhaps." He smiled thinly. "Lubeda Madji, king of the Djero city Murijenaja, has sent warriors to the village Najhadende at the edge of Kurasi territory. He says that since many of its inhabitants are Djero, not Kurasi, the village must pay tribute to him, not Yagana. Ourassi and Menekuya, King Biratha's oldest sons, want to fight, of course. Biratha is old but still full-blooded. He's sent a messenger to King Lubeda with what most of us think is a challenge. We're waiting for a reply."

They could be going to war soon? Jeneba sucked in her cheeks and glanced sideways at Tshemba. In the heat of battle, with no time to think about anything but the enemy and self-defense, he would certainly give himself away by fighting in Tomo's style. Of course, he might be killed, too, or she might. She frowned.

One of the Kurasi brought a bow and an arrow from his room. Using the arrow laid against the string to alter the tone, he plucked an accompaniment to himself while he sang about a beautiful but sad queen and the heroic warrior who died to make her laugh.

The bowharp reminded Jeneba of the ones in the market which had been only musical instruments. On impulse, she said, "Do you know the song about Bisiri's harp?" There must be one.

The harp-player hesitated before shaking his head. "I

know the story, of course, but only bards learn the song. It's very long."

"Tell the story, then," the Tou warrior said.

Around the courtyard other warriors nodded eagerly. "Yes, tell the story." The harp-player grinned in the flickering lamplight and, laying down his bow, settled himself on his stool with great show.

Like every other storyteller she knew, Jeneba reflected with amusement.

"In ancient times," he began, "a king named Dininko ruled Yagana. Dininko had many sons and among the youngest was Bisiri, who was very unhappy. He knew he would never carry the king's shield and spear, nor was he a great warrior like many of his older brothers. We Kurasi have a saying: no man is truly dead until he is forgotten. Bisiri feared that because he excelled in nothing, he would be forgotten and therefore die true death. This preyed on him so much that he went to a wise man of Yagana and asked, 'What can I do that all generations yet unborn will remember Bisiri?' The wise man said, 'If you make a bowharp from a rib given to you by its owner, you will become immortal. But Yagana will be lost.' Bisiri scoffed that anything could destroy Yagana, and set about finding a rib to make his bowharp. But he couldn't find one. A rib does not come from a living creature, nor can an animal talk to make a gift of its bones. So he couldn't slaughter a cow or sheep for it. If a person gave him a rib, though, he would have to wait for them to die. He went to all his oldest kin . . . but they refused their ribs. 'We have heard it will destroy Yagana,' they said. Bisiri wept in disappointment and dispair.

"Now he had a very dear friend Bujhada, who was as close to him as a twin. Bujhada couldn't bear to see his friend so sad. He said, 'You may have my rib, dear brother.' That hardly consoled Bisiri, though. He could only think of how many years he would have to wait for Bujhada to die. He could not eat or sleep or laugh, only weep bitterly. It broke Bujhada's heart, and so while they were hunting wild sheep in the mountains, Bujhada fell on his spear. 'Now you have your rib,' he said, and died.

"Bisiri rejoiced and removed a rib even as he wept at the

loss of his friend. He buried Bujhada in a nearby village, then cleaned the rib, carved it with the image of a snake coiled around it, and polished it to the gleam of ivory. He strung it to make a bow. When he plucked the single string, the bow began to sing on its own. It sang of Yagana, of her greatness, of the heroism of her warriors, of the wisdom of her kings, of the beauty of her women, and Bisiri's bowharp sang that Yagana, built by the sons of the first man Jhokete, is too good for men and that because of the weakness of men it would go to sleep and be lost, the first time for vanity, the second for falsehood, the third for greed, and the fourth for dissension. It sang on and on, making many prophecies. In triumph, Bisiri returned to Yagana, but when he arrived he found only bare ground where the city had stood. His vanity had lost the city."

The harp-player's voice died away. Jeneba let out her breath. "What brought it back?"

He shrugged. "No one knows, but one day many years later it reappeared. It's been lost and regained a second time, too, but that's another story."

Jeneba glanced around the courtyard and thought of the palace and city spreading beyond, so solid, so seemingly unmovable.

But as she told Ngmengo the following afternoon, "Suddenly it felt as solid as morning mist."

The bush-man stopped gnawing at the leg of cooked goat she had brought him and stared out through the trees toward the valley. The bellow of a crocodile carried up on the breeze from the basking reptiles scattered like logs on Lake Kujhata's shore. "Perhaps it's wise not to stay in Yagana too long."

The thought followed her down to spear practice.

The army exercised in the meadows outside Yagana's walls. Groups lining up across from each other threw blunted spears at the opposing line and used long, oval shields painted with two interlocking spirals to stop spears thrown at them. The gibber of voices and war cries swirled around Jeneba, mixed with the thunk of spears off shields and the scents of sweat, crushed grass, and the oil the warriors rubbed on themselves. An exhilarating mixture. Jeneba's blood raced in response to it even while she concentrated on watching Tshemba each time his group took its turn. Did he move as Tomo used to? She raked through her memory, trying to recall the practice fighting in Kiba.

The boom of a drum interrupted her concentration. It stopped everything. In a breath, the meadow froze into silence. She turned in the direction of the drum sound to see Jhirazi and an older man dressed in striped white, indigo, and red-ochre standing at the mouth of the gate tunnel.

"King Biratha," someone near Jeneba breathed.

Jeneba felt she would have recognized him even without being told. Not only did he look like his sons Ourassi and Menekuya, who she had met during the army's morning run around the valley, but his pride and dignity of bearing surpassed even her uncle's. Of course, he was older than Mseluku; Ourassi, his eldest son and heir to the spear and shield, had sons of his own. Even aging, Biratha remained vigorous looking. He bent only a little, remaining as tall as his sons, and almost as muscular. Like Ourassi, he wore his hair braided in neat rows from the forehead back, pigtails on the neck laced with small beads of the same bright yellow metal Jhirazi wore. Scars sweeping from his forehead around the outside of his eyes to his nose turned back to spiral on his cheeks.

From their groups beyond Jeneba, Biratha's sons hurried past her to join their father. Menekuya moved with a springing stride, grinning. Ourassi stalked, his eyes as intense as Jhirazi's had been watching while Jeneba wrestled, and glittering with something else Jeneba could not quite name.

Biratha began speaking. Jeneba understood none of the words but she liked the clear, strong voice.

Laughter spread across the meadow.

"What's he saying?" she asked the warrior next to her.

"We're going to fight King Lubeda."

She blinked. Eagerness she could understand, and anticipation, but ... amusement? "Is he such a ridiculous opponent?"

The fringe of pigtails across the warrior's forehead jumped as he jerked around to raise brows at her. "What?

Oh." He grinned. "No. The laughter is in appreciation of our king's wit. Biratha said that at first he intended to send Lubeda an image of Inyabe." Her unfamiliarity with the name must have shown in her face. He whispered, "Inyabe is the messenger spirit who comes for the dead. He's a head with arms and legs. Instead of the threat, though, Biratha had his messenger say that King Biratha wanted to marry 'Princess Lubeda.' Meaning that the king considers Lubeda weak and womanly. Weak as some women, that is," he amended hastily with a glance up at Jeneba.

She bit back a laugh. "What was Lubeda's reply?"

The warrior chuckled. "That the 'princess' is interested in the proposal and will bring a negotiating party to Najhadende to discuss the bride price. Lubeda may be greedy, but he does have the intelligence and humor to respond in kind."

What made her look in Tshemba's direction she did not know, perhaps to see if he understood the joke. But the sight of his face, of the savage eagerness, the fierce longing burning there shocked all laughter out of her. And left her shaken, even more uncertain than ever about his identity. Tomo relished battle. She had often seen him grin in anticipation of a skirmish. Never, though, had he shown this *hunger*.

"The king is aging. I expect Ourassi will be asked to lead our 'negotiators,'" the warrior whispered on. "That should please him. Commanding the army is almost as important as being king."

Another warrior snorted. "Nothing but kinghood itself will satisfy Ourassi."

The one talking to Jeneba frowned in disapproval at the other warrior, then stopped, the fringe of pigtails on his forehead twitching as his attention snapped back to the king. "Hoooh! Biratha himself will lead us."

From the cheers, it appeared to be a popular decision. The king's sons looked startled, though, and leaning close to their father, spoke rapidly. He shook his head. Jhirazi whispered to him, too, and when he shook his head again, turned away with eyes like bottomless holes in the tight mask of her face.

The warrior caught his breath.

"What is it?" Jeneba asked.

He glanced up at her. "It's said by some that the reason the king listens to her isn't because she serves Kuma but because she can see the future. I wonder what she sees now?"

That made two remarks from the day to echo in Jeneba's head.

The army left for Najhadende at dawn, a long line of horses and excited riders trotting out the east gate, shattering the silence of the misty, still-shadowed valley as they crossed it and clattered up the road over the east hills into the light. The Tou warrior rode beside Jeneba. His voice rolled around her, a stream of speculation on Djero fighting ability and the humiliating defeat Biratha's army would hand the invaders, but between the churning thoughts in her head and watching Tshemba's back several horses ahead, Jeneba barely heard. If she were affecting him, he might try to slip away from the army. But was she affecting him? As far as she could tell, he cared about nothing except the battle. The hunger had glittered even more brightly in his eyes while mounting up this morning.

Wrapping her kadoru tighter against the dawn chill, the charms around her neck rubbed together, and for a moment, she forgot Tshemba in a rush of other thoughts. Biratha obviously believed in the ability of his chief witch doctor, but she could not help wondering if Kurasi charms—one to wear around her neck to neutralize any charms the Djero used, the other a skin pouch containing ointment to rub on before the battle to make her invulnerable to Djero spears— worked for Dasa.

But the other charm disturbed her more. She slipped a hand under her kadoru to rub the slim piece of horn hanging around her neck with the neutralizing charm and her buffalo talisman.

The priests of Kuma had held a ceremony for the warriors last night. Sacred drums beat out the rhythm while priests and priestesses first made offerings on the altars to Kuma, Inyabe, and Chudimu, their god of battle, in the god-house on the corner east from the palace, then danced on the west common in the masks and costumes of the gods. As the huge head of the death messenger Inyabe whirled past Jeneba, someone touched her arm.

She turned to find Jhirazi beckoning to her. The priestess pulled Jeneba onto the deserted heroes' terrace, where she held out the horn charm. "Take this."

The piece of horn felt smooth and warm in Jeneba's hand. She peered at it. "The witch doctor has already given me one."

"Against the Djero. This is different. As long as you wear it, you will have no blood-days."

Jeneba stared. She had never heard of such a charm before. Ngmengo would have appreciated it on the journey here, though, when her blood-days made it taboo for him to eat any food cooked by her and forced him to travel far enough from her that he would not be contaminated by her uncleanliness. "It really works?"

For an answer, Jhirazi pulled at a cord around her neck and held out an identical charm. "What use is a priestess who spends part of the month unable to perform her duties because she is unclean and taboo? The same can be said of a warrior."

The words of the warrior in the meadow about the priestess being a seer echoed in Jeneba's head. She rubbed her thumb across the charm. "Do you see a battle that long?"

But the priestess's eyes had been unreadable in the shadow of the heroes' terrace. "The future has many roads. One should be prepared to walk any of them."

Slipping out of the city later, Jeneba had gone up into the woods and searched, calling, until she found Ngmengo and told him what happened. "I couldn't leave without telling you. I'll miss you."

In the shimmering gray of darkness a tear sliding down his cheek glistened like liquid fire.

Guilt and concern stabbed her. "Will you be all right?"

He started, blinking, then laughed, a short sound as sharp as his thorns. "The gods of the wild look after their monsters. But . . . I'll miss the cooked meat, and your company."

"Maybe this will help." She held out a bone flute she had bought in the market after spear practice.

His breath caught. An eager hand reached for the instru-

ment. He played a few notes and night turned the sounds so
piercingly clear Jenebe felt the music in her bones. Even
night birds' cries and the creaking voices of insects stopped
to listen.

"You can be the bard of the wild."

Ngmengo grinned. "No, a praise-singer, and I shall play
in praise of beautiful women like you, who have three parts
generous—hips, breasts, and eyes—and three parts fine—a
small fine head, long thin neck, and narrow waist—and
whose skin is so smooth the waist is a hundred-year trip for
a louse."

Jeneba raised an inquiring brow.

His grin broadened. "Because its feet can find no grip and
it keeps sliding off."

She shook her head. "I think you're lucky that wizard
didn't turn himself into a hyena and bite off your—" She
laughed at his interrupting yelp of dismay. But the laugh
bounced the charms hanging around her neck and amusement quickly died. Her fingers wrapped around Jhirazi's
charm. "Why is she so concerned about me? What use does
she expect me to be to her?"

The bush-man's eyes glistened above the pale tube of the
flute. "Perhaps there are roads only a leopard's daughter can
walk."

Riding through the dawn, Jeneba huddled deeper in her
kadoru and frowned. She intended to walk no roads for Biratha's daughter. As soon as she could be sure Tshemba was
Tomo Silla, they would both be going back to Kiba.

The seven days of the ride to Najhadende gave her plenty
of time to ponder the problem of making Tomo come with
her. After all, he had nothing to gain and much to lose. Her
mind churned endlessly, but no answer presented itself, no
enticement, no argument, nothing except force, carrying him
back bound, a prisoner. An unsatisfactory solution. She viv-
idly imagined her people's reaction to seeing their dead hero
dragged in tied on the back of a horse. It would negate
everything she hoped to accomplish.

While she wrestled with the problem, Jeneba watched
Tshemba. To her consternation, every day he seemed less

and less like Tomo. He rode like one in a dream, or a seer in the grip of a vision, eyes hot with hunger. He ate little and spent rest periods testing the points of his spears and the edge on his knife.

"Do you love battle so much?" she asked him at one watering stop.

For a moment he did not answer and she wondered if he even heard. Then he looked around, smiling thinly. "It's the greatest pleasure of my life, and the harder and bloodier the fight, the greater my joy."

His fervor knotted her gut. What about style and elegance in fighting? And honor? All so important to Tomo. She remounted unhappily

As the mountains loomed ever higher and closer, the country rose and dried. The woods vanished, replaced by open grass, but grass shorter and less green than around Kiba. Lakes and water holes all showed a muddy or weed-choked margin from shrinkage. Late in the afternoon of the seventh day they reached Najhadende.

The village lay at the foot of the Bumala Mountains, a cluster of circular compounds atop one of the area's rocky, plateau-broad hills. Sideless tents had been set up east of it.

Jenebe sniffed. Cooking meat. Her stomach snarled in longing. As the horses reached the top of the hill, she saw the source of the smell . . . two firepits with the whole carcass of a cow roasting over each.

The men around the pits straightened and turned . . . stocky, yellow-brown people, narrow-nosed, their heads shaved on the sides and the rest of the hair oiled and powdered with ochre into a stiff red crest. Long sheepskins wrapped around their waists or draped over one shoulder and under the opposite arm.

A man with the highest, thickest hair crest of all rose from his stool under the largest tent and moved to stand by one of its supporting poles. A tattooed red snake coiled across his face from one cheek up across his forehead to the other cheek. King Lubeda?

Two Djero warriors trotted out to the riders at the head of the Kurasi line. "The princess Lubeda welcomes her suitor and invites the negotiators to enjoy our hospitality tonight."

Biratha glanced at Ourassi. His son replied stiffly, "The negotiators accept with pleasure and will join you as soon as we've tended our horses and greeted Najhadende's chief."

Memories of Imbu rushed back at Jeneba. Nykoro had entertained Mseluku's party and the Keoru warriors the night before their battle, too, and those destined to kill each other in the morning had eaten, riddled, wrestled, and danced together through the night. Even as they laughed, however, the two groups eyed each other, taking measure, politely testing. She almost asked Tshemba if he remembered, too, then caught herself. Tomo was too clever for such an obvious trap.

So she drifted at the edge of the activities and watched him instead, waiting for some betraying reaction. For once, she did not mind being just a spectator. Her own personal riddle needed too much concentration to leave room for those told by the warriors.

"A thing leaves naked, but returning, the body is covered with clothes," a Kurasi said.

"Guess you: some men who are many and form a row; they dance the wedding dance, adorned in white hip dresses," the Djero came back.

She would never have guessed *corn* and *teeth*, as the Tou warrior did. Some of the warriors preferred wrestling to riddles. A wickedly grinning Ododo and Chomba tried their best to prod the Djero into challenging her, but to her relief, everyone refused.

"A man only wrestles a woman when courting her," Lubeda's warriors snapped.

Tshemba also sat out of the wrestling, though not for lack of opponents. He declined several challenges with the sharpest tone she had heard him use: "I didn't come to play games like a child."

Unlike Tomo, who loved to demonstrate his wrestling ability.

But perhaps the refusals would bring Tshemba what he *had* come for. Judging by the offended expressions as the challengers stalked away, and the subsequent whispering, frowning, and pointing toward Tshemba, he had made enemies who would give him as hard and bloody a battle as he claimed to want.

The king's sons both wrestled, and did well. Neither king tried, though, choosing instead to sit on a ground cloth in Lubeda's tent playing stones-and-cups. Their conversation drifted to Jeneba through the noise of the wrestling.

"It's such a small village to cause trouble, and so far from civilized centers," Lubeda said. He dropped round red stones into the double row of hollows in the game board. "Can you truly say it's even in Kurasi territory? I've seen more old Burdamu camps than in the Kurasi settlements area and the village isn't laid out in the Kurasi fashion."

Biratha raised a brow. "Nor the Djero fashion. If you want to assign ownership on the basis of architecture, perhaps Najhadende owes tribute to the Burdamu. It's built over an old nomad camp, copying the buildings and fences in stone." He took his turn dropping playing stones in hollows around the board.

Lubeda's face hardened. "The villagers are Djero. They belong to me."

Biratha eyed him a moment, then said mildly, "Well, our armies can decide that in the morning. For now..." He emptied most of the hollows on Lubeda's side of the board. "It would seem this game belongs to me."

Wrestling gave way to dancing. Turning from watching it, Jeneba looked around and discovered that Tshemba had disappeared.

Hissing through her teeth in dismay, she ran out of the Djero camp to peer into the night. Mala's half-closed eye gave her more than enough light to see by, but Tshemba's tall figure showed nowhere around the camp or on the rocky slope below. Cold flooded her. Where could he have gone!

Then she spotted him... west of the village and beyond the Kurasi camp, wrapped in a kadoru and squatting motionless on the rimrock at the edge of the hilltop. She wrapped herself in her own kadoru and settled down near the hobbled horses where she had a clear view of him.

As far as she could tell he did not move the rest of the night. She dozed off, but when the boom of the war drum jerked her awake at dawn, Tshemba still sat on the rimrock.

He moved only when Duaffa yelled, calling them both to come watch Biratha make offerings to Kuma and Chudimu.

She and Tshemba joined the other warriors, but after the king finished, Jeneba carried her breakfast portion of fruit and grain paste out to the western rimrock where Tshemba had sat and offered them to her own gods, to Mala-Lesa and Kuta. Then with the war drum reverberating in her bones, she opened the pouch Biratha's witch doctor had given her and untied her tsara to spread on the magic ointment.

The last traces of sleepiness washed away in a fiery rush of excitement that jerked her nerves taut as a bowstring. Her senses sang, so keenly aware she could almost hear the heartbeat of her fellow warriors. The scents of ointments and acid sweat swirled around her.

"Weapons!" Menekuya yelled.

Tshemba snatched up his shield and spears, eyes smoldering with eagerness.

The drum thundered like a racing heart now. Yelling, everyone charged out of the camp and down the hill into the valley. From east of the village, the Djero ran before the throb of their own drums.

The two armies halted five or six spear lengths apart.

Abruptly, the drums stopped. For a moment that seemed to stretch out to forever the long lines faced each other in total silence, and even the hills seemed to hold their breath, waiting.

Then: "Kurasi!" Biratha called. "Yagana!"

In the rear line of his warriors, Lubeda's head flung up. "Heeee! Djero!"

Spears hissed through the air.

As in a dream Jeneba watched the first of hers leave her hand and float up over the warriors in front toward the Djero line. Djero spears glided toward her. She saw the coppery gleam of the freshly sharpened points, the thin hide strips binding the shaft to the head. Some never arrived, colliding with Kurasi spears and falling short. Others sailed on to be deflected by Kurasi shields or stick in them, or in warriors. A man in front of her went down impaled through the stomach. The Tou warrior caught a spear in his thigh. A fiery-cold rush of fear washed through Jeneba. The protection magic had failed.

But Kurasi spears found targets, too. Fear became a leopard snarl of elation. Lubeda's and Biratha's witch doctors neutralized each other's magic. That left victory to be decided on fighting prowess alone.

Time leaped forward again. Whooping, Jeneba sprang into the front line, careful to move around the fallen warriors. Perhaps Kurasi were not weakened by a woman stepping over them, but why take a risk with wounded men. She hurled her second spear. The point ran through and out the far side of a Djero's neck. At the same time, her shield deflected one spear aimed at her and caught two more. She pulled them loose and returned them to the Djero point first.

More spears from both sides found victims. Some warriors lay where they fell, dead or badly wounded. Others fought on with blood streaming down arms or shoulders or legs. The hot, salty scent of it filled Jeneba's nose. None was hers, though, and for a moment she wondered wryly whether the witch doctor's magic worked so well for her or if it was Jhirazi's charm against blood-days preventing blood of any kind from flowing out of her body.

The thought ended as a tall figure hurled past her at the Djero line. Tshemba . . . shieldless, carrying only the shorter stabbing spear. Her pulse leaped. Madman! He would be killed . . . and she might never know whether he was Tomo or not.

She dashed after him. Her shield knocked aside one spear threatening him. She sank her stabbing spear into the shoulder of another Djero aiming at his back. Then the shield became a battering instrument to sweep aside a third warrior. Gradually, though, Jeneba wondered why she bothered. Nothing touched Tshemba. The battle was breaking up into small groups and pairs of combatants, and no matter how wildly Tshemba threw himself into the most desperately struggling groups, he emerged unscathed. His spear drew blood time after time but the stabbing spears always missed him in return.

Jeneba stared in awe. A very powerful witch doctor must have made his charms.

They did not appear to please him, however. He flung away from each fallen warrior screaming in what sounded like anger and...disappointment? Surely she misunderstood, yet once, when he turned his head in her direction, she saw that the hunger in his eyes burned more fiercely than ever.

Could he be cursed? Jeneba wondered. *You will fight and win but never taste victory.*

She swung her shield just in time to smash it into the face and body of a warrior aiming for her with his stabbing spear.

Or could his curse be a different kind, and his protection far greater than that any mere witch doctor could provide? Fighting without caution or a shield that way...might he be seeking something other than victory, something that the gods denied him?

"Tomo!" she called in Dase. "Won't Ello open his arms to you?"

He stopped the spin toward her too late. His reaction to the name had already betrayed him. Snarling, he whirled away and plunged toward a circle of warriors around Lubeda.

She called after him, "The gods won't let you escape me that easily!"

Tomo whirled, face twisted. "Then you kill me." He spread his arms wide, exposing his chest. "I don't know how you found me, and I thought that with this battle sure to come I could keep you from being sure of me while I died honorably, fighting, but...take the vengeance you came for."

"I didn't come for vengeance." Not that kind. She blocked a Djero's stab with her shield and ran him through the belly with her spear, then whirled as she pulled it out to smash the shaft across another warrior's throat. "I'm taking you back to Kiba, to confess your treachery to those you betrayed."

Emotions surged across his face almost too fast for her to follow...horror, anger, anguish. But what she saw clearly was the tightening of his hand around his stabbing spear, and the twitch in the muscles of the arm holding it. He was going to attack!

"I won't fight you, Tomo."

"And I won't go back to Kiba!"

"You will." She stared him hard in the eyes. His very refusal to face Kiba gave her the answer how to make him go back, though she took no satisfaction in using it. "You'll go or the Kurasi will learn who and what the hero Tshemba Diasi really is."

The thunderous beat of a drum interrupted them. It cut through all the cries and yells of the battle. *Stop*, it boomed. *Silence. Parlay.*

The war cries and clash of spears against shields died away, until only the groans of the wounded and dying disturbed the hush.

Menekuya stepped from among the Kurasi warriors, tears streaming down his face.

Lubeda came from the Djero to face him. "Do you wish to surrender?"

Menekuya's chin rose. "Not surrender. Never. However, we wish to stop the battle for now." He turned and pointed.

Out of the warriors came Birtha's bard with his face paled to the color of cream, then Ourassi . . . carrying a slack and bloody Biratha.

Kurasi warriors wailed and slashed their arms with their spears and knives.

In the sky, dark clouds slid across the sun.

"King Biratha has been killed," Ourassi shouted above the wailing. "Allow us to take him back to Yagana and observe proper rites for him. After his shield and spear have been taken up by a successor, we'll return and finish the battle."

The head and tail of the snake tattooed on Lubeda's face twitched. "How long will you need?"

"One cycle of the moon."

The king stared at Biratha's body for several moments, then nodded. "I'll return in a month, then, but if you aren't here, be warned: I'll come to Yagana."

A not-so-subtle threat, and as if to emphasize it, thunder rolled in the distance.

* * *

By the time the army broke camp, clouds blackened the sky, drooping in thick, low folds, darkening the day to twilight. Lightning stabbed through them and thunder crashed and boomed. But no rain fell, not a drop all the seven days of the ride back to Yagana. There was only the ceaseless thunder and lightning, and air pressing down on them, hot and heavy and still. Jeneba patted her bay endlessly, trying in vain to soothe him. Like the other horses, he picked his way on the tips of his toes, ears twitching, eyes rolling, shying at every shadow and movement. Her own nerves crackled like the lightning. Biratha's death had certainly upset the gods.

They arrived at the valley by night with thunder pounding like some great drum and lightning brightening the landscape in brief, stark flashes. With relief, Jeneba guided the bay down into Yagana's valley.

But suddenly the line halted.

"What is it?" someone asked.

In answer, lightning lit up the valley for one blinding bright moment, and in that moment cold flooded Jeneba's bones. For the one moment, she had been able to see everything...lake, pastures, fruit groves, crop fields, the meadows where they practiced with the spears. But in the center of those meadows lay...nothing.

Lightning flashed again, confirming the unbelievable. Nothing. Where Yagana's massive walls should have risen lay only barren ground. The city had vanished.

CHAPTER

SIX

Yagana gone. Jeneba's gut churned. All that magnificence
...extinguished. The flickering gloom of day only con-
firmed last night's nightmare. The warriors had camped in
the meadow and from their expressions of disbelief as they
stumbled across the barren ground of the city site, Jeneba
suspected many had expected to find Yagana's walls high
and solid above them again when they woke. But there was
only pale red dust.

A paleness the Kurasi echoed, skins gone from copper to
ivory, faces drawn tight over the bones of their skulls.

Thunder rumbled overhead. The Tou warrior whispered to
Jeneba, "It isn't just a story, then."

She frowned. Just a story? No. But...

"Why has it gone now?" Tomo asked hoarsely.

Her exact thought. She puzzled even more, however, at
Tomo's tone and the tortured glitter in his eyes. As though
he felt personally responsible for the city's loss.

Could it be his fault? she wondered suddenly. According
to the Kurasi warrior's story that evening in the Warrior's
Court, Bisiri's harp had prophesied Yagana would be lost
once through falsehood. Also according to the warrior,
though, that had already happened. The third loss should be
from greed.

Someone shouted on a warning note. The warriors
whirled, those still in the meadow snatching up their spears.

Jeneba's fingers released the shaft of hers almost as soon
as they touched it, however. "Don't attack! It's my friend the
bush-man." She ran to meet the lone figure jogging across
the valley toward them. "Ngmengo! Yagana..."

He nodded, eyes grave. "Yes. I saw it happen."

Behind Jeneba, Menekuya's voice said, "Tell us."

The V scars on the bush-man's forehead creased. "I was looking down at the city about midmorning seven days ago. Suddenly it . . . rippled—like hot air on the plains at noon—and just faded away."

Duaffa murmured something in Kurra.

Menekuya said, "I think we should speak Burda so everyone can understand, but yes, that would be when my father died."

"Killed by Lubeda's greed," Ourassi hissed. "And that greed has robbed us of our city." He shook both clenched fists at the rumbling sky. "Djero blood will flow like a river for this!"

Lightning flashed. The warriors shook their spears and howled.

"No!" a voice shouted.

Jeneba spun toward the voice and stared with everyone else. From among the warriors came Biratha's bard.

He turned to face everyone and raised his voice. "Greed has killed Biratha and taken away Yagana, yes, but not Lubeda's. Remember the songs. Yagana has always been lost from within."

"Whose greed, then?" Menekuya demanded.

"Jhirazi came to me before the army left, because her father was fond of me and might listen to me, she said, and if not, then as a bard I wouldn't be actually fighting and would probably survive. The future has many roads, she said, but among the certainties was that if Biratha fought, he would die, with terrible consequences. I told the king that, but he insisted on fighting."

"My father wouldn't run from danger. What's that to do with whose greed killed him and lost Yagana?" Menekuya snapped.

The bard took a deep breath. "I stood on the hillside to watch the battle and compose a song about it, but I watched the king especially, because I was afraid for him. He was fighting two Djero. He could have handled twice the number without difficulty in his youth, but he was no longer young, while the Djero warriors were, with all a youth's strength and quickness. As valiantly as he battled, they began overpowering him. You couldn't know that, Menekuya, because you were busy holding off three Djero yourself. Ourassi saw, though." The bard stared accusingly at Biratha's eldest son.

Breath caught around Jeneba. Someone among the warriors muttered.

Ourassi frowned. "That isn't true. If I'd seen my father in trouble, I'd have gone to his aid."

"No," the bard said quietly, sadly. "I watched you while I was running down the hill. You had disabled one opponent and were looking around for another. You looked straight at your father. You even took a step toward him. Then you stopped and turned away."

Ourassi's face went cream-pale. "No! I never saw him! Why would I leave him to die?" But Jeneba caught the same acid scent of fear from him that Tomo Silla had after the half-men captured Mseluku.

Other warriors did not believe him, either. They shouted in Kurra, shaking spears.

The Tou warrior spat in Burda, "Because you hunger for the shield and spear of the king! I've seen it in your face and eyes, and I have heard the whispers . . . that you feared you might never be king, that the vigor of your father would let him live so long he wouldn't die until you were old yourself and he would make a younger son his successor."

Ourassi's knife appeared in his hand. He leaped for the Tou.

Duaffa intercepted, shouting. He used his own language but the tone told Jeneba he challenged Ourassi.

Menekuya shoved between in turn, shouting even louder, and pushed Duaffa back. The copper beads at the end of the pigtails on his forehead clicked together. "Wait! Listen to me! *Silence!*"

He kept on yelling until all other voices had stopped and the only sound in the meadow was the growl of thunder.

Menekuya held out his hands. "This is not the Kurasi way. Or the way of civilized men anywhere," he added with a glance at the Tou warrior. "I know you want someone to blame for our loss, but don't judge too hastily, because you might be wrong, and right or wrong, tearing him apart won't bring back Yagana. And it must be Yagana we think about now, for her sake and for our own. She is the strength and soul of the Kurasi and a part of us is lost with her."

Jeneba eyed them . . . the pale color, the drawn faces and prominent bones . . . a people suddenly thinner . . . diminished.

"There are those like Lubeda who hunger after our empire," Menekuya continued. "If they hear of Yagana's disappearance they'll fall on us like lions and hyenas on a wildebeest herd at calving time . . . take us slaves, sack our cities, and destroy all that Yagana has built through the generations. Remember what the songs say of the dark years while Yagana slept before?"

They remembered. Jeneba read dismay in eyes and faces. The warriors shuddered.

Menekuya paced up and down before them. "We don't have time to blame anyone. We must recover Yagana, and soon. Don't forget, if we're not back at Najhadende a month from now, Lubeda will come here."

And see the city gone, Jeneba reflected. How the snake on the Djero king's face would writhe for joy then. And how Kurasi blood would flow with their strength and soul gone. She and Tomo would fight with them, of course. Honor required that; they had pledged to defend the city while they remained guest warriors. Just two of them, even with Tomo's death-seeking fighting frenzy, would not stand off an army, though.

Menekuya swung to the bard. "What do the songs say about how we found Yagana before?"

"Nothing about the first time." The bard frowned. "After he lost Yagana, Bisiri vanished. We don't know what made Yagana reappear years later. The second time the wise man Yobanna told Kotote, grandson of the treacherous Lurre, to hunt for the war drum Borru. Finding and playing it brought back the city. That won't work this time, though, because Borru is inside Yagana."

Menekuya frowned. "Then we must ride to all the villages and cities of the empire. Somewhere there is a wise man or seer who can advise us as Yobanna did Kotote."

"Seer." Vine-patterned scarring on the bard's forehead

wrinkled as he frowned in a suddenly thoughtful expression. "A mountain seer."

Menekuya looked around at him. "What?"

"We need to find a mountain seer," the bard said. "I just remembered a song one of my predecessors composed about a prophecy made after the city was recovered the second time. It's full of praises for Kotote's bravery and the recovered glories of Yagana, then starts quoting a seer who in the midst of the celebrations reminds everyone that Yagana is still endangered by greed and dissension. That's when the seer says:

> "Remember, children.
> Remember, children of your children's children,
> When Yagana sleeps again,
> Wail not.
> Slash not your skin for grief.
> Seek your soul instead.
> Seek her in the mountains,
> Seek the seer whose visions
> Grow clear in the high, shining air."

"But we have no cities in the mountains," Duaffa said.

"I've heard of a mountain seer," Ngmengo said. "Travelers around their fires at night talk about a seer named Idju who lives in Kanjuna in the Bumala Mountains. It's said he knows all things."

Menekuya swung toward the bush-man. "Do you know where in the Bumala Mountains? We don't have time to waste on a long search."

Ngmengo nodded. "I can guide you. I once planned to visit him myself and frightened a traveler into telling me the way."

"The Bumala Mountains are Djero territory," Duaffa said.

Since the bard began quoting the song, Jeneba had noticed a growing light in Tomo's eyes. Now it blazed with a fierce brightness that suffused his whole face. He stepped past Jeneba. "Then any Kurasi seen there will arouse suspicion. Let me go."

Jeneba hissed. Had he lost *all* honor to risk Yagana in his courtship of Ello? No, she realized a moment later, suddenly understanding that blaze in his eyes. It was hope. He *sought* honor, the honor helping recover the city would bring.

But if he went and failed, he might simply keep going. She would lose him. "I'll go, too."

That would serve honor twice, letting her discharge her duty to the Kurasi and Yagana while keeping track of Tomo. Action appealed to her more than waiting for Lubeda anyway.

Tomo whirled, scowling.

Menekuya shook his head. "I thank you both very much, but Yagana is Kurasi, lost through Kurasi greed. The task of recovering her belongs to Kurasi."

"Not entirely, majesty," the bard said. "Yagana is more than the soul of the Kurasi. She is a city of all men, a shadow in the mind and a longing of her children. She is a strength carried in the heart, a perfection for which all strive. It is only fitting that foreigners also help recover her."

The blood-days charm suddenly dragged at Jeneba's neck. Was this the road the priestess wanted the leopard's daughter to walk? But . . . why her? Why not the Tou or another of the foreigners already guest warriors in Yagana's army, warriors who would not have to use charms to keep from being taboo?

"*Help* recover her," Menekuya said. "The responsibility is still Kurasi. I'll welcome the aid and companionship of the guest warriors, however."

Duaffa said, "Someone must command the army. We prefer you, majesty, and since your brother lost the city, isn't it fitting that he seek to restore it?"

Fury blazed in Ourassi's eyes. "*I* can't go. If Lubeda and the other Djero kings see me, they'll attack or capture me, and they'll certainly send their armies here to find out why I'm not burying my father and becoming the new king."

Menekuya rubbed his temples. "He's right. It's too much risk for him to go."

What foolishness, Jeneba thought irritably. "Ourassi is in danger only if he can be recognized. Disguise him." She glanced at Tomo as she said it. He looked away. "Different dress and a change of hairstyle will make him look like another person."

"And I know of nuts whose shells can be boiled for a dye to darken his skin and hair so no one will ever guess their real color," Ngmengo said.

Ourassi's mouth thinned. "Disguise! I won't sneak through Djero territory like a thief! The gods once took away Yagana for falsehood. How can you be fool enough to think they'll return her for the same offense?"

The words reverberated around them. Jeneba sucked in her cheeks. All the teaching of her life agreed; there could be no victory in a battle fought with dishonor. From the discomfort in the faces of Menekuya, the bard, and the other warriors, she suspected they must be thinking something similar.

And yet, a soft voice in her head whispered, the road which looked "honorable" wound through so many dangers that it might destroy any chance they had of learning how to recover the city.

She tried to shut the voice out. It sounded like the leopard she met when the half-men attacked. What other choice did the Kurasi have between safety and honor if safety meant deceit? One could not be both deceitful and honorable.

Kuva Myebo was, the voice purred.

She caught her breath. Kuva Myebo, the Dasan hero who pretended to be poor and cowardly yet saved a city and won a bride and a ruling Stool.

Jeneba leaned close to the bard. "Do you have any songs about heroes who performed noble deeds through disguise?" she whispered.

The bard started and stared up at her. On the other side of the bard, Ngmengo grinned. "Like Kuva Myebo? The Kurasi have the same legend, except they call the hero Doka-Ma-Boda."

The bard sucked in his breath. "Of course. Majesties, remember Doka-Ma-Boda."

Menekuya's head snapped around. Other warriors' eyes widened. Heads nodded.

Ourassi began, "This isn't the same—"

But the warriors were all looking at Menekuya. Duaffa said, "What shall we do, majesty?"

Ourassi's mouth closed in a tight line.

Menekuya looked slowly around, eyes widening, then with an apologetic glance at his elder brother, took a deep breath and turned to Ngmengo. "Find the nuts, please."

They buried Biratha in the bare earth where Yagana used to stand, stretched out in a long chamber at the bottom of a narrow shaft with a few food offerings but little ceremony, no drinking and wrestling, no riddling . . . no time for anything but a simple praise-poem. Some warriors headed for Kurasi cities hunting wise men, in case the Djero seer failed them. The rest surrounded the valley under Menekuya and Duaffa's command to turn back travelers and keep them from discovering the city had vanished.

Jeneba reflected with satisfaction that no one would recognize Ourassi among the three riders and bush-man who hurried east under finally clearing skies. His skin now looked dark yellow-brown and his hair a dull near-black. Unbraiding the hair and gathering it on top of his head in a Burdamu-style horse tail changed his appearance still more, as did switching his tunic for Tomo's tsara after both had also been darkened in the nutshell dye. A faint bulge at his waist marked a bag of copper and yellow-metal arm bands Menekuya had collected from the warriors and given them in case they needed to trade for anything.

Ourassi scowled down at himself, however, and when his horse, kicked into a trot, almost ran over Ngmengo, he snapped at the bush-man, "Why don't you just tell us how to find the seer so I won't have to waste time worrying about matching your pace?"

The sharp retort rising in Jeneba's throat died as Ngmengo sent her a grin before looking up solemnly at Ourassi. "There's no need to worry, majesty. I'll keep slow enough for the horses to stay with me."

While Ourassi sputtered, Ngmengo trotted off ahead of the group. Jeneba bit back a grin. On the journey to Yagana she had soon learned not to pity the bush-man for being forced to walk. He might seem slow, but like a pack of wild dogs, Ngmengo could jog all day, and day after day.

Ourassi discovered that endurance, too. Ngmengo set a pace that in five days took them—sometimes riding, often running beside the horses to rest them without stopping—farther than the army had gone in seven. The broad-topped hills grew steeper and rockier, and scrubby brush appeared among the grass and scattered trees. Trotting beside Ngmengo, enjoying the liquid grace and bottomless well of power that carried her tirelessly forward, Jeneba glanced back past her bay at the men. Ourassi's impatience had given way to a baffled frown which rippled the pattern of scarring on his forehead.

She raised a brow. "I don't think he's pleased to find himself struggling to keep up with you."

Ngmengo glanced back, too, then shook his head in a rattle of branches. "That look is for you, not me. A monster is expected to have unusual strength, but you puzzle him. You keep going when both he and Tomo are exhausted. I think he may envy you."

Envy her? she thought in astonishment. Really? That added an extra measure of pleasure to the run. And what did Tomo feel? She eyed him. Hunger burned in his eyes again. Hunger to recover his honor by recovering Yagana? Or did he hope to battle their way to the seer and die in the attempt so he would not have to return to Kiba? She set her jaw. She would just have to make sure that that did not happen.

They jogged on in silence for a while, she lost in her thoughts, Ngmengo looking around, then he sighed. "So dry. And this used to be such green country."

She raised her brows. "You've been here before?"

"Many times." He grimaced. "I've wandered far since I stopped being a man. It was just a half month's journey south of here I first heard about Idju. I started—"

He broke off, sniffing the air. Jeneba's nostrils flared. She smelled it, too. With a shift in the late afternoon breeze from west to east, the air no longer carried the scents of wild herds but that of goats and sheep, and another odor, mixed among the animals' . . . men. Different from the scents she had smelled around the Kurasi villages they passed. "Djero?"

The bush-man nodded. "There." He pointed.

South of them the tips of cone-shaped roofs showed above a hilltop.

They circled well around the village, avoiding, too, the grazing flocks of sheep and goats, each attended by a boy with hair combed up into a miniature red crest.

All pleasure in running evaporated. Jeneba's nerves stretched taut, flinging her senses out to test the air for the scents and sounds around them, alert for any indication Djero had seen them. The men stiffened and began scanning the hills, too, heads and eyes in constant motion.

At sunset they camped cautiously on the shore of a small lake. From across the water came the scents of animals and men.

"There's a village on the far side," she said. "We'd better keep the fire small."

Ngmengo nodded agreement.

Ourassi's eyes narrowed. "What are you, Jeneba Karamoke? Not human."

She snapped around angrily. "My blood *is* human!"

"Not to Kurasi," Tomo said. "They believe both the mother and father contribute blood, but the father's is most important. To Kurasi, your leopard-man father makes you a leopard-woman."

For the moment, she wished she were, with claws to rake down some handy tree trunk, ripping the bark again and again, until it hung in shreds. Tight-lipped, she waited for Ourassi's reaction. If he ordered her to leave, she would not argue, unless he sneered, then she would challenge him before going, but in either case she would follow the party, keeping watch on Tomo.

Ourassi shrugged. "No wonder you outrun and outwrestle our warriors." Gaze swinging toward the lake, he picked up his spear. "I think I'll catch fish for our supper."

Ngmengo grinned and, pulling his flute out from among his branches, played a few soft notes. Jeneba, though, stared in astonishment while Ourassi strolled to the shore and peered cautiously into the water before stepping close to it. He did not care what she was!

"Surrounded by demons, one almost welcomes a ghost," Tomo said.

A flare of anger at having her thoughts guessed guttered out almost instantly. "Ah? You consider yourself a demon?"

He stiffened. Before he could answer, however, a flicker of movement jerked Jeneba's attention toward the lake . . . a long, pale hand snaking up out of the water by Ourassi's feet.

"Water spirit!" she shouted, and raced for the Kurasi.

Just then the hand clamped around Ourassi's ankle and jerked. He went down, screaming.

She caught one arm before he vanished completely under the water. Yelling for Ngmengo and Tomo, Jeneba dug her heels into the ground and locked her fingers around Ourassi's wrist to pull against the water spirit.

Almost in vain. Ourassi's head went under. She had never felt such power before, even in the half-man, nothing except maybe the uchami. Snarling, calling aloud on Mala and all her own leopard strength, Jeneba hauled at the arm.

Ourassi's head reappeared, sputtering. He shouted curses.

"Kick!" Jeneba screamed. "Kick it in the face!"

The water churned to foam around him as he flailed with his free foot and arm. Past the end of his other foot the spirit's face appeared above the water, pale as foam under hair like a tangle of water weeds, eyes gleaming red in the dying light.

An arm closed around Jeneba's waist. Tomo. At the edge of her vision, she saw that Ngmengo had locked wrists with Tomo's other arm. Finally.

Her relief did not last long, though. The three of them pulling together managed little better than she had alone, just keeping Ourassi's head above water. The harder they tugged, the harder the spirit wrenched back. And Jeneba's gut knotted as her feet slipped forward.

"Kill it!" Ourassi yelled.

How? With wood, like the uchami?

"Ngmengo, break the head off a spear and throw the shaft at the spirit."

"Do I dare let go?"

"Try it."

But the moment the bush-man and Tomo released each other's wrists, Jeneba slipped closer to the water. Ourassi's head went under again. Ngmengo hastily grabbed Tomo's arm again and the three of them scrambled backward enough to pull the Kurasi up where he could breathe again.

Now what?

"Let go, spirit!" she called.

It just bared its teeth.

Her feet slipped again. She fought backward. "Please, spirit. He's my husband. If you eat him, his mother and sisters will throw me and his children out of our house."

The spirit pulled harder.

Jeneba's thoughts raced. How had the heroes of legend dealt with spirits?

"Sometimes spirits can be bribed," Ngmengo said.

"Release him and we'll give you other food," Jeneba called.

The red eyes flashed with interest. "What other food?"

What indeed. Not fish; it could catch all of those it wanted for itself. They needed something the spirit, unable to leave the water, could not normally obtain.

"We have grain paste."

The spirit's lip curled. "The villagers pour grain in the water for me."

Jeneba's feet slipped more, skidding in the mud at the lake's edge. All of Ourassi but the arm she held disappeared under the water, and this time all the pulling of the three of them could not regain the lost ground.

Food, Jeneba thought desperately. Something the spirit never had the chance to eat. Meat? But they had none at the moment, and the spirit probably captured enough of the animals coming to the lake to water that it had no burning hunger for meat.

She slid another foot-length closer to the water.

Fruit? "Ngmengo," she hissed back over her shoulder. "We took some oranges from that grove we passed through outside of Solillo. Have we eaten them all?"

The bush-man slid a hand into his branches. "There are two left."

She slipped again. "Hold one up! Spirit," she called. "Look at this fruit!"

The spirit's attention snapped toward the orange sphere the bush-man held. Ngmengo tossed the fruit out into the lake beyond the spirit.

The creature flung itself after the fruit. Scrambling desperately, they dragged Ourassi out onto the bank and well away from the water where he lay choking, coughing up water. The rest of them dropped panting to the ground around him.

"I don't know where it came from. I looked into the water and didn't see anything," he gasped.

Ngmengo shrugged. "They're sly. We got you back, though. The spirit may be happy, too. I think I smell it eating the orange."

A sweet-sharp citrus odor floated in from the water. But other scents came, too. Man-smells . . . stronger than they had been earlier. Water splashed.

Jeneba spun around and up into a crouch, hissing. Their shouting had attracted attention. A line of canoes headed toward them through the twilight. Strength poured back through her in a jolt of icy fire. She leaped to her feet to run . . . but stopped there. Tomo and Ourassi could not hope to follow. Running would mean leaving them behind, unacceptable in one case, dishonorable in the other. And what would become of Yagana? So she stood motionless while the canoes touched shore and Djero swarmed up from them to surround the party with a circle of spears.

CHAPTER

SEVEN

They grouped back-to-back in the twilight while the Djero watched them narrow-eyed. How suspicious they must look through Djero eyes, Jeneba reflected . . . members of three different tribes and a monster. What could such a strange group be doing together except outlawry?

"Who are you?" demanded a warrior with black birds tattooed on his arms. "Why are you in Djero lands?"

Ourassi drew in a breath like someone preparing to speak.

Jeneba caught hers. Mala give him the wisdom not to tell the truth; she had no way to caution him aloud without arousing the Djero's suspicion.

He said nothing, though, and Jeneba heard the click of his teeth as he closed his mouth.

She felt tension ripple through Tomo, smelled a sudden acid scent, and heard his breathing quicken. Bracing to fight? The Djero seemed to think so. The grip on their spears tightened. The snakes and birds on arms and jaws twitched with the movement of muscles beneath.

He must not be given the chance to die. She said hastily, "We mean no harm. We're simple travelers, accompanying this bush-man to visit the seer Idju."

"Fool," Tomo hissed in Dase. "You'll give everything away."

Inwardly she cringed, but she kept her voice calm. "Wait and see."

The Djero warrior frowned in disbelief. "Accompanying the bush-man! Do you take us for children?"

She looked down into his eyes. "The bush-man was once a man. We were prisoners of Burdamu outlaws, on our way to be sold into slavery. He saw the camp, mistook this man"

—she pointed at Tomo—"for a certan witch doctor, and rescued us to ask how he might reverse the bewitchment that made him a bush-man. When we couldn't help, he asked us to accompany him to a seer he'd heard of in the Bumala Mountains."

"I know nothing about a seer named Idju," the warrior said.

Ngmengo replied, "He lives in the village of Kanjuna."

The Djero's frown deepened. "I've never heard of a village by that name, either."

One of the other warriors spoke in his own language.

The first listened, then pointed at Ourassi. "What tribe is that one?"

"Apazi," she replied promptly. The Dase word for copper. "They live west, beyond Malekuro territory."

"He wears Kurasi scarring."

Jeneba thought furiously. Mala, what did she say to that?

"I've visited Yagana," Ourassi replied. "Visitors there often add decorative scarring in the local pattern. See, Tshemba has some, too, on his arms."

Several of the warriors talked back and forth. The speaker listened, then nodded and turned back to Jeneba. "Come with us to our village."

Jeneba's gut knotted. Tomo was tensing again, and a quick glance around at him found that hunger burning in his eyes. He *did* want to fight! "Of course. We'll ask your elders about the seer." Mala grant she sounded and looked more confident than she felt. The Djero knowing nothing about the seer and his village gave her a very uneasy feeling.

She caught the eyes of the others, and held them until they nodded.

Some Djero took the canoes back across the lake. Others led the horses. The rest marched the party around the lake.

Their village stretched out over the water on tall stilts. Villagers poured out of the wooden huts, running lightly across narrow walkways to the shore in a rattling click of wooden, stone, and ivory beads piled strand on strand around their necks. Strutting, the warriors led their captives out across one of the walkways to a solitary hut, and after stationing a spearman at the shore end of the walkway, gathered with the rest of the villagers on shore.

Jeneba grimaced. The voices reached her clearly, but she understood nothing they said. Then she noticed Ngmengo . . . squatting with head titled, his lips pressing into a grim line. "Do you understand what they're saying?"

His branches rattled sharply. "An elder has suggested that since you three were to be sold into slavery, it is your fate and the village might as well profit from it. They plan to destroy me and take all of you to the market in Murijenaja."

Ourassi hissed in dismay. "Lubeda's city! When this dye wears off and I'm recognized, my people are doomed!"

"You had to mention slavery," Tomo snapped at Jeneba.

This time she refused to let him make her feel like a fool. "It seemed the only believable reason for people of different tribes to be together in one place at the same time. Don't you think we'd spend our time better finding a way to escape?"

She swung around, examining the hut. The Djero had taken their knives as well as the spears, but the weapons were useless for attacking the guard anyway, not with the rest of the village milling beyond him where they would see anyone from the hut trying to cross the walkway. Jeneba sucked in her cheeks. The only other possibility seemed to be down. She dropped to her knees and tore at the grass matting covering the floor.

A piece came up to reveal wrist-thick poles laid close together. Poles too thick to break through without an axe. The walls, though, were another matter. Grass mats lined them, too, but pulled away to reveal rows of thin wood strips lashed across the heavy upright posts that made the stilts and supported the roof. With little effort she broke out the bottom three strips between two uprights on the lake side of the hut, producing an opening large enough to squeeze through.

Ourassi snorted. "We can't swim away!"

She glanced up. "That's what the Djero think. I wasn't thinking of swimming, though. Ngmengo, would the water spirits bother you?"

The bush-man's mouth twisted wryly. "Monsters prey on men, not one another."

"Then could you swim after a canoe for us?" When he did not respond, she prompted, "Ngmengo?"

He hung his head. "I can't swim."

What! "But Burdamu take their herds across rivers all the time."

"I always held on to a cow."

She groaned in dismay. Now what? They needed that canoe.

"Maybe the spirits won't bother a leopard-woman, either," Tomo said.

Jeneba flung up her head. Ello take him! "I'm not—" she hissed, but broke off to eye the poles of the floor, an idea forming. Maybe it was unnecessary to swim. Experimentally, she reached between two of the poles. Her hand slipped through. She sucked in her cheeks. It might work. "All right, I'll go for the canoe."

Crawling out through the hole, Jeneba slid down one of the supporting posts and swung in under the hut. A forest of stilts supported it. Light from the thick crescent of Mala's eye made it a forest of shadow as well, gray to her but hopefully impenetrable darkness to human eyes. She worked her way toward the walkway along the flooring poles. To keep above anything reaching up from the water, she wedged her toes between the poles, too, or when possible, clung to the stilts.

"That only takes you to shore," Ourassi hissed through the grass mat flooring. "What will you do then?"

Use her father's spirit. It might as well be useful after being responsible for bringing her to this situation in the first place. "I'll try not to be seen."

The walkway offered less shadow. She could only cling as close to the poles as possible and pray that by moonlight the color of her fingers reaching up around the poles did not appear too much darker than that of the weathered wood.

But the light was brightening to dancing red. Her pulse leaped. Fire. Lit in celebration of wealth to come from selling three slaves, no doubt. Grimly, she slid faster along the poles.

Only to freeze as feet padded along the wood above her. Someone headed for the hut! If they found her gone—

A foot coming down on her fingers cut off the thought. She bit her lip to keep from crying out. Then the whisper of footsteps halted a heartbeat after lifting off her fingers and a figure visible through the spaces between the poles turned, bending over. All pain vanished, forgotten in a surge of fear. The Djero had felt her fingers under his foot!

Jeneba snatched both hands free and flung herself at one of the supporting posts. Wrapping around it, she pressed into the wood and held her breath, willing herself to look like part of it, praying the Djero could see nothing in the shadows under the walkway.

The guard spoke questioningly. The Djero above her rubbed his foot back and forth along the walkway. He made some reply that brought another question, one with a note of surprise. The guard came out and knelt down to rub his hand on the wood, too. He said something short. The other Djero replied sharply.

Cold ate into Jeneba. Any moment now one of them would lean over the edge to peer under the walkway. Water lapped at her toes. Every instinct in her body recoiled from it, skin twitching at the imagined feel of pale, cold fingers closing around her ankle, but she forced herself to slide down the post into the lake. Mala grant that her son Abbe, the god of water, kept his demon children away from the village.

Above, the Djero who had stepped on her leaned over the edge of the walkway. Jeneba hurriedly sighted on the nearest hut, and submerging, swam for its walkway.

What seemed like an eternity passed until her fingers touched posts. Reaching them, though, she swung to the inside and used the walkway's shadow to hide her scramble for shore. Never had mud felt so welcome. Crouched on it, panting, she gave thanks for her safe passage.

The Djero at the hut she left had given up trying to find what he felt underfoot. Now he stood outside the door of the hut, a doorway blocked by Ngmengo.

"I would speak to the men," the Djero said.

"I lead the humans. Speak to me."

Jeneba could not see the Djero's face but his tone snarled. "Address men with respect, monster, or—" He broke off.

Ngmengo stared down at the shorter Djero. "You threaten?" he purred.

The Djero said, too quickly, "Of course not. I come with an invitation. Our chief asks for the honor of sharing his food with you."

Jeneba grimaced. Food with what in it? Something their witch doctor added to weaken them and prevent them from trying to escape on the journey to the slave market? She slipped away without listening to the bush-man's reply. There was no polite way of declining the hospitality. They needed that canoe quickly.

She crept along the shore, running ever more crouched as the fire above blazed brighter, freezing at every suspicious sound. Where were the canoes?

With relief she finally saw several pulled up on shore beyond the next walkway. She huddled beneath the walkway for a few moments while someone ran overhead, then with one last look around for anyone possibly watching, crawled out to the nearest canoe. Pushing it into the water forced her to risk standing, but though her back muscles twitched, feeling eyes and spears, no cry of alarm followed her as the canoe slid out into the lake. For lack of paddles she had to use her hands, too, and each time she dipped into the water, she shuddered, expecting to feel spirit fingers closing around her wrist.

"Praise Kuma," Ourassi breathed when she arrived beneath the hole in the hut wall. "What kept you so long? Their chief wants to come and share a meal with us. We tried pretending we'd already eaten, but the chief's linquist acted insulted and started looking suspicious that maybe we knew what they intend, so to keep from being put under close guard and maybe even bound, we had to accept. The chief will be here anytime."

He scrambled down a stilt post into the canoe. Tomo followed. Ngmengo, however, stuck in the hole, his branches snagging.

"Break off the interfering things," Ourassi snarled.

Ngmengo recoiled. "They're a part of me. It would be like cutting off a finger or ear!"

"I'll help him," Tomo said.

But Jeneba was already shinnying up the post. She broke out two more wood strips from the wall. That enlarged the opening enough for him to work through. While the bushman climbed down, she used a little more of their precious escape time to rip loose more squares of grass mat. Folded around the pieces of wood from the walls for rigidity, they made two paddles, crude but safer than hands.

"I hate abandoning the horses and weapons," Ourassi muttered.

So did Jeneba. She tossed the makeshift paddles down to the canoe. "I'll get them." Somehow.

The scars on Ngmengo's forehead rippled. "How? The Djero have our weapons and the horses are in a pen where everyone in the village can see."

She knew. Her gut knotted. "And I am noble and a Dasa. I'll meet you at the east end of the lake."

Tomo frowned. "You brought the canoe. Let me try for the horses."

She made no move to climb down. "I'm not trying to rob you of a chance to do a heroic deed," she said in Dase, "but you can't be as stealthy as I can." Before any of them could argue further, or she lose her courage, she backed into the hut.

The canoe left. Jeneba edged up to the hut door to study the guard. He did not watch the hut closely. The dancers interested him more. She waited, and the next time he looked away, she slid through the opening and somersaulted down over the edge of the walkway into its shadows for a second time. And swung hand-over-hand along the poles as fast as she could. That left her feet dangling uncomfortably near the water. Mala grant that her luck with the spirits lasted a while longer.

The guard spoke, answered by a resonant voice. Feet whispered against the wood of the walkway.

Icy fire flushed her veins. The chief!

Jeneba gave one last swing and let go. And landed silently

in the mud at the waterline. Creeping up beneath the guard's feet, she huddled to wait.

A portly man draped in sheepskin strode across the walkway, followed by two women carrying basket-trays.

His bellow at finding the hut empty rattled the walkway. Jeneba pressed into the ground and wood, making herself as small and invisible as possible. She understood none of the furious shouting above her, but an imagined translation ran through her head.

A hole in the lake side of the hut? But they couldn't swim away. Even foreigners wouldn't be that stupid.

Well, if they did, they're gone; the spirits have them.

I won't believe that. See, a canoe is gone. Spread out! Search all around the lake!

Howling, every man in the village snatched up a spear. Some raced east or west along the shore of the lake. Others piled into canoes to pursue by water. Jeneba heard no hoofbeats to indicate anyone had taken the horses, however. Possibly they knew nothing about riding. She had seen no other horses in the village when they arrived, no enclosures suitable for anything but sheep and goats.

When the noise had quieted and footsteps across the walkways told her the women and children left behind had gone into their huts, Jeneba peeked out. The village looked deserted, except for a boy guarding each sheep and goat pen. The horses stood alone in their pen.

She tried as never before to feel like a leopard . . . to move like one. Hunching low and keeping outside the circle of light cast by the dying fire, she crept across to the pen and slid through the low fence.

The bay flicked his ears in recognition. Her kadoru and bridle lay in a pile with the others' in a corner of the pen. There was no time to bridle up, though. Every moment she delayed leaving increased the risk of being seen. Gathering up the bridles, she slung them across her chest and back and bundled the kadorus under one arm. Then she vaulted on the bay. Pointing him at the fence, she dug in her heels.

He lifted off his hocks to clear it cleanly. The other horses followed.

A yell told her she had been seen, but now she only grinned. Let them try to stop her.

Led by her bay, the three horses thundered past the fire, past women and boys racing from the lake huts with spears, and out into the night.

Once away from the village, she halted long enough to bridle the horses, then raced the three of them east, swinging wide around the lake to avoid the Djero. How were the others doing? she wondered. Had they kept ahead of the pursuing canoes? Had they avoided any warriors on shore? Mala's crescent eye sliding behind the horizon still provided plenty of light to see by when she reached the east end of the lake, but . . . neither men nor bush-man appeared among the trees and brush. There was only moonlight and the whisper of the chilly night wind.

Shivering, she wrapped in her kadoru. Recaptured! Or could they have fallen prey to the spirits? Only surely Ngmengo would not—

The thought chopped off. She sniffed the breeze, sorting out its load of odors. Among those of plants and animals lay human scents. And one not-quite-human. Her pulse jumped in a quick surge of hope.

"Ngmengo?" she whispered.

A bush sprouted arms, feet, and a head. The men crawled out from under other bushes. "We were afraid you'd been caught."

"We will be if we stay here much longer." She tossed them their reins. "I smell Djero coming."

Tomo tossed her something in return before he vaulted on his horse.

As her fingers closed around the objects, she stared in astonished delight. A spear and knife! "Where did you get these?"

Ourassi bared his teeth. "From warriors who made the mistake of being alone when their canoe overtook us." He kicked his horse into a trot.

They all followed his example, anxious to put distance between them and the Djero. They kept moving even when moonset plunged the countryside into total darkenss, only slowing to a walk. Jeneba and Ngmengo led the way.

"We're lucky to have a leopard-woman along," Ourassi said. "You see in the dark and I'll admit I probably couldn't have reached the canoe or horses without being caught, or been so fast thinking up that story you gave the Djero."

"Deceit is the nature of a cat," Tomo said.

Anger flared in Jeneba. The hyena! "So is tearing out throats," she hissed.

Ngmengo pinched her leg. "It's a truer story than you know, your majesty. I've planned several times to visit Idju to ask about curing my bewitchment. Maybe this time I'll reach him without distractions."

Jeneba took a deep breath. The bush-man was right; she should not let him goad her.

"I'm bothered why those Djero haven't heard about this seer," Ourassi said.

She wondered about that, too. What bothered her even more was the villagers not having heard of Idju's village. It stirred something else, too, soft whispers in her head . . . bits of conversation, remarks that whispered at the back of her mind until she tried to listen, then, maddeningly, faded to silence.

The whispers continued to plague her for the next four days . . . four days of pushing the horses as hard as they could without killing the beasts, of paths through ever-steepening hills becoming narrow mountain trails they must lead the horses up, of growing cold . . . four days of trying to avoid any further contact with Djero, four days of nerves stretched singing-taut, eyes, nose, and ears alert for everything around her.

Jeneba raked fingers through the short fuzz on her head in frustration. Was a god trying to talk to her, or the ghost of some ancestor? And what could he be trying to say?

She still had no answers when late the fourth day she heard Ngmengo whoop and, looking up in the direction of his pointing finger, saw a village above them.

"Kanjuna!" Ngmengo crowed.

It sat tucked into a large hollow in a cliff, round stone

huts rising from the rocky shelf beneath to the rock hanging overhead.

Relief quickly became apprehension, however. She saw no movement in the village. No voices came down on the breeze, no human odors. And as they climbed nearer the base of the cliff, cold crawled up her spine. Some of the huts showed gaps in their walls. One had collapsed in a heap of rubble.

A path wound up the rock face, so narrow they had to lead the horses. At the top of it, her heart dropped. The village lay empty, a ruin, inhabited only by scattered and broken bones, some human, the rest those of mountain sheep left by—Jeneba sniffed, tasting the smells of the place—left by a leopard which had laired there.

She stared around, heartsick. There was no seer here to consult. Now where would they learn how to recover Yagana?

Ourassi groaned. "Deserted. *Deserted!*" he whirled on Ngmengo in fury. "I should have known better than to trust a monster!"

"I didn't—" the bush-man began, face and eyes stricken.

Ourassi spat back, "There's no time to hunt for another seer either! The half-moon was three nights ago. The next half-moon Lubeda will be at Najhadende, when we aren't there he'll come to Yagana. My people are doomed!" He gripped his spear as though about to throw it at Ngmengo.

The whispers in Jeneba's head came together, remarks about starting for the seer several times, and having been through the country when it was much greener. That had to be many years ago. Or even generations? She grabbed Ourassi's arm. "If the Kurasi are doomed, don't blame Ngmengo."

He whirled on her. *"I didn't leave my father to die!"*

Ah? Her brows rose. When someone calls, "Witch, witch," those who are not witches do not turn around. This was hardly the time to argue guilt, though. "I meant the bush-man didn't lie. He just doesn't feel time as we do, do you, Ngmengo? Can you remember how long ago you heard about Idju?"

Ngmengo's head hung. "I never thought to consider it."

Ourassi scowled. "I don't understand."

"Immortals don't count the years. Or are bush-men merely very long-lived?" she added, glancing at Ngmengo.

The men stared.

Ngmengo sighed. "I don't know . . . but the grandsons of my age-set have grown old and died while I remain almost unchanged." His face twisted in anguish. "I'm still a fool!"

The anger went out of Ourassi like a fire doused with water. He slumped and dropped the spear.

Tomo's lip curled. "You're defeated by one failure? What a sorry king you would have made. *I* intend to go on looking for that seer."

What a spear-bladed tongue Tomo had grown, Jeneba thought angrily.

Ourassi stiffened but only replied bitterly, "There's no time. We have to go help fight Lubeda and the other hyena armies that will fall on us, and hope enough of my people survive to make another search in some other generation. We'll start back in the morning."

CHAPTER

EIGHT

They made a bleak camp in the ruins of Kanjuna. Tomo speared fish from a nearby stream while Jeneba cut grass in a meadow below the cliff face protecting the village and Ngmengo gathered roots in the woods, but no one except the horses, stalled in what must have been a sheep or goat pen, ate much, and no one spoke, only sat picking at the food and staring into the fire. Jeneba eyed them . . . Ourassi sunk in despair, Ngmengo anguished at the edge of the firelight, Tomo with an angry, desperate gleam in his eyes. And what did she look like? Jeneba wondered. Unbelieving? Rebellious? She refused to believe their search could end so emptily. They might have the wrong wise man as Ourassi suggested, but when they needed to find a seer, Ngmengo had known of one. That was too opportune to be wrong. Nor, surely, would the prophecy bring them to a long-dead seer in an abandoned village without reason.

Jeneba gathered up the uneaten food. Automatically, she tossed some on the ground as offerings to pacify local ghosts, then realized what she was doing and stared at the bits thoughtfully. Ghosts. Could— But no; the village had probably been empty long enough for all the ghosts to have sunk to whatever underground claimed unfed Djero shades. Certainly the seer's ghost would have left. She rolled the rest of the food up in her tsara and wrapped herself in her kadoru against the chilly night.

Ngmengo stood watch as usual. After a while Tomo and Ourassi fell into restless sleep, but Jeneba felt as wide awake as the bush-man. She sat curled by the fading heat of the fire, listening to the horses munch the grass she had cut for them, her mind churning.

Perhaps the prophecy was true but misdirection had come from the gods. She sucked in her cheeks unhappily. They might have been judged unfit to learn how to recover Yagana. Heroic deeds belonged to heroes, after all, and what were they . . . a coward and traitor, a man who coveted his father's kinghood so much he let his father die, a monster, and a fool of a leopard's daughter.

Ngmengo groaned. "How could I have been so stupid! I never even *thought* to consider how long ago I heard about Idju!" He tore at his hair and wrenched branches as though to rip them off. "I should have left hunting seers to men and just sung my praise-songs as Jhirazi suggested."

"Jhirazi suggested?" Jeneba peered across the dying fire at him in surprise. "When?"

"After the army left for Najhadende." He stared out at the western sky. "She brought cooked meat out to me every evening. She said she knew you'd been doing it. Then she would stay for a while to listen to me sing and play the flute. She kept looking down at Yagana as though about to cry. 'She shouldn't be allowed to die,' she said the night before the city disappeared. She turned to look at me with eyes that burned to my heart. 'Yagana can live as long as people remember her. Will you promise me to make praise-songs about her and sing them everywhere you go as long as you live?'" He grimaced bitterly. "She must have known what a fool I'd be."

Indignation flared in Jeneba. He had no reason to blame himself like this, certainly not if the gods had used him to misdirect Ourassi's hunting party. "If you'd said nothing, we'd be no better off, just wandering around the mountains hunting a seer without any idea where to start. I think Jhirazi was trying to insure that all the roads of the future would lead back to Yagana. If the city isn't recovered right away, she wanted to make sure someone keeps reminding the Kurasi of their soul so they can survive until Yagana is found again."

His branches scraped sharply together. "I should have been content with that. If I'd said nothing, you'd have asked wise men in Kurasi cities and villages about mountain seers and learned where the right one was. I *am* a fool. I always

have been and always will be!" Jumping to his feet, he
scrambled away from the cliff trail and into the woods
below.

Jeneba started to follow, but stopped, glancing back at Tomo
and Ourassi groaning and twitching in their sleep. Someone
had to stand watch. Then again, which was more important,
protecting these two jackals or comforting her friend? Besides,
the mountainside lay brightly lit by moonlight, a hunter's
night, and the cool breeze carried a tantalizing load of scents.
She sucked in a deep breath, reading them. Plants, game
animal smells, leopard odor. They called to her, tempting her
to come out and prowl the dark, tasting its wonders.

Jeneba caught herself with a start halfway down the trail.
What was she doing . . . abandoning duty, finding beauty in
the deadly night and actually longing to walk around in it?
Madness! She set her jaw and made herself climb back up to
the village. Her father's spirit *would not* dominate her!

Huddled in her kadoru by the coals of the fire, she continued to ache for Ngmengo, and for Yagana, Menekuya, Jhirazi, remaining behind when she knew that might happen,
and all the Kurasi who had lost families and their soul and
strength. She could almost pity Ourassi, too. What must it
be like to see such devastation result from one's action? His
greed had not just endangered a group of warriors as Tomo's
moment of cowardice had done but destroyed a whole people and a center of civilization.

She had known that since they left Yagana's valley but
somehow it had not struck her as keenly as it did now. They
must find the city. Jeneba lifted her chin. By Mala, they
would, somehow. She refused to believe the leopard's
daughter had been set on a road that led nowhere.

Assuming, then, that the prophecy in the bard's song
brought them here for a purpose and had not misled them,
the answer they sought must be near. She strained to remember the exact words the bard quoted.

> *Seek your soul instead.*
> *Seek her in the mountains.*
> *Seek the seer whose visions*
> *Grow clear in the high, shining air.*

* * *

Jeneba stiffened. Seek the seer. *Seek* the seer. The prophecy said nothing about finding him or asking him anything! Excitement bubbled up in her. Their answer lay in the seeking, then, or . . . in the dead village itself? Idju could have seen they would be coming and left a message!

Scrambling to her feet, she ducked through the low doorway of the closest hut. Drifts of dust and broken pottery littered the floor. Jeneba pawed through them. What form would a message take? An object? A drawing? She examined the walls. Drawings circled the interior, painted in colors turned gray and black by her night visions: bushbuck, mountain sheep, great birds, lizards. A second hut displayed more animal drawings. So did the next four.

Then, in a hut in the center of the village, the bushbuck and wild sheep ran among drawings of dancing people. Her heart leaped. She peered closely at the paintings, but to her disappointment the clothing and hairstyles looked Djero, and the drawings depicted skin decorations of birds and lizards. None of the people could be Kurasi or Dasa. Still, she continued to explore the tower, pawing through the rubble of stone from the hut's partially collapsed walls. There must be a message *somewhere*.

Under the stones lay a pile of crushed bodies, two adults huddled over the smaller forms of four children . . . all shrunken, dried stiff and hard, dusty smelling. Sunken eye sockets gaped at her and withered lips peeled back from teeth in silent screams. Their hair still stood in crests and bird and lizard tattoos remained visible on the leathery skin. The broken shaft of an arrow protruded from the shoulder of one adult, who also clutched a knife in his claw-like hand.

Jeneba scrambled backward out of the hut, heart slamming against her ribs. Kanjuna had not been abandoned, it would appear, but slaughtered. The discovery brought a disquieting thought. Seers sometimes failed to see personal tragedies. What if Idju had left a verbal message, something passed from father to son to be given to the strangers when they arrived?

Nothing suggestive of a message appeared in any of the

other huts, either. Jeneba came out of the last and raised her hands to the shining oval of Mala's eye. "Creator, tell me what to do. Show me our message hasn't been lost with whatever marauding outlaws or bribesmen attacked this village." Perhaps she had misinterpreted something, or overlooked—

The throaty growl of a big cat rumbled behind her. She spun, heart jumping. A leopard stood between two of the huts, dragging the carcass of a young mountain sheep so freshly dead blood still dripped from its neck. The warm, salty scent of it drifted to Jeneba, curled tantalizingly around her.

The leopard's tail lashed.

Jeneba said hurriedly, "Greetings, sister. Have we trespassed in your lair? I'm sorry. We'll be gone in the morning."

The leopard stared back unblinking for a long, taut moment before dropping the carcass. "Ah?" She sniffed the air, then bent to lick at the blood on the sheep's throat. "What are Dasa doing here in Djero lands at all?"

"Hunting the seer Idju . . . only we came too late."

"Yes. Men have been gone from here so long I and my mother and my mother's mother have all used these little caves for birthing our cubs." She tore at the carcass.

Caves? The word echoed in Jeneba's head, followed by a phrase from the bard's song. *Seek her in the mountains.* She caught her breath. Could that mean they should seek actually *in* the mountains? She eyed the leopard. How had the animal come into the village? Not by the trail up the cliff face. Even being used to her scent, the horses would have given an alarm if a leopard passed.

"Is there another way into this village, say through a cave in the mountain?" Though she shuddered at the idea of exploring a cave. They were entrances to the underground world of the dead.

The leopard lifted her head. "There's a tunnel leading to the top of the cliff."

"Where's the entrance?"

The leopard's eyes narrowed. "What do you seek here?"

Jeneba hesitated, then told the leopard about Yagana and

the prophecy that brought them to Kanjuna. "Would you happen to know the answer we need?"

"No." The leopard eyed her across the carcass of the sheep. "But as you are my sister I can tell you this: you'll never learn the answer by asking men for it."

Picking up the sheep, she dragged it away behind the huts.

Jeneba scowled after her. Must leopards always talk in riddles?

While she puzzled over the riddle by the embers of the fire, Ngmengo slunk back into camp. He said nothing, only squatted dejectedly next to her.

Jeneba smiled at him. "You brought us to the right place." She told him her thoughts on the prophecy in the bard's song, and about her conversation with the leopard.

Instead of looking relieved, though, he groaned and pounded his forehead with his fist. "Oh, no!"

The men thrashed in their sleep. Ourassi echoed the groan.

Jeneba frowned. "Now what's wrong?"

He grimaced. "I found another village, an inhabited one, and tore apart a hut to capture some Djero and terrorize them into telling me the names of all the seers in the area they'd heard about. Until yesterday I thought I was doing something helpful and important. I felt almost like a man again. But I'm just the monster that wizard made me after all."

Tomo turned over, whimpering. "Don't eat me. Please. I can tell you where there's meat enough to feed your whole village."

Jeneba's jaw tightened. "Everyone else here is a monster trying to act like a man, too. Help me. If men can't give us the answer to recovering Yagana, who do we ask?"

They debated the answer the rest of the night. The gods? But none of the group was a priest, or a mount, someone a god possessed and spoke through. Ask some monster? The Little People brought good luck if dealt with correctly. It usually consisted of long life or wealth or education in healing herbs, though. That applied to defeating half-men in wrestling, too. Jeneba had never heard of either half-man or Little People dispensing wisdom. Nor had Ngmengo. Nogama, uchami, and other demons were malevolent and incapable of speech, and perhaps not even able to think above the level of hunting strategies.

"Some water spirits can be friendly," Ngmengo said, "after they've been appeased with food."

Since Lakes were often entrances to the underworld, perhaps spirits had contact with shades. Perhaps a spirit had met Idju's shade. That suggested another possibility, too. "What about asking ghosts?"

Ngmengo shook his head. "I once had an uncle whose ghost appeared to frighten away outlaws about to abduct two of his grandchildren, but I've never heard of a ghost willing to help anyone beyond its immediate family."

"And most won't even help family members." She sighed. "I know." They envied the living, and resented having to depend on descendants for offerings to sustain their existence. Jeneba hugged her knees. "I think Biratha should be eager to help recover Yagana, though."

"He's back in the valley," Ngmengo said. "Why would the prophecy bring us here if Biratha knows the answer?"

The next day Jeneba left the food remaining from breakfast at a crossroad as an offering for Mala-Lesa, but still no answer seemed the right one. Vivid memories of the last time she admitted talking to a leopard kept her from telling Tomo and Ourassi about the meeting or asking them for suggestions.

"We'll try a water spirit first," she told Ngmengo finally.

He grinned. "And then anything that isn't a man."

Lesa's eyes vanished behind the horizon. Ourassi had ridden ahead to scout out a campsite. Now he came galloping back around the hill. "There's a village ahead. We'll swing wide and keep going until we're past it."

"Past it?" Tomo's eyes glittered. "Why not use it? I'll go in and ask about seers."

"I don't think they're welcoming strangers. They either have sickness or they've just finished a battle. There's a whole line of bodies outside the village." Ourassi pointed at birds circling in the sky.

Jeneba caught her breath. "Djero put their dead out?"

Ourassi glanced around and down at her. "Yes. Why?"

Jeneba whirled to Ngmengo. "We forgot about hyenas! Ourassi, wait here. I want to talk to the hyenas." She handed her spear and reins to Ngmengo and started in the direction the Kurasi had come.

"Talk to the hyenas?" Ourassi called after her.

"Can you understand them?" Ngmengo asked.

She glanced back. "Hyenas are part cat, aren't they?" But she touched her heart four times for luck. "You tell them about the leopard, Ngmengo."

Hyenas. She raced around the hill and over the adjoining one, picking her way through the stones and brush toward the circling birds. How could she have forgotten the hyenas, and their magic staff that woke the dead? Chikura was the reason Dasa buried their dead, in sealed jars preferably. But if Djero, like Burdamu, let scavengers dispose of corpses, that meant the hyenas questioned almost every Djero born. Including Idju. Jeneba's pulse quickened.

At the broad top of the hill she dropped flat and crawled through the wiry grass and scrubby brush to the far side. The village sat on top of the next hill, two rows of low, broad houses with conical grass roofs. Below them on the slope eight bodies lay in a row, each curled on its slide with the head pointing east. Some appeared to be women and children. Jeneba's neck prickled. The village had disease, then. She must be careful not to touch the bodies.

The scavengers had no such qualms. Vultures and marabou storks dropped like spears on the corpses. A pair of jackals appeared out of the brush to drag away a young child. Jeneba sucked in her cheeks. Where were the hyenas?

Coming, she realized moments later. A familiar hooting sounded off in the brush, sharpening to a gleeful chuckle. Spotted bodies shambled out of the twilight to charge whooping at the scavenger birds. Squawking and flapping their wings in protest, the storks and vultures yielded, but did not leave. Grouping noisily just beyond reach of the hyenas' snapping jaws, they waited to dart in at the first opportunity. More jackals appeared. The hyenas chased them back, too.

It occurred to Jeneba that she was likely to receive the same welcome. She glanced back up at Mala's eye high in the eastern sky. "Great Mother, protect this foolish leopard's daughter." Touching her heart four times, she stood, straightened the drape of her tsara, and strolled down the hill. "Greetings, cousins."

The hyenas whirled, baring sharp, catlike teeth. Tails hoisted, bristling.

Jeneba stopped short. That put her among the birds, but she kicked a stork that pecked at her bare legs, and backed off two vultures by mimicking a leopard's snarl.

Several hyenas giggled.

Another of them, grizzled, one eye a blind white, shouldered through the birds and jackals toward her and stood staring up, sniffing. He was as large as a leopard. Jeneba forced herself to meet his eyes calmly, though her heart pounded amid all the tearing beaks and powerful jaws. Finally the hyena said, "Leopard. Yes cousin." His tail whisked. "What why, leopard-woman?"

Dismay trickled through her. Maybe Ngmengo had been right to question whether she would be able to understand hyenas. She licked her lips. "I don't mean to interrupt your inquisition and meal, wise one, but I have a question only you may be able to answer."

One-eye sat back. "Ah yes?"

"Years ago there was a seer named Idju in the village of Kanjuna. I need to know if when your people questioned him after his death he said anything about the city of Yagana."

"Yagana?"

One of the hyenas giggled shrilly.

One-eye bared his teeth. The giggle chopped off.

Cold slid down Jeneba's spine. Had they head about Yagana? If they knew, did Lubeda? Urgency stabbed her. "Can you tell me anything about the seer?"

"Is that—" a whisper began, only to stop abruptly when One-eye laid back his ears.

He turned to her and yawned. "How, ah? Kanjuna never territory ours, no."

No, it would not be. Still... "I thought perhaps you talked about interesting interrogations with other clans."

"Clans enemies."

She had seen enough skirmishes between hyena clans to know that was usually the case, but the cut-off whisper, something in his tone, and the lack of bristle in his tail as he mentioned the enmity told her he was lying. The question was: could he be cajoled into admitting clans did talk sometimes?

One-eye fixed her with his sighted eye. "Interest why Djero seer?"

"Because I have friends in Yagana." She hoped she understood him correctly. "You've heard about Yagana."

The hyena leader shrugged. "Maybe yes. Concern no. Night's children us denied sun's children Kurasi."

What? Oh. He meant hyena had no chance to question and eat Kurasi. Kurasi buried their dead, too. "It concerns me, though. But since you know nothing about the seer, I beg your pardon for interrupting you. I'll go talk to one of the mountain clans."

She started to back away. And stopped, breath catching. Sometime while she talked to One-eye, two of the hyenas had slipped around behind her.

"Ah?" One-eye smiled. The show of teeth contained no humor.

Her heart had raced before. Now it slammed against her ribs as though trying to escape from her chest. She forced herself to breathe slowly, fighting panic. "I have a duty to find the city. I must talk to whoever can help me."

"Help you why? Benefit us, how, ah?"

Hope flared. If profit concerned him, he *did* know something! She straightened. "I'm the leopard's daughter, a superior hunter. I can bring down a big kill for you."

Around her, hyena eyes flared in the dying light. One of them whooped. But One-eye's bared teeth brought silence again. "Buffalo?"

Her gut tightened. "The buffalo is my totem, taboo for me to kill." She licked her lips. "Is there anything else that would make helping me worth your trouble?"

One-eye grinned. "Yes maybe." His sighted eye gleamed red. "Kurasi dead."

Revulsion jolted her. "You—" she began, only to stop. If he did have a message that would tell them how to bring

back Yagana, perhaps the Kurasi would willingly pay his
price. Then again, he might have very little. In either case,
though, Ourassi would have to be consulted. "I can't decide
for another people. If you'll give me a hint what you know,
I'll ask a Kurasi." Not that she considered Ourassi an ideal
representative, but he was the only Kurasi at hand.

One-eye hesitated only a moment. "Tell everything seer
said what how yagana. Decide you yes no. Now."

The hyenas behind Jeneba giggled. She frowned. He had
told her nothing. "Everything" could be a great deal, one
word, or nothing. Could she bluff him into more? "You'll
have to be more definite or there's no bargain."

"Ah? So." With a switch of his tail he turned away.

So much for bluffing a hyena. Or was One-eye bluffing,
too? She gritted her teeth to keep from calling him back, to
make herself wait on what he would do next.

He stopped. She bit back a grin just in time. Looking over
his shoulder he said, "Denied us Dasa, too. Dasa you. Dasa
for Yagana?"

The hyenas giggled hysterically. Anger blazed up in her.
"No!" No matter what her duty to Yagana, it was a foreign
city, after all, not worth more than her own people.

"Loss you."

He turned away again and this time kept going. Driving
aside the press of birds, he shambled to the nearest corpse, a
man, and muttered deep in his throat. The air before him
swirled, like a glowing dust-devil, then a short, bone-white
staff appeared at his feet. Chikura! He picked it up in his
mouth and tapped the corpse four times with the end. On the
last touch the Djero opened his eyes. One-eye laid down the
staff and growled something unintelligible at the dead man.

Jeneba sucked in her cheeks. No bargain. The bluff had
failed. But perhaps she had no need for his bargain. One
might be made on her terms.

She turned away, staring down the two hyenas behind her.
"Try to stop me from leaving and my next war tsara will be
hyena-skin."

Their gazes shifted past her to the corpse sitting up shak-
ily. Giggling in anticipation, they trotted to join the rest of
the clan around their victim.

The birds had lost interest in her, too. Jeneba dropped to her belly. Using the deepening dusk and every clump of grass and piece of brush as cover, she crawled along behind them. They did not form a solid line but clustered in ever-shifting groups beyond the teeth of the hyenas. At the first good break between groups, Jeneba wiggled through toward the corpses. A stork noticed her and stretched out its beak for an experimental touch . . . only to jump back squawking at the rumble of a leopard's snarl in her throat.

Within arm's reach of a corpse, Jeneba stopped between two clumps of brush and gathered her legs under her. Then she waited.

The corpses spoke their own language so she understood none of their answers to the hyena's questions. She recognized the tearing sounds beneath the giggling and chuckles at the end of each inquisition, however, and the crack of bones splintered by strong hyena jaws. The breeze brought her the musky smell of the hyenas and a strong, sour scent like that she had smelled around diseased people before. As the light faded, the sounds came closer until with the sky completely black, the group reach the body by Jeneba.

She peered cautiously around the brush. Mala's almost fully opened eye shone brightly on blood-matted coats and reflected like fire in hyena eyes. One-eye still carried the staff. He touched it to the dead man four times. The body stirred. Then just as he had at the first body, One-eye laid down the staff.

Jeneba held her breath. Twisting and bending forward so that her arm lay almost flat on the ground, she reached out of the brush, slowly, cautiously.

The hyenas chortled at the dead man. One-eye asked a question. The dead man muttered thickly.

Her fingers touched the end of the staff. Straddling the tip with two fingers, she began dragging the staff toward her.

A hyena's tone sharpened. The dead man's reply sounded sullen.

Now she could wrap her hand around the shaft. The tip was almost in the brush.

Then One-eye lifted his head. Through the brush she saw him turn away from the dead man, sniffing. A chill slid up her back and a danger cry sounded in her head. Moments later she recognized why . . . the breeze was changing!

One-eye's good eye flared. "Leopard." He looked around, searching, sniffing. And froze, good eye staring at the ground by her bush. "Chikura!"

He had seen! Jeneba leaped to her feet, swinging the staff. It caught One-eye squarely under the jaw. He went down in a crack of meeting teeth. Another hyena rushed her. She clubbed that one on the side of the head, then spinning, bolted away up the hill.

She did not look back. Whoops and hysterical chuckles behind told her the whole clan was in pursuit.

Her father's spirit had been tested wrestling the half-man and uchami, but never running this way. Here was no sprint against a fellow warrior. She ran for Yagana, and for the Kurasi. And she ran for her life.

Reaching deep for all the leopard strength and speed her father had bestowed, Jeneba stretched her stride as long as muscle and bone would allow. She pounded over the hill, down it, around the next to where she had left the others. The wiry grass and brush sliced at her legs. Air burned down her throat to her lungs with each breath.

The hyenas howled close behind.

She rounded the hill. "Ngmengo! I have—"

But the bush-man was not where she had left him. She stumbled to a stop, staring around in disbelieving horror. Everyone had gone, men, horses, even her little bay.

"Ngmengo!" she yelled. "Ourassi! Tomo!"

No one answered.

No. *No!* She gasped for breath. What had happened? Had the men laughed at the idea of taking advice from a leopard and convinced Ngmengo to go on? Had they waited awhile but when dark came decided she must have been killed?

The first hyena appeared around the hill.

She leaped forward again, racing up the slope. Maybe she could see a campfire from there, or find a convenient hole to stuff the staff down and hide it.

The hyenas scrambled after her, eyes flaming.

"Ngmengo!" she yelled again.

"Jeneba," a voice called back.

She turned her head, desperately trying to locate the source. "Ngmengo!"

The hyenas were only spear lengths behind.

"Down here."

Then she saw the campfire, down between two hills beside a spring. She scrambled for it.

"Have Dasa us now," One-eye snarled.

Maybe not. She waved the staff. "Ngmengo! Catch! And don't give it to anyone else." She hurled it at him like a spear.

He plucked it neatly from the air.

Several of the hyenas plunged past her toward the bushman, but did not attack, only circled him, whooping. The rest surrounded the camp. Over her shoulder Jeneba saw One-eye gather to spring at her.

She whirled into a crouch. "Kill me and you'll never have Chikura again."

The hyena stopped.

The two men jumped up where they had been squatting by the fire. "What have you done now?" Tomo snapped.

"That staff is Chikura."

At the edge of her vision she saw the men stare. Ourassi's eyes lighted. "We can bring my father back to life, and the warriors killed in the battle. We can chase away Inyabe forever."

He stepped around the fire, reaching for the staff.

Even before Ngmengo evaded the Kurasi, however, Tomo jumped in Ourassi's path. "No! We can't banish death! Give the staff back, Jeneba."

"Return us," One-eye snarled.

"First we talk," she replied. She straightened and breathed deeply until she stopped panting. "What did the seer Idju tell your people when questioned?"

The hyena's good eye flamed. "Give Chikura us!"

"When I've heard what you know, I promise. No sooner."

The hyenas whooped and giggled and chuckled back and forth. One-eye glared at her. Jeneba waited. Finally One-eye said, "Stone Mountain clan told. Passed story, dam, cubs, generations. Seer said, 'One day many years from now people will come to Kanjuna. I know not what they'll look like or how they call themselves, but they'll be looking for me, and talking about a city called Yagana. Tell them they must find Bisiri's harp and play it where the city stood.'" One-eye bristled his tail. "All. Give Chikura us now."

She whirled toward Ourassi. "We're supposed to find Bisiri's harp."

His eyes snapped away from the staff, the light in them dying to dismay. "It's been lost for generations."

Jeneba looked back at One-eye. "Find it where? How?"

"Me you tell all. Problem you," the hyena replied. "Give Chikura us."

Jeneba frowned at him, but he met her eyes with the unblinking directness of truth. She sighed. "Give it to him, Ngmengo."

"No!" Ourassi howled.

The bush-man tossed it at the hyenas. Tomo sighed in what sounded like relief. One-eye leaped up to snap the staff out of the air and the entire clan raced away whooping.

"You fool!" Ourassi snarled. "Don't you realize the power that staff would give us?"

She had had just about enough of being called that. "Would it bring back Yagana?" she snapped.

He bit his lip.

"It bought us information, though. Think about Bisiri's harp. Don't you have any idea where we can find it?"

He rolled his eyes. "I told you, it disappeared generations ago."

There must be some way to track it, some clue in the words of either Idju or the seer in Yagana. *Seek her in the mountains.* She kept coming back to that. In the mountains . . . in caves? In the entrances to the underworld?

As though guessing her thoughts, Ngmengo said, "Maybe we can bribe a water spirit to talk to Bisiri's shade and ask him where it is."

Ourassi scowled. "I wouldn't trust a spirit. Bisiri could only tell us where it was when he died, anyway. If he even had it then."

"It isn't as if the harp is one of his own ribs," Tomo said, and sucked in a sudden, sharp breath.

Jeneba felt the same shock. "Bujhada," she breathed. *That*

was the answer . . . Bisiri's sacrificing friend. A man always knew where his bones lay.

She met the men's eyes. Both pairs glittered with excitement. Ourassi had had the thought, too.

Only Ngmengo frowned at them in puzzlement. "I don't understand."

No, not coming from a tribe that let the hyenas eat its dead. There were no bones left. Quickly, she explained.

He grinned. "We'll bribe a water spirit to talk to Bujhada's shade."

No, a water spirit would not do. The words of the seer in Yagana echoed again in Jeneba's mind and its meaning rang clear. They must seek Yagana in the mountains, in the entrances to the underworld. If they wanted to find the harp, they must go down to the world of the dead and ask Bujhada where his rib was.

CHAPTER

NINE

The cave entrance looked unimpressive, a low hole in the mountainside nearly hidden behind a tangle of brush and vines. They might have overlooked it except for a faint path to it and the offerings before it, a pot of fermented milk surrounded by hot peppers, yams, dates, and a pasty dough like busumwo.

Jeneba arched her brows. It hardly seemed like an entrance likely to lead to the underworld. The local villagers they talked to, though, had claimed to see ghosts around it all the time. The offerings supported at least the belief that they had. One old man had told them, too, about two of his age-set who dared to go into the cave years before when they were all boys.

They said it goes down so far they couldn't reach the bottom though they climbed all day, the old man said. *And all around them the whole time they felt shades brushing against them and heard their sighs and groans. Soon after coming out, they both sickened and died.*

Remembering that sent a chill down Jeneba's spine. By venturing into the underworld, they might be condemning themselves to death. But what other choice did they have? Bujhada must be found.

"We don't know how long we'll be gone," Ourassi said. "Jeneba, you stay here and look after the horses."

"Let me," Ngmengo said. "I'm not suited for climbing." He shook his branches. "Predators and monsters won't attack me, either."

Ourassi shrugged.

They lit two of the stock of torches made from tree branches. Gathering up the spare torches and stepping carefully over the offerings, they ducked in through the cave mouth.

A narrow passage beyond sloped downward away from the bright afternoon light. Into darkness.

Ngmengo's voice followed them. "Ntolo go with you."

Twists of the passage soon blocked out the light from the entrance. They moved along the slowly broadening passage with only the torches to see by. Then even that failed as walls and roof vanished. All the torches showed was the floor plunging steeply downward. Tomo hurled a stone out into the yawning darkness. It seemed forever before the rattle of its landing came echoing back to them from far out and below.

"We'd better mark our path," Ourassi said.

The floor softened into scree, mud and stones washed from the entrance by rainwater. They slid and skidded down it, pausing frequently to pile stones for markers or scratch lines on larger boulders with the points of their knives. The air hung heavy and stale, but not motionless. Touches as light as cobwebs slid time and again along Jeneba's arms, neck, and legs, and once she swore fingers traced the tribal scar across her cheek. Angry hisses spat in her ears. From the way the men started and brushed at themselves, they felt the same thing.

Occasionally light reflected back at the torches from out in the blackness, in glints or a pale vertical strip, and as they reached the bottom, Jeneba saw why. Stone hung down from above or jutted up in long cones from pools of water so still and clear that the reflected stone seemed to stretch downward into an infinity of darkness, too. One row where hanging rock matched projections coming up from below reminded Jeneba uncomfortably of monstrous teeth. Some places the teeth met and fused into a single pillar.

They carefully marked the floor and stone pillars as they threaded their way between pools across the cavern.

The wall on the far side rippled downward in a glossy stone waterfall gleaming in a rainbow of colors. As though a section of the Rainbow Serpent had been buried. Jeneba ran her fingers across the surface. It felt as slick and smooth as glazed pottery.

A tall, archlike opening through the wall opened into another passage, this one with the countless stone spears from its roof tangled in a mass of filaments like roots turned to stone. The passage led steadily downward, turning and twisting until it emptied into a series of ever deeper and colder caverns. Jeneba regretted having left her kadoru on the back of the horse. And all the while, the cobweb touches continued. The hissing in her ears became more and more clearly voices, and more and more shrill, though speaking no language she understood.

Despite her shivers and the suffocating swirl of ghosts, Jeneba found herself fascinated by the caverns . . . the massive stone pillars, jeweled grottoes, curtains and waterfalls of stone shining or glinting in the torchlight.

Most amazing of all, though, after a while, the deeper they went, the better she saw. Even details high on the cavern roofs and well beyond the edge of the torchlight were visible. Details the men could not see.

Ourassi held his dimming torch out at arm's length and peered frowning into the darkness beyond. "These burn too fast. We'd better find something soon or we'll be using the torches we need to get back up."

And what happened when they reached that point? Jeneba wondered. Go back when the underworld might lie just beyond the next cavern? Go on though it would mean they might have to find their way out blind . . . which would probably mean never getting out at all?

"There are two openings out of this cavern," she said. "One to our left has water running into it so it must go down."

"Left where?" He squinted past the torch. "I wish I had your leopard's eyes. I can't see anything."

"I think I do," Tomo said.

He proved it by heading straight for the opening.

A short passage beyond led into yet another cavern, which dropped in a series of broad water-filled steps to a great underground lake filling most of the rest of the cavern. They had to work their way around the sides, climbing through a forest of cones growing up from the floor. The chill of the stone ate into Jeneba.

Ourassi stared around him with a grin. "I can see, too."
He raised his voice above the howl of ghosts. "This is beautiful!"

But the torches were nearly out. How could any of them
see? Her skin prickled with more than cold. Even her vision
was too good. She could even distinguish color. Some of the
rock had a reddish tone. So did Ourassi's dyed skin.

Jeneba blinked. Ourassi, too? She stared harder at him,
and at the rock. Her breath caught. It was the light, not
Ourassi, that was red. But the torches glowed yellow.

What light was she seeing?

Ghost voices screamed.

In the next chamber the color and flicker of the light became more pronounced, and in the one after that a tunnel on
the far side pulsed with red light.

Ourassi stared at it. Jeneba heard his sharp intake of
breath, even through the ghost voices. "Fire. We're almost
there."

She frowned at him. "There's no fire in the underworld.
Each level is darker than the last."

"In your Dasan underworld, yes, mortal, but you've come
hunting Kurasi dead."

The voice whispered, its sibilance overriding the ghost
voices so that as the sound of it faded, the ghosts, too, fell
silent. It spoke no language she knew, not Burda or Sifri, the
Keoru language, nor any dialect of Dase, yet she understood
it perfectly.

"All men understand death's language, mortal."

Jeneba whirled. Behind them stood a great head, as tall as
a man, with arms coming out his ears and legs protruding
where his neck should be. Scars spiraled on the broad copper
cheeks; black and bright red beads decorated thin coppery
braids dangling down the forehead.

"Inyabe," Ourassi breathed. Whooping, he ran for the red
tunnel.

But the Kurasi messenger of death leaped over their heads
to come down blocking the way. His voice hissed. "Only the
dead may enter."

Ourassi protested in his own language, saying something
that used the names of Bujhada, Bisiri, and Yagana. He

tossed his head and reached out as though to push the messenger aside.

Inyabe evaded while remaining between Ourassi and the glowing tunnel. "I know you consider your mission urgent, but you must go back to the upper world, where living men belong."

A surge of desperation knotted Jeneba's gut. They could not come this far to find themselves on yet another lost road? Only Bujhada could help them find the harp. The god must know that. How could he—

The thought broke off in a sudden idea. Inyabe was not a true god. "Does death's messenger rule the underworld?"

Ourassi glanced sidelong at her, then focused back on Inyabe. "He does not," he said in Burda. "Amurangi sits in power here. Take me to him, messenger."

Inyabe frowned. "It's he who instructed me to turn you back."

Ourassi drew himself up. "If he wants obedience, let Amurangi himself command me."

"Hear me, then, Ourassi Ijhelo," a new voice boomed. It reverberated around the cavern, echoing back and forth until it seemed that a chorus of voices shouted. "You *cannot enter*."

Ourassi whirled, obviously searching the shadows of the cavern for the speaker. "Amurangi, great master of fire, ruler of the underworld, hear me. Without the harp made from Bujhada's rib, my people will be destroyed. I refuse to allow that!"

"You refuse to allow that." Laughter boomed, mocking laughter so thunderous Jeneba clapped her hands over her ears against the pain of it. "What a pretty speech." The light in the tunnel flickered as a shadow moved across it, the giant silhouette of a man. "Were you so concerned about your people when you let your father die?"

Ourassi's head snapped up. *"I didn't—"*

More mocking laughter interrupted him. Ourassi went stone stiff. Amurangi hissed, "In your greed for power, you *did* abandon your father to certain death. There are no lies here. Only in the world of living men may one deceive others, and himself."

Ourassi's mouth worked, but no sound came out. After a moment, he closed his mouth and turned away, shoulders slumping. Jeneba thought she heard a sob.

Tomo drew himself up. "If the living can't enter, kill me. I'll enter as a shade, learn what we need from Bujhada, and come back to tell you."

Amurangi chuckled. "Yes, you'd like that, Tomo Silla. Dying would satisfy you very well. You could not be returned to Kiba, and the Kurasi would believe you sacrificed yourself for Yagana. But the dead you joined would know better."

Now Tomo stiffened.

The god turned toward Jeneba. Even against the light streaming around Amurangi, his skin and hair glowed light, bright copper with flame chasing across them. None of his features showed, however, nothing except eyes that gleamed like an animal's in firelight. The eyes pierced to her soul. "What about you, leopard's daughter? Will you, too, offer to die for Yagana . . . or is duty and honor less important to you than living to go home and vindicate yourself in the eyes of your people?"

The gibe stung, but his sneering tone also struck a spark of anger that overrode her rush of shame. And through the anger she saw a flaw in his question. "How could I aid Yagana by dying? I'm Dasa; this is the Kurasi underworld."

This time his laughter carried genuine amusement. "Very good. You're right. Only Ourassi's shade can come in."

Anger flared hotter in her. "I thought you said there are no lies here. My people have many stories about visiting the underworld. I think we could all come in as living people if you'd let us."

Red light pulsed behind the god. Flames chased down his arms and body. He himself stood very still, however.

Tomo and Ourassi stirred. Ourassi turned back, blinking like a waking sleeper. He wiped tears from his cheeks. "We have such stories, too. In the name of Yagana, I comm— I beg you to let us pass!"

The flames around Amurangi jumped higher. "It's dangerous. The sight of living people will excite much resentment. You may be attacked."

Ourassi sucked in a deep breath. "Perhaps it would be just punishment. There's no risk too great for Yagana."

"Risk?" Tomo snorted. "We felt and heard ghosts all the way down here. They were harmless."

The glowing eyes narrowed, then Amurangi moved to one side of the tunnel. "Enter, then. Inyabe will guide you. Remember, however: this is your world; beyond me you enter theirs."

A chill seeped through Jeneba. She reached under her tsara for the haft of her knife . . . then let go, grimacing. A blade offered no protection against the dead.

They followed Inyabe past Amurangi.

Into another great cavern. Flame flickered everywhere, blue across pools in the floor, red down the roof and walls and rock formations. Yet it gave off little light, no more than twilight dimness, and no heat. Jeneba hugged herself, shivering.

Or was it the cold she shivered from? All around them moved shades, sitting in groups on rocks, swimming in the flaming pools, Kurasi with the brightness of their copper hair and skin faded, gone dull as spear points seen in the gray light before sunrise. All except their eyes. Those gleamed with the brightness of flame as the shades turned to watch the visitors.

Several leaned toward companions, whispering. The sound reached Jeneba as a hiss. Shades on the rocks climbed down and those in the pools crawled out . . . never taking their eyes from the visitors. They fell in line behind the party.

Jeneba edged closer to Tomo and Ourassi.

Ourassi glanced backward. "How far before we reach Bujhada?"

Inyabe raised a broad brow. "Awhile. Newcomers pushed older shades into farther caverns and Bujhada died many generations ago. Do you want to go back?"

Ourassi eyed the shades again. He shook his head.

Awhile? A long while, Jeneba reflected grimly. They followed him through one cavern after another in endless succession. Each looked the same. Rocks and water burned.

Shades stared with smoldering eyes, to whisper and stand
... to join the group trailing the party.

Or stalking them. The hissing whispers grew slowly
louder, angrier.

"What are they saying?" Tomo asked Ourassi.

Inyabe replied, "They want to know why living men have
been allowed to enter, especially foreigners and a Kurasi so
ashamed of his blood that he darkens his skin and hair."

Ourassi stopped and spun to face the shades behind them.
He called out something.

Inyabe interrupted him. "They don't understand you. The
Kurasi language of their lifetime is different from yours."

The shades shuffled closer. A murmur like the rumble of
thunder ran through them.

Ourassi stiffened his back and spoke again.

Inyabe smiled thinly. "I could be your linguist, yes, but do
you really want them to know who you are and why you're
here? However much they resent the living, they still love
Yagana. They feel the emptiness where their soul should be.
If they knew who lost her, they would tear him apart. A just
punishment, perhaps, as you said, but would that help recover Yagana?"

A shade stalked a step closer yet toward them, teeth
bared. Another shade followed, and another.

Tomo drew his knife.

"No!" Jeneba shouted, but the warning drowned beneath
a deafening howl.

The mob of shades surged forward.

Shadows could not hurt someone, she told herself, but the
nails of one raked Jeneba's face and opened the skin. Another tore at her arm. She shrieked in pain. Somewhere in
the press she could hear Ourassi and Tomo screaming, too.
The touch of the shades seared, so cold it burned like fire,
withering her flesh even as their nails ripped her. With blood
running hot down her face and arm she flung sideways to
escape. But the shades were everywhere, and they closed in
with the predatory grins of hyenas.

No! They were dead, immaterial shades. How could they
feel so solid? How could they press around her, snarling,
slashing, tearing? When Jeneba tried to strike back, though,

her hands passed through them. In desperation, she clawed out her knife, but of course it had no effect, either. They only walked through the blade to pound and rip at her. Her tsara shredded. Shade nails left gash after seared, bleeding gash in the flesh beneath. She screamed again and again at each wave of scalding cold, and whirled, lashing out in vain at the maddened mob pressing around her. She must not fall, she warned herself. She might never get up again.

"Mala, help us," she screamed. Surely Mala-Lesa could see her even in the Kurasi's fiery underworld.

If the High God did, though, Mala chose not to interfere. No great force swept away the shades.

Jeneba felt strength draining with her blood. In its place came despair. Amurangi had warned them about the underworld. Now they were going to die down here.

The thought also brought a brief flash of bitter amusement. Die in the world of the dead, killed by shades. Yet her own shade would still have a long journey, first back to the surface and then, soon, because no one would know she was dead and sustain her with offerings, down to join the warikile, older ghosts, in the shadows of the Dasan middle underworld.

Her flesh felt as though it were charred, ready to drop from her bones. But by now she screamed less in pain than fury and frustration. Was there *no* way to fight back? Must she, a good warrior, die unable to inflict any injuries on these savage copper shadows?

Stone roughened underfoot. Jeneba stumbled . . . and staggered backward, arms flailing desperately to help regain her balance. Her back bumped against stone. A fleeting glance around identified it as one of the stone spikes. Cold flames licked down it. She whirled, shoved the knife between her teeth, and began climbing. The rippled stone had the glassy smoothness of glazed pottery but it also dripped in strings and folds, and each offered toe and fingerholds . . . precarious but still they were holds. The flames lapping at her felt no colder than the touch of the shades. With weakness came less awareness of pain in general, a creeping numbness she wearily welcomed. Long-nailed hands from below caught at her legs and ankles. Since kicking no more dislodged them then slashing with her knife had driven back shades on the cave floor, she set her jaw and dragged them up the stone with her. Leopards climbed with a load all the time. So could she.

A foot slipped. She dug her toes into the stone . . . felt skin scrape from the ends with the force of her grip, felt the sticky warmth of blood. Still, she dragged herself higher.

The spike rose all the way to the ceiling. Once she reached the top, there would be nowhere else to go. The shades could climb up and pull her off. At the moment Jeneba did not care, though. Falling was a quicker, better death than being torn apart and having the flesh burned from her bones.

She looked down. Now she could see Ourassi and Tomo. Ourassi stood with his back to stone and one arm raised to protect his face while he whipped the other back and forth through the shades tearing at him. He bled from as many slashes as she did. Shades completely surrounded Tomo, who threw himself at each charging shade, snarling as furiously as they did.

Jeneba almost lost her grip on the stone. She stared down at Tomo. He showed not a single wound, and each time a shade collided with him, it bounced off. Then both Tomo and the shade screamed. In disappointment. Tomo was still courting Ello, with the same disappointing results.

She caught her breath. The shades could not harm Tomo. Why? Because the gods chose to make him live? Because he wanted to die? Or maybe some other reason.

If a man wanted to die, he would not fear that which might kill him. They had felt the shades but not been hurt by them on the climb down through the caverns. There had been no injuries until after Amurangi implied there was danger in meeting shades in their own world.

Even if Tomo had given her a way to fight the shades, however, the three of them still needed a guide through the underworld. She peered around the cavern, searching for Inyabe . . . and saw him finally, lounging against a stone spike at the far end of the cavern.

Jeneba slid down the stone.

Shade hands snatched at her. Their touch seared as agonizingly as ever, but fear still ran through her, too. She forced herself to keep climbing down, right into the thick of them. They could harm only those who feared them, she told herself firmly. If her hands and knife passed through them, she should be able to walk right through them, too, to go anywhere she wished.

Jumping the last short distance down from the stone, she shoved her knife back into its sheath and hurled herself into the mass of shades, wading toward Ourassi. Shade nails raked her. She made herself ignore the pain, as she shut out the agony of her ripped and burn-withered skin. Maybe each new touch hurt a little less than the last.

"Ourassi! Don't fight!" she called. "Just walk through them and don't be afraid. They're only hurting us because Amurangi made us think they could!"

The nails of a shade dragged down her arm, but this time no pain came. Another shade leaped at her, a woman's. She brushed by like the touch of a feather. No new pain! Whooping in triumph, Jeneba pushed through to Ourassi and grabbed his arm. "Inyabe is this way." She towed him toward where she had seen death's messenger. "Run at them. They're as harmless as they were in the caverns on the way down. Tomo, you come, too," she called to him in Dase. "They can't kill you, either."

Lighted by the dim red light of the flames, the shades continued to attack, screaming, in wave after furious wave. Jeneba shed them like shadows and strode on to where Inyabe lounged.

The messenger started at the sight of them. After a moment he smiled. A gesture without humor. "You're braver and cleverer than we thought. I suppose you insist on going on? This way."

Jeneba lost track of time. They seemed to follow the messenger forever, though without growing hungry or feeling any need to sleep. Along the way shades hissed and glowered, but never tried attacking again. One followed them, though, a man's, groaning and sighing and pleading. Unlike all the others, he had shaved his head nearly bare, leaving only a little fringe around the hairline, just enough to let him tie on blue and white beads. As Nbaba did. He wore Nbaban scar patterns on his calves, too.

Tomo frowned back at him. "What's he saying?"

Ourassi shrugged. "I don't know. I can't understand his language."

"It's Bisiri," Inyabe said. "He asks you to give Bujhada a message, that Bisiri loves him and begs his forgiveness."

Bisiri!

Ourassi stared at the shade. "I know how he feels." His voice caught. "I would give my father the same message."

Uneasiness slid down Jeneba's spine. "Why doesn't he tell Bujhada himself?"

The humorless smile twisted Inyabe's mouth again. "You'll see."

They reached a vast, shallow lake swept by sheets of blue flame. Inyabe waded through it to one of several small islands rising in the center. A shade sat on the stone bank, dangling his feet in the icy fire of the water. Snakelike scars crossed his cheeks and his hair had been twisted into thin ropes gathered in a knot on top of his head. He scrambled to his feet at the sight of them, staring, nostrils flaring.

Inyabe pointed at him. "This is the one you seek."

"Bujhada," Ourassi breathed. He held out his hands to the shade. "Inyabe, tell him I am so honored to meet him, then tell him why we're here."

Jeneba disliked the sardonic quirk of the messenger's mouth as he gave Bujhada's shade a brief story of Yagana's fate and the search to recover the city. The shade's bitter laugh as he listened disturbed her even more.

At the end of the recitation, the shade muttered to Inyabe and turned away.

Inyabe grimaced. "He asks me to take you away. He refuses to speak to you."

"No! He can't!" Ourassi protested.

"He says he was a fool to love Bisiri so much, and an even bigger fool to sacrifice his life for that love. He wishes to have nothing more ever to do with any living men, particularly one who like Bisiri thinks only of himself, who takes all from others for his own profit. Come. We'll go back."

"Wait!" Ourassi cried. "Appeal to his honor. Tell him how much his city needs him."

Inyabe chuckled. "The dead have no honor. What use is it?"

"There must be some way to make him talk to us. It's the only way we can find his rib."

Inyabe cocked a broad brow. "The dead cannot be *made* to do anything."

"Try bribery," Tomo said.

"How?" Ourassi asked bitterly. "A chinu, one of the dead upon the earth, is one thing. It will do anything for food offerings. But the lummachinu, the dead below the earth, are beyond touch."

Jeneba pursed her lips, remembering the story about Bisiri and Bujhada the warrior told. "Maybe not. Wouldn't they still like to live? We can offer life of a kind . . . immortality."

Tomo scowled. "What?"

Jeneba turned to Inyabe. "Remind him of his people's saying: a man is never dead until he is forgotten. Tell him that the harp will make him live again as it sings to his people of him in new epics and praise-songs. All Kurasi will know that his love of his people and city has lasted even through death. His selflessness will be an inspiration to everyone."

Tomo snorted, but when Inyabe repeated her words, Bujhada glanced around.

Ourassi sucked in a quick, excited breath. "Yes. Can you make up a praise-poem for him now?"

Jeneba hesitated. "Why don't you?"

He grimaced. "My brother Towejho is a poet, not me."

And Mseluku had been the best after the bard in the court at Kiba. Mala! If only Ngmengo were here.

Jeneba thought frantically, trying to remember all the praise-poems she knew, hunting inspiration.

"Bujhada!" Tomo began.

Steadfast.
Most selfless of men.
You gave all to friendship.
You—you—

Jeneba's gut squeezed as he floundered. She said hurriedly, "I bow in awe."

> I weep.
> How could such sacrifice
> Bloom into tragedy?
> Bujhada!
> Immortal.
> Smooth bow of bone,
> Coil of snake
> Ivory-gleaming.
> In vanity strung,
> What music you make:
> Epics, love songs, dirges,
> And over and over
> Notes sweetest of all sing:
> Bujhada. Bujhada! Hoooh! Bujhada!

Inyabe echoed her. Bujhada's shade turned around, eyes gleaming. It whispered.

"Do you promise that praises of him will be sung all across the empire?" Inyabe said.

"Across the world. I promise," Ourassi said.

The shade stared hard into Ourassi for a long time, then sighed heavily. Through Inyabe he said, "The rest of my bones are dust in that mountain grave. Bring what is left of me home to Yagana. Souraka Chimbua has it."

Jeneba had never heard the name before.

"Who is he?" Ourassi asked. "Where do we find him?"

"To the south and east, in the plains below the Mburi highlands."

"Nbaba and Tou territory. Which is this Souraka?" Ourassi asked.

But as Inyabe translated, the shade's gaze jumped to stare past them. His eyes flared. Hissing, he whirled and dashed away. Jeneba looked around to see Bisiri's shade wading through the blue fire of the lake toward them.

"Bujhada," the shade cried pitifully.

"Resign yourself," Inyabe said. "He refuses to forgive

you. Come," he told the rest of them. "Now you must go back to your world."

They left Bisiri's shade weeping against a stone spire rising from the water.

Tomo's lip curled. "After all this time, he still cries when he doesn't have what he wants."

Anger flared in Jeneba. "You've certainly become quick to condemn the faults of others."

His eyes slid toward her and away again. "No more than I condemn my own."

"But Bisiri has atoned for his weakness," Inyabe said back at them. "After Yagana was lost, he wandered many months and long distances across the world, searching for the way to regain the city. A camp of Nbaba found him ill and starving. Not knowing who he was or what he had done, they nursed him back to health. He confessed to the chief about himself, but the Nbaba allowed him to remain with them. The chief became his blood brother and consulted many wise men and seers about how to recover Yagana. None could provide more of an answer than that one day Bisiri himself would discover the way if he were patient. So Bisiri became the camp bard, making praise-songs for all occasions and accompanying himself on his harp. He never let it sing of Yagana, though, for fear his heart would break hearing of it. He died fighting with his adopted people."

"Then he never found how to recover Yagana," Tomo said. A smug satisfaction in his voice made Jeneba want to claw out his heart.

Inyabe smiled thinly. "But he did. In the battle he gave his life to save the chief's. At the moment Bisiri sacrificed himself for his friend without thought of reward or immortality, Yagana reappeared." He paused, gaze boring into Tomo. "What will you do?"

Tomo opened his mouth but before he could speak, death's messenger waved his hand. Jeneba hurled into searing heat and blinding bright light. Where were they now? But the pain of the light would not let her open her eyes enough to see.

"Jeneba!" a voice said in surprise. "How did you come out of the cave without me seeing you?"

Her heart jumped. Ngmengo! Cautiously, she forced her eyes open a crack. They stood in mountain woods at the mouth of the cave. What she had taken to be some new torture was simply the normal temperature and light of the upper world.

Ourassi blinked around. Anxiety edged his voice. "How many days have we been gone? How much time have we lost?"

"Days?" Now Ngmengo blinked. "The sun's traveled barely a spear length across the sky."

Jeneba felt her jaw drop. The men looked dumbfounded, too. All that time going down and following Inyabe through the underworld without time passing? But more than that, she realized belatedly that all their wounds had vanished. Even their clothing had become whole again.

Ourassi ran for the hobbled horses. "Mount up, quickly!"

"What did you learn?" Ngmengo called after him. "Where are we going?"

"South," he flung back over his shoulder, "to find someone named Souraka Chimbua. If we ride hard, maybe we still have time to find the harp and reach Yagana before Lubeda does."

CHAPTER

TEN

They rode hard...the rest of the day, straight through to dawn, and through the next several days and nights while the wide eye of Mala lighted their way all night. Stops were brief and infrequent, just enough for some sleep while the horses watered and rested or while they found food for themselves. They rode fast, trotting a great deal, often running beside the horses, cantering when the horses seemed fresh enough. The hoofbeats rapped out the name of the man they hunted. Souraka Chimbua. Souraka. Souraka. He must be Tou, Jeneba decided. She had met a few Nbaba and the name did not sound like theirs.

Ourassi watched the moon with grim eyes. She could almost hear his thoughts. In eight days Lubeda would be in Najhadende.

In seven. The same thought reverberated through her head.

In six days. Five. And still the villages were Djero. She watched his hands whiten around his reins.

Why she felt compelled to offer encouragement Jeneba did not quite understand. Perhaps because she found herself disliking him less. But she felt the press of time, too, so maybe the words were as much for her own benefit as his. "Lubeda might wait a day before he decides your army isn't coming," she said during one watering stop. "The march to Yagana will take seven more. That gives us until—"

"The dark of the moon to be back," Ourassi finished. "I know." He stared past her our across the hills. "Kuma grant that's enough. I'm beginning to wonder how long we'll need to find people in this country."

Jeneba wondered how people lived. It had become bleak

landscape ... dry, blistering hot, vegetation so sparse that
bare soil spread between patches of scrubby brush and withered, wiry grass. Broad expanses of cracked earth surrounded every lake. Many had dried up completely. Blowing
weeds and dust rattled against the crumbling stilts of abandoned lake villages while hippo and crocodile bones protruded from the hard-baked earth. They saw none of the
herds she was used to seeing on the plains. A few antelope,
some wild sheep ... jackals, hyenas, and vultures, too, but
in small groups. No buffalo, no wildebeest, no zebra or giraffe.

The party drank long and deep whenever they found
water, and filled the water bags. Tomo had scoffed when
Ngmengo urged them to risk visiting a Djero village to trade
some of Ourassi's arm bands for the pig stomachs. Now they
were grateful for his insistence.

"The sand is coming for Yagana," Ourassi whispered.

Though only halfway to zenith, Lesa's eye had already
bleached the sky and heated the hills so that the air danced
and shimmered before them, and blue pools rippled among
the brush. Demon pools, evaporating before the riders
reached them. Jeneba shivered. Would the green plains
around Kiba look like this one day, too?

Ngmengo whooped. "There's a village that looks inhabited."

Jeneba saw it, though "camp" might be a better description. The Nbaba appeared to have just returned to being
nomads. Brush-fenced pens and flat-topped tents of woven
grass mats clustered beside the remnant of what must have
once been a huge lake. Their cattle and sheep spread out
across the surrounding slopes.

A lone villager appeared as they rode up to the camp, an
old man, slender and dark yellow-brown, his hips wrapped
in yellow-and-indigo striped cloth, his face and arms painted
red-ochre with tribal scars highlighted in white. Jeneba
heard others inside the grass-mat tents, though, and smelled
them ... the acid tang of fear-sweat. She sucked in her
cheeks. What had happened to these people besides drought?
The Nbaba she had met from farther south and west, where

their lands bordered Dasan territory, had been friendly, laughing people.

This old man did not even smile. He stood solemn, head high, the red beads in his fringe of hair ticking against each other in the hot wind. His only flicker of expression, betraying amazement and uncertainty, came when his gaze wandered across Ngmengo. But Jeneba did not think the bush-man accounted for the undertone of fear in his voice. "I am Mafala, son of Bomela of the clan Ufuno, chief of this village," he said in Burda. "Who are you? What do you want here?"

Jeneba caught a flash of motion past the narrow opening of one tent, motion and a gleam of light on a copper edge. Someone inside stood ready with a spear.

She noticed Ourassi eyeing the tents, too. "I am Ourassi, grandfather, son of—" He choked suddenly on the words . . . sat gripping his reins white-knuckled and breathing hard for several heartbeats. He finally continued in a strained voice. "Son of Biratha of the clan Ijhelo of the Kurasi. We seek a man named Souraka Chimbua. Can you tell us where to find him?"

The chief stared up at him in silence a long while before replying. "I don't know him myself but travelers have brought many stories. That Tou has a bad belly."

The Nbaba way of saying this Souraka was an evil person. Jeneba sucked in her cheeks.

"He has something which belongs to my people," Ourassi said.

The chief nodded. "He claims to be a king building a kingdom, but he's only an outlaw, demanding tribute from camps, Tou as well as Nbaba, and attacking if he doesn't receive it. Survivors are sold to the Djero and Chullo. It's said he protects his warriors with powerful charms. It would be safer to let him keep your property."

Ourassi regarded him solemnly. "I must recover it, grandfather."

Tomo sniffed. "Only old men and women worry about safety," he said in Nbaba. Impatience edged his voice. "Do the stories say where Souraka is?"

Jeneba started in dismay. Even tired and desperate as they

were, how could Tomo speak to an elder without the respect and honorifics simple courtesy required? She caught expressions of embarrassment on Ngmengo's face. And Ourassi's; even if the Kurasi did not understand the words, Tomo's tone was unmistakable.

The chief's eyes narrowed. "Travel south and east. If the stories are correct, you will soon find his spoor. Or he may find you, cousin."

Discomfort became a grin Jeneba swallowed. The old man used the term for father's brother's son, a minor kinsman among the matriarchal Nbaba, hardly of account. The tightening of Tomo's jaw told her he recognized the reproof in the choice. He said nothing, however, only wheeled his horse toward the water.

"We thank you, grandfather," Jeneba replied for him in Nbaba.

They and the horses drank deeply at the lake and refilled the water bags.

After the camp disappeared behind them, Jeneba reined her bay back beside Tomo. "Is that how Malekuro speak to chiefs and elders?"

Tomo stared silently ahead.

"*Is* he Malekuro?" Ourassi asked. He turned on his horse to stare back at the two of them. "You and Amurangi call him by a different name and talk of returning to Kiba. The god says he wants to die. Inyabe asks how will he atone. What have you done, one-who-calls-himself-Tshemba?"

Tomo stiffened. "It won't interfere with finding the harp."

Ourassi's eyes narrowed. He glanced questioningly at Jeneba. "Will you tell me? Has it something to do with the reason you must vindicate yourself to your people?"

"It's a personal matter between Tomo and me." No need to tell the world about his treachery. "But Yagana's recovery comes first."

Ourassi shifted his gaze back and forth between them then up to the bush-man ahead and sighed. "Great Kuma. Why should Jhirazi maneuver to send such as we on so important a search?"

Ngmengo looked back with a wry smile. "I think the

many roads of the future must be stranger than any of us realize."

They rode the rest of that day and two more, impatient at the time used for every step, asking about Souraka in the camps they passed—three Nbaba and one Tou—once someone would be talked out of hiding. All four camps had heard of him. None knew more than rumors of where he might be found.

Ruined stationary villages lay much closer together, some simply abandoned and weathering away, others burned to the dusty ground. Jeneba eyed each with gut knotting. There was obviously a battle going on for this country, often fierce. No wonder everyone hid with spears.

Toward evening a game trail with fresh antelope tracks led them to a spring. They backed away as soon as they spotted the pool beyond a rock outcropping, though. Four antelope still stood drinking. A lucky number.

"Supper," Ngmengo whispered.

Ourassi frowned from his spear to the rocks. "Can either of you throw left-handed?"

A left-handed throw would let the thrower remain mostly in cover, lessening the chance of the antelope seeing him and bolting.

Tomo shook his head.

Jeneba never threw left-handed, either.

"Could a leopard reach one of them from the rocks?" Ngmengo raised a brow at her.

Ourassi turned to look at her, too.

Leopard. She shrugged. "I'll try."

She vaulted off her bay and edged along the rocks to peer around them at the spring, measuring the distance with her eyes.

"Kujhimbe, god of the animals, takes animal forms," Ourassi hissed after her, "so be sure to ask the antelope if he's Kujhimbe before you kill him."

Crawling up the rocks, she scooted along the top of them on her belly. The spring lay below, with the antelope playfully butting each other and nibbling at the patches of green grass around the banks. Jeneba reached under her tsara for her knife, then carefully drew up her knees, gathering, muscles coiling. The leopard in her snarled eagerly.

An antelope flung up its head, nostrils and ears twitching. Jeneba froze.

After several moments the antelope dropped its head to the water again.

She sprang.

The surge of power carried her up and out from the rocks. With it came exhilaration, pure joy in the strength and grace of her body. The leap brought its own pleasure, too. She felt as thought she floated, gliding with dreamlike slowness, able to hang above the antelope forever.

The animals moved at the same speed. They reminded her of the warriors and spears in the battle at Najhadende. One bawled in warning. The others' heads drifted up. Hindquarters bunched for the first great bound away.

Too late. She dropped on one. Her weight carried them both to the ground, and before the animal could recover enough to struggle, she slashed its throat. Kujhimbe was Ourassi's god, not hers.

But for safety, she murmured, "If you're Kujhimbe, forgive me for killing you. We need you to eat."

Then somewhere close, a child cried. It was muffled almost instantly, but not before Jeneba looked up in the direction of the sound.

An Nbaba woman jumped back among the rocks on the slope above the other side of the spring. Not quickly enough to avoid being seen. She had companions among the rocks with her, too, Jeneba saw. An eye showed here, a glimpse of hair or fingers there. Too few to be an entire encampment, she judged. Ten or twelve at most, women and children. From the woman's face, drawn and unpainted, and the way she had clutched a bow she carried, Jeneba wondered if they might not be refugees from some battle like the ones that destroyed the villages she had been seeing.

"Share with us," she called up in Nbaba, slapping the carcass. "It's too much for just my companions and me."

The woman's head reappeared, expression suspicious. Then a man's voice murmured . . . too low for even Jeneba to catch more than a word or two, something to do with food.

Hunger overcame suspicion. One by one the hiders left cover.

Jeneba saw she had miscounted. They also had two men, one very old, the other with a bloody arm wrapped in a bandage of dry grass.

The two groups shared not only the meat and cluster of rocks for the night but some roots and dried fruit the Nbaba had with them. The Nbaba eyed Ngmengo warily at first, a fear that ebbed finally when the bush-man pulled out his flute and began playing and singing.

Only to return abruptly when Ourassi asked about Souraka. Eyes went white-rimmed. The women clutched their children.

"Yes, we know him," the old man said bitterly. "He attacked and destroyed our camp a month ago. We're all who managed to escape."

Jeneba's heart jumped in dismay. A month! They were still that far from the harp?

But Ourassi moved around the campfire to squat by the old man. "Grandfather, please tell me how to find your camp. I seek this Souraka."

The old man's eyes rolled. "You have a good belly, cousin. Don't spoil your head. Souraka is death and slavery."

"I'm not nearly as kind as you think, grandfather," Ourassi sighed, "and I cannot spoil my head. Even if I *had* luck to lose, for the sake of my people, I must find this man."

The old man regarded him solemnly. "Then the gods go with you."

They left halfway through the night, slipping away with a wave to the young woman and boy standing watch, riding as fast as Ngmengo could run along the Nbabas' back trail.

Ourassi eyed the thinning moon. "I'd hoped Souraka would be closer. In three days it will be a month since the battle."

As though any of them needed to be reminded. Jeneba's stomach knotted. Only three days and they did not even have the harp yet.

Three days. The distance across the hills seemed endless.

She found herself counting every beat of the horses' hooves, every step of her own feet when she ran beside the bay. It seemed as if they never moved.

Two days. Over every crest lay the same dry earth rolling away to the Mburi highlands that never grew closer, the same hot wind, the same struggling remnants of grass and brush. The same decaying village ruins.

One day and a night to go.

Mala's eye would rise just before midnight. Between dark and then, when they would have traveling light, they rested themselves and the horses. The men slept with the unmoving stillness of death but despite her exhaustion, Jeneba found a restlessness keeping her awake. One dawn from now Lubeda would be in Najhadende. He might even arrive there today. Where was Menekuya? What was he doing?

She sat wrapped in her kadoru against the night chill, watching Ngmengo move across the rocky slope below, spreading the bones of the vulture Tomo's spear had brought down earlier. Presently he climbed back up to sit down near her and pull his flute out of his branches.

"Tomo won't be happy," Jeneba said. "There was almost enough meat left for another meal."

Ngmengo glanced sideways with a smile. "Let the gods or any wandering ghosts have it. Perhaps the gods will smile."

He blew a few notes.

Movement down the slope caught her attention. Jeneba tensed. But the first visitor to the bones was a scavenger, not a ghost . . . a caracal, though the glinting paleness her night vision made of the tawny little cat gave it a ghostly appearance.

"That meat was put out for gods and ghosts," she called in a whisper.

The caracal looked up, her tufted ears flicking. "There are no ghosts around here, and do you really wish to insult a god with leavings?"

Ngmengo chuckled. Jeneba grinned. "Then, welcome, cousin."

A pair of jackals appeared out of the rocks. The caracal picked up the largest portion of the vulture, its spine and ribs, and dragged it up near Jeneba and Ngmengo, leaving the jackals to make the best of the remaining wings and leg bones. While she rasped the meat off the bones with her tongue, the caracal eyed Jeneba and the bush-man, and the sleeping men and hobbled horses beyond.

"You are an odd group to travel together."

"We're on an odd search," Ngmengo said. "We hunt an ancient harp that once lost a city but is now all that will regain it."

Jeneba grimaced. "If we can get the harp from Souraka."

The caracal's ears flattened. "Cousin, be warned against this Souraka. He already holds one leopard captive."

Jeneba's heart jumped. She leaned toward the caracal. "You know him?"

The tufted ears flicked. "The vultures have been talking about him, anticipating good eating soon. According to them, he almost always makes carrion when he camps near other humans, and he's less than a day's flight south, approaching some Nbaba."

A day's flight south. Praise Mala! With a gleeful glance at each other, Jeneba and Ngmengo leaped to their feet. "Cousin," she said breathlessly, "we thank you with all our hearts. I wish I had a whole vulture to give you in reward."

She ran to rouse the men.

By moonrise they were already on the trail south, all weariness forgotten with the smell of their objective in their nostrils. Even the horses sensed the excitement and stepped out with renewed energy.

They were still moving strongly when Lesa's eye rose in a cloudless sky. With it came a south wind, turning the chilly night to hot day. Jeneba tied her kadoru across the bay's back for a riding pad. By midmorning the sky glared, near colorless, and the brown hills shimmered. The Mburi highlands to the east appeared as though through water... wavering, dancing, dreamlike. The wind smelled of dust.

They passed the ruins of several villages, one of them with brush-fenced pens falling apart before the wind but in better repair than the huts, marking it as having been used recently by a nomad encampment.

From where she walked beside Ngmengo, Jeneba eyed the

fences. "Why do they stay on this land when they have to struggle so to live?"

The bush-man said, "It is their land, and besides that, where would they go? Would you leave part of Dasa territory to them?"

It occurred to her that one day desperation might drive a tribe to take greener lands. Then war would no longer be for glory but survival, a battle without beauty or honor. She shuddered.

"Look!" Ourassi pointed south. "Vultures."

The dark shapes circled just above the horizon, gliding and wheeling in the metal-bright sky. Jeneba's heart leaped. *They're anticipating good eating soon,* the caracal had said.

They kicked the horses into a trot.

Soon Jeneba began to smell their quarry. The wind carried the scents of habitation: people, cooking fires, the pungent odors of goats and manure mixing with the milder one of cattle. Just before midday, cresting a hill, they glimpsed the flat-topped tents of a distant encampment.

Ourassi sucked in his breath. "The Nbaba camp."

"*An* Nbaba camp. It could be just one where there's been sickness killing people," Tomo said.

A possibility that sent a chill of misgiving through Jeneba. "South" was not a very precise direction. It left much room for error. But the vultures remained overhead, which they would not be if bodies had been laid out. They glided in great circles, patiently waiting. The party kept to the low ground between hills as they rode on.

Then the wind carried sound, too, the bleat of goats, shrill fragments of voices. Dismounting, they tied the horses to boulders and ran up the hill. Near the top they crouched, except Ngmengo, who just pulled his head and arms into his branches and casually sidled up to the crest. The rest of them crawled on their bellies, using rocks and brush as cover. Then the sharp hiss of Ngmengo's indrawn breath stopped Jeneba short. She flattened behind him and cautiously peered around the thorny branches. Her heart slammed against her ribs.

On the hilltop opposite sat the grass-mat tents . . . with the

Nbaba gathered on the near side, faces drawn into snarls. The men clutched spears.

After one horrified moment she saw that they looked downhill, not across at her. Rimrock cut off the view of the lower slope of this hill, though, and no brush grew close enough to give her cover for peeking over.

"Ngmengo," Ourassi hissed. "What's down there?"

The bush-man gave Jeneba a chance to slither sideways to cover behind real brush, then edged across the open to the rimrock. "A water hole guarded by Tou warriors," he murmured.

The men's human hearing could not have caught the whisper. Jeneba passed on Ngmengo's answer.

Ourassi frowned. "Guarding the water? I wonder what—"

"This is your last warning," called down an Nbaba man with white-highlighted tribal scars and many necklaces of shells, beads, and animal teeth. He spoke Nbana. "If you don't let us draw water we will have to kill you."

One of the unseen Tou called back up in the same language, "And we tell you again, this water and land all belong to his magnificent majesty King Souraka. No one drinks without his permission."

"So he is here," Tomo murmured. "But where's his camp?"

Maybe that did not matter. Overhead, the vultures cried raucously. Jeneba sucked in her cheeks. Something was about to happen.

It *was* happening. Jeneba's hair raised. As suddenly and silently as though raised by magic, Tou warriors with hips wrapped in animal skins and heads shaved into a variety of skullcaps and pigtail forelocks appeared over the top of and around the hill. Almost before the Nbaba saw them, they had surrounded the taller, darker tribesmen.

The Nbaba lost no time reacting, however. One young warrior went for a Tou with his spear.

"Wait!" a voice shouted.

Everyone froze. Only the vultures moved, wheeling overhead through the glaring sky. Then along the circle of Tou came one more man, this one wearing a hip wrap of leopard skin, complete with tail. A leopard pattern of black spots spread across the white paint on his arms and chest.

He stalked behind the other warriors. "Don't hurry to die, young warrior." He spoke loud enough that his voice carried clearly. "I am King Souraka Chimbua, mightiest warrior in the world, ruler of this land, and I take possession of this camp."

The necklaced Nbaba spat back, "We've heard many stories about you but I, Zabama, son of Maman, chief of this camp, am not afraid. You're no king and we do not belong to you. We belong to no one!"

Even at this distance, Souraka's smile looked arrogant. "Then see my power, Chief Zabama! Pick a warrior to fight for you. Have him choose an opponent from among my warriors . . . any of them. If your man wins, I relinquish all claim on your camp."

At a wave of his hand, his warriors moved around to gather in a group behind Souraka.

Jeneba grimaced. The offer sounded like one which favored the Nbaba, but . . . would an aggressor really make an offer that good?

The vultures squawked above them.

"There's trickery somewhere," Ourassi muttered.

Or magic. Jeneba's skin prickled again at the thought of the way the Tou warriors had appeared.

The chief stared hard at Souraka for a long while, then whirling, pointed at a muscular young man in a scarlet-and-white striped hip wrap. Grinning, the warrior swaggered over to the Tou group. After looking them all up and down, he pointed at a rawboned, loose-jointed warrior.

"Wager," Tomo whispered gleefully. "The Nbaba was meant to choose him. He'll be one of their best warriors; he just looks clumsy."

How could Tomo find amusement in this? Jeneba wondered angrily, then shoved her irritation aside as the two below faced off. The Tou tripped over the shaft of his own spear. Pretense? Jeneba did not think so. The Tou's every movement reflected awkwardness, all the worse, too, in comparison to the lithe grace of the Nbaba . . . like a hyena beside a cheetah.

Souraka appeared unconcerned. He stood watching with his arms folded, grinning.

The grin remained when the Nbaba easily dodged the Tou's spear, and when the Nbaba threw his spear, a throw straight and hard and true. Which veered aside just before striking the Tou to miss him completely. So did the second throw. The Nbaba deflected the Tou's second throw with his shield.

Nbaba and Tou used no stabbing spears. The Nbaba retrieved the Tou's spears to use for himself. He moved with practiced ease and confidence. The Tou stumbled and lurched. Yet the Nbaba could not touch the Tou, for all his superior ability. Time and again the spears slid harmlessly past their target.

Jeneba sucked in her cheeks. Magic.

The grin vanished from the Nbaba's face, replaced by fear and grim determination. But the same pattern continued ... expert defense and offense by the Nbaba, mediocre moves and tactics by the Tou but neither man able to gain an advantage. The fight went on and on under the blaze of Lesa's eye until sweat ran down both men in rivers and their chests heaved ... until weariness slowed the Nbaba's speed and stole away his grace.

A cheetah could outrun the unlovely hyena for only a short time, Jeneba remembered.

The Nbaba stumbled. His opponent charged forward to run his spear through the Nbaba's throat. Staring down at the shaft with an expression of astonishment, the warrior stiffened, he coughed blood, and toppled over. A woman among the Nbaba shrieked in grief.

Tou warriors whooped with triumph.

Souraka yelled, "Behold the strength of my charms! All my warriors and I are no less invincible and invulnerable. If you don't want to be destroyed, if you don't want your people made slaves, you will bow before me and call me king. You will pay tribute ... our choice of your cattle, sheep, and food stores, and your women. I have warriors in need of wives."

Their choice of the herds and food, with no mention of a maximum amount! They could take everything. Jeneba gasped in outrage. Mseluku never asked for anything like that, not even from the richest of his cities, and certainly not from a village as poor as these people's camp must be! What would the Nbaba chief do?

Moving stiffly, as though dragged by invisible ropes, the chief crossed to Souraka and dropped to touch his head to the earth at the Tou's feet.

Ourassi wiggled his way backward. The rest of them followed. Out of sight of the camp, they sat up and grimaced at each other.

Ngmengo said grimly, "That is an unpleasant man."

And he had Bisiri's harp. Jeneba fingered the charms and buffalo talisman around her neck, and touched her heart four times.

CHAPTER

ELEVEN

Souraka left most of his warriors behind to collect the tribute. Only a few marched away with him. Leading the horses and swinging wide around an adjoining hill for cover, Jeneba and the others followed.

His camp lay between nearby hills to the east, in a basin wide and shallow enough that it would give attacking warriors little advantage of high ground yet still offered concealment from anyone beyond the immediate hilltops. A fair amount of grass also grew there, enough to feed Souraka's cattle and goats for a day or two. Lying flat on her belly on the north-side hill with the sun beating hot on her shoulders and legs and flies diving on her, Jeneba could see why the Nbaba had not camped here themselves, though . . . no water. While she watched, the warriors who had come back with Souraka joined women and boys driving the herd in the direction of the spring below the Nbaba.

That left the camp almost empty, a cluster of round-topped, grass-mat tents arranged in a long oval around a common and central tent. Half that central tent stood open on the sides and in its shadow Jeneba saw a cage. Something large moved inside. Pacing. The wind brought a leopard scent among those of goats and cattle. Another even more pungent odor, the reek of excrement and sweating human bodies, almost masked them all, though. The captives Souraka intended to sell as slaves? She wrinkled her nose.

Even the men noticed. Both grimaced. Tomo said, "I think I smell his guest tent."

Probably the one on the far side of the camp with a guard at the entrance. At irregular intervals the warrior looked inside or strolled around the outside, poking at the bottom of the mats with his foot or spear shaft.

"What we need is Souraka's, and that's bound to be the one in the center," Ourassi said. "That's where the harp should be."

"Should be? How do we find out for certain?" Tomo asked sourly. "We can't just ride in and ask."

Ourassi swatted at flies crawling up his face. "Why not? He may care so little about the harp he's willing to trade it. Especially for these." He touched the bulge at his waist that was the bag of metal arm bands. "I can tell him I'm a bard and would like to trade for the beautiful harp I've heard he has."

"You mean you actually intend to go down there?" Tomo snorted. "He'll kill you and take the jewelry. Or what if that's a wizard in the cage instead of a real leopard and knows what you want the harp for?"

"It smells like a leopard," Jeneba said.

A wizard made more sense, however. Where would Souraka have caught a leopard around here? This country made poor hunting for a big cat. And the powers of a wizard or witch explained Souraka's invincibility and invulnerability. Except, only a fool would trust a creature whose pleasure came from harming other men, and why would a wizard consent to remaining caged?

"You can't pass as a bard anyway," Tomo said. "I'll go. I'm safer. I'm as invulnerable as Souraka."

Jeneba frowned. "Are you seeking the harp or a fight?"

"Honor says I should go," Ourassi said with dignity. "You're all brave to join me and I appreciate your help; I couldn't have come this far without you. Since my greed killed my father and lost Yagana, however, my life must be the one risked to recover the harp."

They slipped back down the hill to the horses to wait out the afternoon, all except Ngmengo, who kept watch on the hill with his head and arms pulled in among his black-thorned branches. Draping her kadoru over her head made some shade, but Jeneba still felt as though she were being sucked as dry as the hills around them. She forced herself to stay away from the water bags. They were nearly empty and they needed what was left for the horses, to keep them from colicking feeding on the dry clumps of grass they tore at so voraciously they ripped up roots and all. She eyed them... muzzles searching the dry ground, feet stamping, and tails and shoulder skin constantly in motion to chase off flies. Tonight someone, her probably, needed to risk a trip to the Nbaba's spring to fill the water bags.

Periodically Jeneba ran back up the hill in a crouch for another look at the camp. Why she could not say. The herds came back from water, larger than when they went. Loud wailing marked the arrival of the women taken from the Nbaba. The leopard echoed them with an angry yowl. Otherwise nothing changed over the course of the afternoon. Still... something drew her. Something stirred when she looked down on the tents, a half-formed thought that tantalized her by dodging each time she tried to capture it.

She frowned past Ngmengo's branches. "There's a design in the middle of every mat. Can you tell what it is?"

"No. Do you want me to see if I can work my way closer?"

She shook her head. A new large bush in the bushless basin would draw attention and maybe exploration. "It isn't important."

As Lesa's blazing day eye slipped toward the western horizon, the wailing below faded. In its place the wind brought the smells of smoke and cooking meat. Jeneba licked her lips. Her stomach snarled in reminder of how long ago she had last eaten.

At the bottom of the hill, Ourassi stood and with a wave at her, marched around the hill so he would enter the basin from the east.

Tomo crawled up to join Jeneba and the bush-man. "The fool. We'll never recover the harp by bargaining with Souraka. They never give up something they think someone wants. Fighting is all outlaws like him understand."

"Give Ourassi a chance," Ngmengo said mildly.

They watched him stroll into the basin. The Tou saw him almost as soon as he came around the hill. A party of warriors carrying spears charged out to meet him.

Ourassi stopped and waited for them, leaning on his own spear as though it were a walking stick. Once they reached him the conversation contained mostly sign language but was apparently effective. The warriors escorted him into the camp with every appearance of friendliness, grinning and singing in imitation of a signal drum. Souraka, too—his body still painted with spots but wearing a plain hip wrap now—met Ourassi and led him to a stool by the fire outside the central tent. The warriors brought other stools and joined them. Women, some with the animal skin hip wraps and skull cap head shave of Tou, others wearing the striped fabric and beaded hair fringe of Nbaba, filled bowls from a pot on the fire and served the men. Ourassi had two. One he ate from. The other he placed on the ground for a ghost offering. The women and children ate at other, smaller fires. They all put down ghost offerings, too. One woman carried a pot into the guarded tent.

Jeneba tried not to think about food, but the smell of it curled tantalizingly around her, driving her stomach into a frenzy of snarls.

She longed to be close enough to hear the conversation between Souraka and Ourassi. Or perhaps inquisition characterized it better. Even at this distance Jeneba could see mouths moving and arms waving. Each time the Tou spoke it was something short, but Ourassi always responded with a long speech and much pantomime. No sooner would he finish, either, than Souraka spoke again. At one point the Tou chief stiffened. A chill ran down Jeneba's spine. But Souraka did nothing more, only sat back on his stool and went on talking.

The knots remained in Jeneba's gut, though. Ourassi had made a gesture of plucking a string. Referring to the harp? It obviously disturbed Souraka.

After the meal a number of the warriors wrestled. Souraka leaned toward Ourassi. His teeth gleamed in the firelight. A hand pointed at the wrestlers.

Ourassi nodded and, standing, stepped into the circle of wrestlers. Jeneba sucked in her cheeks. Had Souraka offered the harp if Ourassi won? She touched her heart four times.

The match did not last long. He and his opponent tied up

head to head for the longest part of it, each changing grip on
the other's arms, pushing, testing. Then Ourassi dropped
and twisted. His opponent rolled past. Ourassi came down
on top for the pin.

He faced four other opponents. None lasted any longer.

Jeneba held her breath. Would that win the harp? Souraka's expression was impossible to read at this distance. But
when Ourassi rejoined the Tou by fire, Souraka began pointing at the leopard. With a hand on the other man's shoulder,
he urged him closer to the wooden bars of the cage. Ourassi
went with obvious reluctance.

The leopard snarled and charged the bars. Ourassi held his
ground.

Souraka's teeth flashed in the twilight. As the leopard
lashed out between the bars with a paw, the Tou gestured at a
warrior, who hurried toward the guarded tent.

He reappeared shortly dragging a naked young boy by a
cord around the boy's neck. Souraka pointed at the cage.
The boy screamed.

Jeneba's gut lurched. Mala, no!

She could do nothing. She had to sit and watch while a
warrior poked his spear at the leopard from one end of the
cage, distracting the animal, and the other warriors slid up
the door at the other end to shove in the struggling, screaming boy.

Ourassi tried to act. Shouting, he charged for the cage.
Spears barred his way. Not that he could have saved the boy;
the leopard spun and charged almost before the door could
be dropped again. Clawed forepaws hauled the boy down.
Great teeth closed in his throat, cutting off a shriek of pain
and terror. Then the leopard began feeding.

But Jeneba quickly forgot the boy. The spears that kept
Ourassi from the leopard's cage now pointed straight at him.
Souraka, outside the warrior circle, pantomimed throwing
spears, then gestured first at the hills, then at the guarded
tent. Ourassi stiffened, lifting his chin. Souraka turned and
walked back to his stool.

"I told you," Tomo hissed in Dase, and started to stand.
"We'll have to fight for the harp. He isn't going to give or
trade it to us. And we've left the spears by the horses."

Jeneba pulled him down with a jerk. "No."

He stared at her a moment, then smiled mockingly. "What? Doesn't honor say we must rescue him?"

Conscience urged her to. Every muscle twitched with the longing to charge down into the Tou. But she forced herself to remain lying where she was. "We're here for the harp. That's most important. If we let Souraka know Ourassi has companions, and show him our faces, then we lose any chance of gaining it except by force."

"And you'll let the Kurasi die?"

She clamped her jaw tight. "If necessary."

He eyed her in silence for several moments. "Maybe you aren't as much a fool as we always thought."

She blinked at him. Admiration mixed with bitterness and regret in his voice.

"I don't think they intend to kill him immediately," Ngmengo said in Burda.

While a part of her noted without surprise that the bushman understood Dase, Jeneba peered around his branches. The circle had split and widened into a line well to each side of Ourassi. The right-hand one included Souraka's stool. A Tou tossed Ourassi a shield and spear. Another stepped from the end of the left-hand line to face the Kurasi. Souraka crossed his arms.

Now Jeneba could imagine what he was saying, something like: "Now let's see how skilled a warrior you really are. If you win, you may leave with your life."

She watched with fists clenched. The Tou's first throw passed over Ourassi's head. Ourassi's spear came straight and true, deflected by the Tou's shield. His second would have struck most warriors, but as in the fight at the Nbaba camp, the point skidded aside just before it touched the Tou.

Tomo shook his head. "He can't possibly win. I told you I should have gone."

Ourassi's skill almost equaled Souraka's protective charms. While he could not hit the Tou, none of the other warriors' throws were able to touch him, either. The duel went on and on while twilight died into darkness and the only light came from Souraka's fire, blazing high with dried cow dung the women fed it.

Almost equaled the charms. Skill could not prevent him from tiring. Gradually Ourassi's reactions slowed, until finally, inevitably, a spear slipped past his shield to pierce where his neck joined his left shoulder. He jerked the spear free and hurled it back, but the shield arm had lost its smoothness. The next spear impaled his right thigh. Ourassi fell.

Whooping, the Tou rushed forward, dropping his shield to reach to his waist. The firelight gleamed off a knife blade.

Jeneba bit down on her lower lip to keep from screaming a warning.

Then to her speechless astonishment Souraka leaped off his stool and shoved the warrior aside. He knelt beside Ourassi, examining the wounds. His lips moved. One of the women disappeared into his tent and reappeared with a leather bag. Souraka sorted through smaller pouches inside, chose one. Then while Jeneba stared in disbelief, the Tou chief pulled the spear out of Ourassi's leg and after it had bled a bit, carefully dribbled powder from the pouch into both the leg and neck wounds.

"Mala!" Tomo breathed.

"Maybe it was some kind of test," Ngmengo said.

No. Once the wounds had been treated to his satisfaction, Souraka stood. His warriors jerked Ourassi to his feet and dragged him off to the guarded tent.

Tomo sat up, ghostly gray in the darkness. His mouth twisted. "A practical man. Don't waste what you can trade in the slave market."

"Ourassi's alive anyway," Ngmengo said.

Jeneba nodded. "As soon as the camp quiets, we'll slip down and see if we can sneak him out the back of the tent."

"We?" Tomo's smile went mocking. "You mean me, who can't see by starlight, or Ngmengo, with his branches rattling against each other all the way?"

She sighed. "*I'll* go."

The Tou camp took a lifetime to go to sleep. Jeneba waited biting her lip and toying impatiently with the charms and the buffalo talisman around her neck. Mala's eye would rise at midnight. She had to be in and out before it gave human eyes light to see by.

The eye would be half open, a half-moon Lubeda and the Djero watched at Najhadende, waiting for Yagana's army. Yagana's army watched it tonight, too . . . waiting for the harp.

Urgency drummed at her.

Finally all but the guards vanished into the tents. She jumped up.

Ngmengo reached out to touch her arm. "Ntolo smile on you."

She gave him a fleeting smile, and crouching, slipped down into the basin.

The cattle and goats had been gathered in close to the tents. A direct approach to the guarded tent would take her past them upwind. Too risky with her scent. Instead, she took a longer route, circling east around the camp to keep downwind and well away from the warriors guarding the herds.

Other guards kept watch around the outside of the rest of the camp. Against "subjects" seeking retaliation? She noted them all for caution's sake, though they stood spaced enough that without moonlight for them to see by she could easily slip between. Perhaps she should use the dark to try for Souraka's tent and the harp. But she discarded that thought almost immediately. Souraka had taken one of the new Nbaba women into his tent with him. He would not be sleeping just yet.

Jeneba turned her attention back to the slave tent. A single warrior still guarded the door. She thought she recalled seeing more around it earlier, though. Light glowed inside, too. Dropping on her belly so none of the camp or herd guards would see her silhouetted against the tent, she crawled up to the rear.

A child cried. A man's voice snapped something in a language Jeneba did not understand. Almost immediately the crying faded to a whimper. A woman giggled.

She reached for the bottom of the mat, intending to lift it enough for a peek inside, but the mat would not move. A hurried exploration with her hand along the ground line quickly found why; the mat had been staked down. Mala!

That meant she would either have to pry up a stake or cut the mat to get Ourassi out.

Before risking that, she worked her way across the back, testing the mats until she found one loose enough to raise a little. Pressing the side of her face against the ground, Jeneba peered under . . . and instantly flung herself back, rolling sideways away from the tent into darkness.

The light inside came from a bowl-shaped, animal-oil lamp hanging from the top of the tent. Beneath it cross-legged on the earth floor sat a warrior. She doubted he had seen her. His attention appeared to be divided between watching Ourassi, who sat with neck and hands tied to a stake, and the other prisoners, all children under ten years old, each in a wooden cage, and his game of stones-and-cups with a young Tou woman. The pair of them made it impossible for her to reach Ourassi without someone raising an alarm, though.

Her mind churned. Could all three of them be drawn away? If she set up a diversion on the far side of the camp, would that clear the tent and give her enough time to go in the front to release Ourassi? She sucked in her cheeks. What if he could not walk? And the children. Mala. How could she free Ourassi and abandon the children?

The harp, she reminded herself. They were here for the harp. All else came second. Rescuing the children, and even Ourassi for that matter, would not bring her the harp. Unless . . .

She lay in the dark staring at the slave tent and gnawing a knuckle. Was that too complicated . . . create a diversion so she could free everyone, which would generate even greater confusion, allowing her to reach Souraka's tent? It sounded good except . . . it would mean leaving the others to fend for themselves while she ransacked Souraka's tent. Ourassi would understand, but some of the children were only a couple of years old.

What about using Tomo and Ngmengo? Tomo could handle the first diversion and Ngmengo lead the children away. Only, the original problems with them remained: Tomo remained blind until Mala's eye rose and the Tou would hear he bush-man.

Thinking about the moon sent her glance east. She stiffened. A faint glow showed close to the horizon. The moon! It would be rising soon. There was no time to go for anyone else. Anything to be done she must do herself, and quickly! She frowned at the glow of the slave tent with urgency beating in her.

It was then, staring at the tent, at the design in the center of each backlighted mat, that she *saw* the design. Hair rose on her neck. Leopards. A leopard on every mat, repeated, over and over around each tent. So that was what drew her. The leopard must be their totem. Souraka wore a leopard-skin hip wrap, though, and a totem was supposed to be taboo to hunt.

Still . . . leopards.. The thought that had evaded her earlier rolled out before her. She resisted it. No. She was Dasa and a noble, not a leopard. But it prodded her, and the glow grew in the east. Finally she surrendered with a kind of relief. Yes. That might be just the way to not only lay hands on the harp but save Ourassi and the children. And it was the road that no one but a leopard's daughter could walk.

But first she had to strip down. Hurriedly digging a hole with her knife, she pulled off her arm bands, defense charm, and buffalo talisman, all but the blood-days charm; she could not risk becoming taboo now. She buried them along with her knife and its sheath and covered the spot with rocks. Hopefully she would be back for them sometime. Crouched, moving soundlessly as a shadow, Jeneba slipped into the village, to the leopard's cage.

"Sister, where did you come from?" she whispered.

The leopard started up. "From the south. Chullo captured me."

"Would you like to be free?"

The leopard blinked. "Will you release me, sister?"

"If you'll make me a promise."

The long tail lashed. "What promise?"

"To leave the camp so stealthily no one will know you've gone, and to leave the area before anyone sees you. There's poor hunting for you around here anyway. But before you leave, I need you to go up the north hill. There's a thornbush there which smells manlike. Tell him that I've found the road the leopard's daughter must walk and that I have to remain here awhile. Also ask him to watch Tomo. Will you promise me that, sister?"

The leopard's tail trembled. "As you are my sister and liberator, I promise."

Jeneba pulled loose the locking pegs and raised the door. The leopard sprang out and away into the darkness. Jeneba ducked though into the cage. Lowering the door, she re-pegged it. Then she curled up in a corner with her tsara untied and wrapped around her shoulders like a kadoru, against the night chill. She breathed deeply. The road only the leopard's daughter could walk. Now if only she could walk it skillfully enough.

CHAPTER

TWELVE

Jeneba had all night to wonder if she really knew what she was doing. Mala gave her no chance to retreat. The High God's eye sprang up over a cloudless eastern horizon, a half disk lighting the sky and turning the darkness to twilight. Jeneba easily located the great dark bush on the northern hilltop. Even humans should be able to see well enough to spot someone crossing the basin, no matter how stealthy she might be. That left her nothing to do but sit in the corner farthest from the bones of the child, thinking and doubting.

The leopard being their totem hardly assured her of a welcome, and certainly not of convincing them she was their leopard turned woman. That leopard-skin of Souraka's bothered her the more she thought of it, too. With the uncertainty, though, came another thought . . . of men to the north and west watching this moon, too, with anticipation, with fear, with despair. Depending on her and the others.

Toward dawn Jeneba unwrapped her tsara and, shivering, worked the cloth and cord from the blood-days charm down between the floor poles out of sight. To be believable she must be found naked, no matter how cold it made her. The slim charm itself hid neatly in the passage whose monthly flow it prevented. Preparations made, she curled up tightly on her side on the cage floor to wait for discovery.

Despite the discomfort and the worry chasing knots along her gut, she must have dozed off, because her next awareness was of shrilly chattering voices and something poking her in the back. Whipping over, she swiped irritably at it, and only then woke enough to realize what was happening.

She opened her eyes. Around the cage, Tou backed away. A warrior pulled the butt end of his spear shaft out from between the bars. Jeneba sucked in a deep breath. Now it began. Leopard. She must think and act leopard.

One of the men asked a sharp-toned question. Fortunately he used the Tou language. It let her sit up and blink at him in genuine incomprehension. Someone else repeated the question. But this time Jeneba pretended not to hear. She looked down and gasped as if noticing herself for the first time. She stretched out her arms and legs, explored her face with her hands, grinning.

The Tou burst into shrill babble again. Through it, though, came a louder male voice, demanding. Jeneba turned languidly toward the sound. To her disappointment, he was someone younger and leaner than Souraka. Still, she stared into his eyes, giving him plenty of opportunity to notice the leopard-tawniness of hers. Then moving with the same unhurried grace, she folded her long legs cross-legged. "I don't understand you." She used Dase first, then repeated the sentence in Burda, the Keoru language Sifri, and finally Nbana.

He said in Nbana, "I asked who are you?"

Remembering how the leopards she met had reacted to questions, she stared at him through her lashes, blinking languidly before answering. "I am Jeneba Karamoke, a Dasa and warrior and a noble of Kiba." Never lie if truth served as well.

"What are you doing in there? Where's the king's leopard?"

"*King's* leopard?" She arched a brow. "You're mistaken; I've never belonged to anyone in my life."

"You . . ." With satisfaction she watched his breath catch. "*You're* the leopard?"

She smiled. "It's my other form."

His eyes narrowed. "A leopard-woman? But you've never taken human shape here before."

A good point. Now began the tricky part. "I refused to marry a man in my city that we suspected of being a wizard. He made magic, trapping me in my leopard form. I think he hoped I would be killed for my skin." She laughed softly. "I wish he could see me now, where it is taboo to kill leopards.

He would eat himself in rage. Will you open the door? I want to stretch."

The Tou reached for the pegs.

"I have a question first," another voice said.

The Tou jerked back from the pegs.

Jeneba breathed deeply. He came. Now . . . think leopard. She forced herself to sit motionless and keep her expression unconcerned as Souraka shouldered through the circle of Tou. But she studied him intently. Everything depended on how much he could be influenced. "Souraka," she murmured.

He smiled fleetingly. All the paint had been washed off, revealing skin and the shaved part of his head clean of tattoos and tribal scarring. For jewelry he wore only copper hoops in his ears and beads at the end of the three forelock pigtails dangling about his eyes. A piece of bone etched with the image of a leopard hung around his neck. The smile revealed teeth chipped to points, though, and the gleam of dawn sun off the copper matched a hard glitter in his eyes. "If a wizard's magic forced you to remain a leopard, why have you changed now?"

It was a question she had expected, but her gut still knotted. The answer that had occurred to her could be a dangerous gamble and spears would be impossible to avoid in here if he disliked her answer.

She shrugged. "I don't know. I don't care. All that matters is being able to take human shape again. Now will you unpeg the door or must I do it myself? I've spent enough time in here."

"Stay away from the door," Souraka ordered.

Spears pointed at her. Jeneba pretended to ignore them. With a chill crawling under her skin, she stood as much as the cage allowed. It left her hunched. "You're a daring man, threatening harm to your totem. But then, the Chullo who traded me to you said you seem to know no fear, and I've seen myself that you wear a leopard-skin hip wrap into battle." She reached out through the bars for the pegs.

Souraka slapped her hands away. "I didn't make the kill. I traded for the skin with the same Chullo who captured you." He pulled the pegs himself and lifted the door. "I don't know

if I believe how this happened, but no one could come into
the camp unseen or approach the leopard without it making a
sound. So, welcome, leopard-woman. We're honored by
your presence. Please accept the hospitality of my tent and
my camp."

Without replying, she ducked out the door and straightened, stretching to her full height. The Tou backed away.
For a moment she imagined herself through their eyes, a
good head taller than any of them, lean, tawny-eyed . . . and
long, hard muscles rippling with the tension of superior con-
dition and waiting power. Even Souraka looked a bit intimi-
dated. Mala grant he was, and that he remained so.

They found clothes for her. Given a choice, she picked
not animal skin, which clearly disappointed Souraka, but
striped cloth like the Nbaba. Wrapped under one arm and
tied over the other shoulder, it made a short but acceptable
tsara.

Souraka beckoned to one of the women and murmured.
The woman brought two stools out in front of his tent. Rearing leopards supported the seats.

Souraka nodded toward the stools. "Sit with me."

Women brought food, balls of dough floating in broth
with roots and some meat. The ghost offering went on the
ground at Souraka's feet.

The savory smell set Jeneba's stomach snarling in longing. She tried not to watch the ghost offering slowly disappear. "Does hospitality also include food?"

Souraka glanced across in astonishment. "You're hungry
again already?" He started to beckon a warrior.

"For the food men eat," Jeneba said hurriedly. She refused
to act leopard enough to tear out a child's throat with her
teeth.

His eyes narrowed. "I thought leopard-people preferred
raw meat."

She made herself meet his stare with a dry smile. "Leopards do what they will."

He eyed her a moment longer, while her heart thundered
in her chest, then wiggled his fingers at the women again.
Soon Jeneba sat holding a bowl of her own, gingerly fishing

pieces from the steaming broth with her fingers. The first several bites almost seared her mouth. In her hunger she gulped them down anyway. After the bowl had been drained, the Nbaba women serving them filled it again, this time with honey beer.

Jeneba did not have to pretend delight. Kiba and Yagana made better, but after so long without anything but water, this tasted fine enough.

Thought of Yagana, and then of the bush-man and Tomo up on the hill, possibly hungry and thirsty, dimmed some of her pleasure. In Najhadende Lubeda must be pacing his tent, impatiently waiting for the Kurasi. As the sun rose higher, he would grow angrier. And what of Menekuya? Did he pace, too, staring west, praying for his brother to appear with the harp? Or was he busying himself preparing his army for the battle that must come to Yagana's valley? Her fingers bit into the earthenware bowl. Could they hold off Lubeda until the harp arrived?

Souraka leaned toward her. She dragged her attention back to him.

"If you're Dasa, what were you doing in Chullo territory?"

The reply to that came easily enough. "Running away from the wizard." Warriors gathered on the common, stretching. A pair started to wrestle. Jeneba eyed them. "I've sat in that cage watching you day after day. You really are brave and ambitious to be setting out on conquest with these few warriors."

He smiled. "It's enough to begin. As more villages become mine, there will be more, until I have a great army. Someday I'll own not just Tou and Nbaba lands but others with good grass and water and plentiful game."

Cold crawled through her bones. West and south lay the green plains of Dasa territory.

A fall ended the wrestling match. Another began.

Souraka watched a bit, then glanced sideways at Jeneba. Above his smile, eyes watched her intently. "Leopards are swift and strong. Why don't you join my warriors for their exercise?"

Did he expect her to hesitate? She set down the honey

beer. "Thank you. I'd enjoy some sport, but . . . would it be? I saw what happened to the warrior who threw yours last night."

Souraka's lip curled. "He would have been all right if he'd shown a stomach for blood instead of calling me a hyena when I fed you." He folded his arms. "I would never harm a leopard, would I?"

She made herself smile. "Not if you're wise." Standing, she rewrapped her tsara tight around her hips and strode into the circle of warriors.

The exercise hardly qualified as sport, however. She wrestled eight warriors. Several could have been excellent wrestlers. Could have been, if they worked at it. None had. She threw and pinned each with shameful ease. But after all, why *should* they work at it? With the charms protecting them, where was the need for great warrior skills? They had only to outlast their opponents.

The entire group of them raced, too . . . from Souraka's tent out through the west side of the tent circle, through the scattered grazing cattle and goats to the west side of the basin and back. They ran better than they wrestled, but again Jeneba won easily, crossing the finish line well ahead of the others.

The women and children stared at her, eyes wide. "Tou," they whispered. "Tou." The murmur ran from one to the other in awed tones. Warriors coming across the finish line gaped, too. Some fear showed in their eyes, and, startlingly, fierce joy. What she no longer saw, however, was disbelief.

A young warrior grinned, showing pointed teeth. "You *are* the leopard. No wonder you won. If you fight with us, not even villages with the most powerful witch doctors can stand against King Souraka's army."

A woman cried out: "Tou. Tou, Tou, Tou."

One after another other women, then the warriors, picked up the chant. *Tou, Tou, Tou.* All grinning at her while they shouted.

What? Baffled, Jeneba turned toward Souraka. He regarded her with smug satisfaction. "Haven't you ever guessed? It's our word for *leopard*."

Jeneba knew *she* was staring now. The *tribe* called itself *leopard*? They cheered her because she was leopard, too? *Because* she was leopard.

A strange warmth spread through her. After a puzzled moment, she identified it: delight, joy. Then she saw something else in Souraka's eyes. Hunger. He looked straight at her.

A soft voice in her head whispered there might be value in remembering she was descended from the founding Queen Mother Naruwa. Naruwa had saved her twin brother and killed the village conqueror Korote by sleeping with him. Sleeping with Souraka would give her access to his tent.

Resentment and protest flared. No! Why did she have to think about that just now? Let her first enjoy this new admiration and respect, this approval of her leopard spirit. Was it too much to ask?

Souraka smiled thinly. "But of course you won't be fighting. Tou women aren't warriors and you have more important work."

She started. He could not have meant the final words the way she heard them. They echoed stingingly in her head, reminding her of why she was here.

Jeneba frowned. All *right*. She retied the hip wrap into a tsara. "More important work? What can be more important than fighting?"

The hungry glitter brightened. "You'll see. Will you spend the day at my side?"

She hesitated a moment, as though considering, then gave him the faint, slow smile she had seen other women use with men. "I would be pleased to do so."

It did not please her long. Spending the day at Souraka's side meant not following him to his tent as she hoped but holding court. From the shade of the sideless tent which protected the leopard's cage, he performed the same functions her uncle did . . . directing the camp and mediating its problems. Souraka commanded that everyone use Nbaba for her benefit, then he and a warrior leader decided who would stand watch over the herds and camp that night. Two women came with a dispute over ownership of a goat. A man asked for adultery compensation from a man he accused of sleeping with his wife. A warrior claimed he was still without a wife because another warrior had taken two of the Nbaba girls.

Jeneba chewed the insides of her cheeks in an agony of impatience. The grievances sounded just like those she had heard in countless similar sessions in Mseluku's court. Unlike her uncle, however, who always tried to talk both sides into an agreement, Souraka favored settling disputes with personal combat. Even the women fought, and without the protective charms which prevented the men from inflicting serious injury or death on each other, it became as grim and vicious a wrestling match as Jeneba could remember ever witnessing. One woman broke her arm. Tomo's words from the day before echoed in her head: *Fighting is all outlaws like him understand.*

Lubeda must be furious by this time, perhaps railing at Najhadende's chief, accusing Menekuya and Ourassi of dishonor and cowardice.

An Nbaba woman knelt before Souraka. "Majesty, help me. Every day my head aches with such terrible pain I feel I can't bear it. I went to the healer but she says this is bewitchment. Majesty, I beg you, help me."

Souraka dipped his chin. "Come to me after we eat. We'll identify the wizard or witch responsible and turn the evil back on him."

Jeneba needed all her control to remain relaxed on the stool. The breath stopped in her chest. That kind of request came to a witch doctor, not a chief. Souraka replied like a witch doctor, too. Was he indeed witch doctor as well as chief to his followers?

Witch doctor! Jeneba felt as though she were suffocating. Witch doctor! She might find and take the harp, but what good would that do? Souraka could not help but know who stole it, and his magic could follow it anywhere to destroy them.

Unless she made sure he was powerless before she left. Blood drummed in her ears. The only way she knew to do that was to kill him. Kill the invulnerable Souraka Chimbua! Jeneba sucked in a deep breath. So not only did she need to find the harp, but also learn the secret of his invulnerability.

Toward sunset shouting interrupted the last of the peti-
tioners. Souraka stood, looking in the direction of the noise.
Moments later a warrior came running from the slave tent,
babbling in the Tou language.

Souraka snapped something back, then turned to Jeneba.
"Come with me while I tend to this problem."

She hurried after him. "What kind of problem?"

He said over his shoulder, "The foreign slave tried to
escape."

Her gut knotted.

In the slave tent Ourassi hung between two warriors, his
arms forced up behind his back. One of the warriors bled
from deep slashes across his ribs and the side of his neck.
Ourassi's nose and an ear also dripped blood. Around them
the children crouched in their cages, eyes wide with terror.

Souraka began snapping questions as soon as he stepped
through the door. The warriors gibbered back. Ourassi lifted
his head to glare at Souraka. Jeneba held her breath, but not
by even a flicker of an eye did he look at her or betray that
he knew her.

Souraka scowled.

"What happened?" Jeneba asked.

A mask dropped over his expression. "It would seem the
slave worked his hands loose, untied the neck cord from
around the post, then waited until Segoete's attention . . .
wandered"—He sent a sharp glance at the wounded warrior.
The warrior flinched.—"and grabbed my warrior's spear."
His gaze fastened on Ourassi. "Until last night I could have
threatened you as we do the children: behave and be quiet or
we'll feed you to the leopard. But now the leopard wants
only men's food. Perhaps you have a suggestion what we
should do with him, leopard-woman."

Ourassi stared straight at her, still without showing recognition. Jeneba's mind churned. Did he expect her to plead
for his life? But she could not do that without arousing suspicion. How she wished she dared talk to him, to tell him in
Burda why she was here, and that unfortunately she had still
not located the harp. She blinked slowly at Souraka. "I leave
justice to you. You're the king." She looked around at the

caged children. "These can't be all the prisoners you've taken."

Souraka smiled thinly. "Of course not. The slaves worth trading have already gone to market. These are food for you."

Revulsion boiled up through Jeneba. She fought not to show it.

Souraka turned away. "Beat him, Segoete. Just don't kill or cripple him permanently. I want to trade him for salt and grain."

They left the tent. Jeneba shut her ears to the grunts of pain and smack of spear shafts against flesh.

Lesa's eye rested on the horizon, bloated and bloody. Inside the circle of tents the women spun sticks in tinder to light cooking fires.

What was Lubeda doing now? Jeneba wondered. Planning to start his march to Yagana in the morning? She glanced casually toward the northern hilltop, but no bush showed along the crest.

"Perhaps you wonder why we call ourselves Leopard," Souraka said.

She forced her attention on him. "Because you want the strength of your totem?"

He smiled "We *are* our totem. Many years ago a woman of a chief in a village east across the Tarasi Mountains was seduced by a leopard. She bore twin sons. But the village shunned them because they had leopard blood."

Jeneba's breath caught. How well she knew about that. "So they left and formed this tribe."

"Yes." He stopped to turn and stare intently up at her. "You asked earlier what I meant by more important work for you. The leopard thins in our blood. We need renewal. I want you to be my queen." His eyes glittered. "Together we'll conquer an empire and found a dynasty. The Chimbua clan will be truly leopard once again."

She wanted to destroy someone who shared her leopard breeding? Guilt stabbed like a spear.

He stared at her, eyes narrowing.

Did he read her intentions in her face? she wondered in a

squirt of fear. Hurriedly, she struggled for something to say. "You want me to give up my freedom?"

Souraka bared his pointed teeth. "There has to be a reason the gods released you from the wizard's curse here and now. What else could it be but to become my queen?"

Even with guilt and fear churning in her, a thought whispered that his intended queen would have his trust as well as access to his tent. She met his eyes solemnly. "Perhaps so. Very well; I cannot defy the gods. I'll be your queen."

The evening became a celebration. Everyone ate around Souraka's fire, warriors and women alike. Afterward, they danced.

Souraka disappeared into his tent with the bewitched women. Jeneba tried to follow but Souraka barred the way with his arm. "You dance. I'll come back when this is done."

She joined the dancers around the fire. They stamped their feet and chanted in time to the drumbeat while warriors thumped the butt ends of their spears on the ground. Necklaces piled around both male and female necks clicked in time to the beat, too. Occasionally someone burst up out of the group, leaping high above the others for sheer exuberance.

Jeneba could not share their enjoyment. The warriors had danced the night before the battle at Najhadende. No one danced there tonight, though, or in Yagana's valley. It might be years or even generations before any Kurasi danced again unless she found the harp and learned soon how to counter Souraka's invulnerability.

A screech ripped through the gaiety. The drum stopped abruptly. Tou jostled Jeneba in a hurried retreat.

Why, she saw moments later. A Tou woman writhed in the dust beside the fire, screaming and clutching at her head. Firelight danced red across her. Then while Jeneba watched in horror, blood began pouring from the woman's eyes and ears. She arched backward until her head almost touched her heels. Then with a terrible shriek that felt like a spear running through Jeneba's head, the woman went limp.

Souraka strode around the fire from his tent to kneel be-

side her. The only sound in the camp came from the crackling fire. He touched her bare chest, then looked around at
his followers. "She is dead," he said in Nbana. He stood.
"The senior wife of Kaunou was a witch, and jealous of her
co-wife." He pointed at the bewitched Nbaba woman standing at the entrance to his tent. "Now her evil has turned back
and destroyed her."

Jeneba stared at the dead woman, stomach churning.
Blood still poured from the body in an unslackening stream.
As it did, the body withered, collapsing on itself, skin, ribs
and skull, other bones, until only red-stained dust remained.
Then even that vanished, drunk away by the dry earth.

She looked up to discover that warriors, women, and children had vanished into the darkness. Souraka stood alone
with her by the fire. Jeneba sucked in a deep breath. "I've
never known a chie—king who was also a witch doctor."
Certainly true. She did not have to pretend awe. "And few
witch doctors with such power, either. Where did you
learn?"

"In the southern forests. I hid among the Chullo after—"
A muscle in his jaw twitched. "I lived among the Chullo for
a while. Hunting one day, I found a leopard trapped in a pit.
Chullo kill leopards for their skins, so I dropped rocks and
wood into the pit until the leopard could leap out.

"He spoke to me, calling up thanks in my own language,
and when he was out he explained that he was Onaballo, the
Chullo lord of magic. He'd taken over the leopard's body for
fun, but when he fell into the pit, the animal had become so
frightened that he could no longer control it or use his
magic. As a reward for releasing him, he taught me some of
his magic."

Cold crawled down Jeneba's spine and through her gut.
Souraka used not men's magic but a demigod's. And this
was the man she must destroy before that harp could be
taken to Yagana?

CHAPTER

THIRTEEN

She had to outwit demigod magic. Jeneba fought despair. She forced herself to think of Yagana, of the warriors waiting for the harp, of Lubeda, of her determination to return Tomo to Kiba . . . anything. She must not surrender.

"No wonder you and your warriors resist the charms other witch doctors make," she said with an amusement she did not feel. "I'm sorry everyone's gone to bed. I'd borrow a bowharp and sing praise-songs to you."

The hunger she had seen in his eyes earlier glittered there again. He held out a hand. "Sing them to me alone, then."

She let him lead her around the fire. One of the guards stationed on either side of the tent entrance lifted the grass mat covering the opening. Jeneba ducked under. While Souraka remained outside speaking to the guards, she swiftly fished the blood-days charm from its hiding place and studied the tent's interior. It had little . . . the leopard stools; some baskets sitting against the wall with spears, a shield, and the leopard-skin hip wrap lying on them; a pile of several cowhides for a sleeping mat. Nowhere did she see a harp.

Souraka came in and sat down on the cowhides. "Sing."

She raised a brow at him. "What about the bowharp?"

"There's none for you to use. I'll slap my leg for a drum."

No harp? She stared at him in dismay, then a moment later caught the sly tone in his voice. The blood-days charm bit into her palm as her fist clenched. Souraka lied.

"Oh great warrior king," she purred, "I would not accuse you of untruth, but in fact I know you have a harp. I may not understand your language, but I have observed much from my cage."

Souraka lay back on the cowhides. Light coming from the dying fire outside glinted in his eyes. "I didn't say there was no harp. I said there's none for you to use. No one touches that harp, ever." He paused before going on in a deadly quiet voice. "I would even kill my totem for touching it."

Her heart sank. Had he learned what it was? She sat down on one of the stools. "It's so precious to you?"

Souraka's lip curled. "I detest it. It was a gift from my father."

She felt her jaw drop. "I don't understand."

Souraka jumped to his feet and paced the tent. "Each time one of my brothers became a man, our father gave him cattle from the most recently raided village. Except me. He wouldn't give me any because he said he could never be sure who sired my mother's children. For me there was only a bowharp." His fists clenched. "Oh, he claimed it was valuable. The chief of an Nbaba village supposedly died trying to keep him from taking it. He swore one of the chief's wives said it had been handed down from chief to chief for generations . . . that its song had once destroyed a city."

Jeneba winced at the bitterness in his voice. "Something like that would be more valuable than cattle."

He wheeled on her. "*Nothing* is more valuable than cattle. And the harp has no magic powers. I played it outside our village and not a thing happened. The village didn't collapse. My father didn't even fall ill. I had to strangle him with the harp string to make him die."

Jeneba choked.

He appeared oblivious to her reaction. "I call my clan Chimbua, our word for harp, the symbol of my father's contempt but a name which shall be feared across the world. Being the object of my father's death, it also ties his ghost to me. I feed him well so he'll have to remain on the earth to see me become what neither he nor any of my better-favored brothers were, a great warrior and conqueror."

Also a butcher and slaver, Jeneba reflected. She had to agree with that old Nbaba chief. Leopard breeding or not, Souraka had a bad belly. Aloud, she said, "You must believe there's some magic in it if you won't let anyone touch it."

He smiled thinly. "I believe in caution. Now . . . enough."

Catching her by the upper arms, he pulled her to her feet.
One hand pushed aside her tsara, then loosened his hip wrap
and dropped it to the ground.

Jeneba braced herself. Blood drummed in her ears. She
had slept with men before, but always friends.

His eyes raked her hungrily. "Tou," he whispered in a
triumphant voice, and jerked her to him.

The touch of him brought a wave of revulsion . . . the
clutching hands, sweaty chest pressed roughly against hers,
his breath hot on the hollow of her throat. Impulse shrieked
for her to claw free. She made herself wrap her arms around
him. Naruwa had done this, and so could she.

Not with enjoyment, however. Rhino coupled with more
gentleness and elegance. His arms locked around her back
so hard her ribs creaked in protest, and when they went
down on the cowhides, he threw her, landing heavily on top.
Something hard and edged under the cowhides at the level of
her neck added further to the discomfort, too. She clutched
the blood-days charm and thought of other men she had
known, of missed chances with the Kurasi warriors Ododo
and Chomba. She thought about Yagana. Frustration hissed
through her. She still had no idea where the harp was.

Or did she? Catching her breath, she turned concentration
on the object under the cowhides. It felt curved behind her.

Souraka finished in a final convulsive heave and rolled
off, frowning. "You don't couple like a leopard. I expected
scratching and biting. Fighting makes strong babies."

She raised a brow. "You haven't watched leopards. The
male does the biting and that's on the back of the female's
neck so he can mount her." Which sounded like something
Souraka would enjoy. Jeneba rolled on her side to throw an
arm and leg across him. If only there were water enough to
bathe, water heated steaming hot and poured over her, with
plenty of soap leaves to scrub her skin clean of him. "You
speak of babies. If I'm to bear yours, I want to know you'll
be here to defend them. No magic is perfect. Tell me what
endangers you so I can watch for it and warn you."

He patted her arm. "Don't worry. Nothing around here
can harm me."

He grabbed her again. This time she took pleasure in obliging him by sinking her teeth into his shoulder. He fell asleep almost immediately afterward.

Jeneba lay awake, brooding. A cautious exploration under the cowhides found the object there wrapped in soft-tanned skin. She dared not slide it out. Each time she moved it, Souraka stirred, muttering, as though sensing her intention, but what she could feel through the wrapping had the edged curve of a rib. Daytime, when he was out of the tent, would be a better time to examine it.

That did nothing to help her learn about the magic protecting him, though, and in the morning Lubeda would leave Najhadende for Yagana.

Jeneba wished she dared visit the slave tent to see what had happened to Ourassi, or run up to the black bush atop the northern hill, but the eyes of the camp followed her everywhere. They might wonder at her interest in a slave and a bush. So she lounged on her stool beside Souraka, watching the Tou warriors wrestle, wondering if the Kurasi were still alive. Hoping Tomo and Ngmengo were still all right. Had they gotten water? Food?

"I want to see you wrestle," Souraka said.

Anger flared at his peremptory tone. With an effort, though, she kept her reply lazily mild. "Leopards don't obey orders, majesty." Then she rose to challenge the warriors again. Reluctantly.

As they had the day before, the warriors lost and accepted defeat with delight. Guilt stabbed her. They liked her, and more, *approved* of her. And she was lying and plotting against them.

"How can you enjoy losing to me?" she asked a young warrior, helping him to his feet after pinning him.

He blinked at her surprise. "How can we *not* when it proves what a powerful totem we have?" He dusted himself off, grinning. "You'll surely bring us much luck."

Another warrior said, "And there's no danger. Nothing can harm us."

Other men echoed him.

But Jeneba heard a soft snort from outside the circle of warriors.

The sound came from three Tou women kneeling grinding grain. Jeneba slipped out of the warrior group and strolled over to them. "Who believes the warrior is wrong?"

Two of the women started and kept bent over their grinding stones. The third looked up, then went on without missing a push of the round grinding stone over the concave base stone.

Jeneba squatted before her. "You?"

The woman glanced quickly at her two companions. The morning sun gleamed off her scalp, shaved except for a skullcap of short fuzz. "His majesty Souraka has said nothing can harm them, and who am I to doubt him? The one who said the warriors are fools to believe all they're told is dead. She used to sleep with Souraka before he tired of her and gave her to Kaunou. She said he spoke of something that counters the charm."

Dead. Gave her to Kaunou. That would be the witch of last night. Jeneba leaned forward eagerly. "Did she say what? I want to make sure such a thing can never be used on him."

The woman looked up again. Her eyes searched Jeneba's intently. After a moment, she shrugged. "Daua was always looking over thornbushes and thorn trees. I don't think she found what she wanted, though."

Excitement stirred in Jeneba. Wood could neutralize some magic. If the witch were interested in thorn trees and bushes, then thorns, not just wood, must be necessary to pierce Souraka's protection, and thorns of a particular kind. How might Souraka react to hearing that someone knew so much about his charm?

She brought it up casually after submitting to him that night. "I heard something about that witch today. The women say she claimed to know something that would counter your invulnerability, and that she was very interested in thorn trees and bushes."

His arm across her chest tensed. "She couldn't know."

In the dark, Jeneba smiled in satisfaction. "She told the women you told her."

He rolled away and sat up. "I tell no one about my magic, especially a woman!"

"But if she was examining thorn trees—"

"She was a witch," he interrupted sharply. "Somehow she used her powers to learn a few things."

"Like what?" Jeneba sat up, too, and pressed against his back, wrapping her arms around him. His shoulders felt hard as stone. "If she knows, other witches and wizards might, too. I'm frightened for you."

The tension went out of him. Chuckling, he lay back, pulling her to the cowhides with him. "There's no need to be. She could never have found what she was looking for."

Jeneba lay listening to his breathing deepen into the regularity of sleep. She hissed in disgust. Still no useful information. If only she had spent some of her childhood watching her mother instead of caring only about becoming a warrior. Sia Nyiba could charm anything she wanted from a man.

The lump made by the harp pressed into the back of her neck. Jeneba traced its curve with her hand until it disappeared under Souraka. Perhaps she should just take the harp and trust to the gods to protect her long enough to reach Yagana. Or maybe she could take it, free Ourassi to carry it back, and remain here until she learned how to destroy him. Even if the gods helped the harp reach Yagana safely, something must be done to protect the Tou and Nbaba, and, ultimately, the Dasa, from his predations.

"What do I have to do to make you tell me?" she whispered at him.

Souraka stirred. "Never tell anyone," he muttered.

Jeneba's heart lurched. He had heard her? "But what if—"

She broke off. His breathing remained deep and even. He was still asleep.

Then her breath caught. What was it the grain-grinding woman had said? *She said he spoke of something that counters the charm.* Spoke of something. An odd choice of words. The Tou woman had assumed that the witch meant Souraka had told her something, but it could refer to overhearing something, and Daua used to sleep with Souraka.

Pulse thundering, Jeneba leaned close to his ear and whispered, "What was the witch hunting?"

The reply came as almost a sigh. "Black thorns."

Tightness in her chest released like a cut cord. No wonder he felt safe. All the thorns she had seen in this country were brown or green ... except Ngmengo's. "Black thorns neutralize your protection?"

He grunted. The sound had the quality of a laugh. "No."

Her stomach dropped. No! "What does she want the thorns for, then."

"Husband. Other warriors."

She sucked in her cheeks. He answered exactly what she asked, no more. "Black thorns will kill the warriors but not you?"

"Yes."

Slowly, she asked, "What will kill you?"

He rolled over. Her heart jumped. Was he waking? Paralyzed, she waited for him to open his eyes and demand what she was doing.

He only threw an arm across her and went still again.

Licking her lips, Jeneba repeated the question.

His arm tightened. He grimaced, muttering unintelligibly.

Fear and urgency set her blood pounding. All her will went into keeping a soft, patient voice. "Majesty, if black thorns kill your warriors, what kills you?"

He groaned, "Black thorn dipped in the burned bones of a pure black yearling bull."

Triumph sang through her, but tempered by the knowledge that she still had to tell what she knew to someone who could collect the thorns and make the bone powder. Carefully, she slid out from under his arm, though instead of circling around the hides, she deliberately stepped over Souraka on her way toward the tent entrance. See if his magic could also withstand the weakening effect of a woman crossing over him.

"Where are you going?"

Mala! If her heart stopped like this one more time tonight, it might not start again. Jeneba turned. "Would you prefer to have me soil a corner of the tent?"

He turned over. "Don't be long."

"No."

Wrapping her tsara around her shoulders, she ducked under the entrance mat.

"Greetings, lady leopard," one of the guards said.

The camp lay in total darkness. Mala's eye rose after midnight, but she still had to work fast, before Souraka began wondering what kept her out so long.

Jeneba sauntered around the tent. Though she felt sure the guards could see little, she made sure she was out of sight before racing silently across the common and slipping between two tents out of the camp.

Finding the cache of her belongings was harder than she anticipated, though. Stones scattered across most of the basin, ghostly gray stones all about the same size and shape, and she had been in a hurry when she buried everything. She moved fifteen or twenty before finally uncovering the cache. The knife was all she wanted, however. The Kurasi charm and her buffalo talisman went back in the hole.

No light showed in the slave tent tonight. By listening and slipping around to the front to observe, she decided only the outside guard remained, too. She heard nothing inside but harsh, rattling breath. Since Souraka's magic left her knife usless for killing, she used it to pry up two stakes holding a tent mat, enough to let her slide underneath.

The children slept curled in their cages. Ourassi sat with his back to a tent wall, arms stretched wide and tied to separate frame poles. Bruises and weals crisscrossed his chest. His head hung forward, bobbing with each labored breath.

Putting a hand over his mouth to muffle any involuntary sound, she breathed his name in his ear. The hand proved unnecessary. He woke silently, and instantly slumped slack against a tent pole one moment, lifting his head the next. She saw why he breathed with so much difficulty. His nose lay flat on his face. Both eyes were blackened and swelled almost shut. Beneath her hand his mouth felt distorted, short of teeth.

She removed the hand and cut the thongs binding his wrists. Bending to his ear she whispered, "Can you walk?"

His arms hung limp. With great effort he dragged one to his wounded leg. His swollen jaw knotted as he nodded.

When he tried to stand, though, the leg gave way. Jeneba sighed in dismay.

Ourassi clutched at her arm. "I'll...be...fine. Need time."

She pointed his feet toward the loosened mat. "See if you can slide under without making a sound."

To her amazement, he did. Outside she pushed the stakes back into place. "Try again."

He stood this time. He limped laboriously, but he walked, and by moving slowly he managed to make little noise.

"Can you see well enough?" she whispered.

His bruised lips twisted in a smile. "I'll feel my way straight out of the basin. When the moon comes up is time enough to work my way around to Ngmengo and Tomo."

She gave him the knife, for all the good it would do against the warriors' charms, and told him what she had learned from Souraka.

Ourassi sighed. "The gods are finally smiling. Now all we have to do is find a black yearling bull."

"Send Ngmengo with the thorn when it's ready."

Nodding, he limped away into the darkness. Jeneba touched her heart four times and hurried back to Souraka.

CHAPTER

FOURTEEN

One of the entrance guards woke them in the gray light before dawn, bursting into the tent babbling shrilly. Jeneba started, heart drumming, then forced herself to lie still and open just one eye a slit. Souraka leaped off the cowhides, firing back questions as he wrapped his hip cloth.

"What is it?" she asked.

He was already running out of the tent.

Jeneba tied her tsara and followed at the lazy pace of someone curious but unconcerned. If she had not known what the problem was, she could have guessed easily. Everyone in the camp clustered around the slave tent. They moved aside to let her through.

A guard crouched wailing before Souraka. Souraka spat something back. Catching sight of Jeneba, he said, "When you went out last night, did you see a guard at the slave tent?"

She eyed the terrified warrior. "Yes. Why?"

Another warrior spoke, one of the pair who guarded Souraka's tent during the night.

Souraka listened, frowning. "It's impossible," he said to Jeneba. "The guard swears he never left the tent unguarded. You say you saw him here. My own guards swear they called back and forth to him all night. Yet the slave has vanished."

Jeneba arched her brows. "He obviously went out the back of the tent."

"The tent is undisturbed."

He spun away, shouting. Everyone scrambled to search the camp perimeter for Ourassi's trail.

"He came from the east. Maybe he left that way, too," Jeneba suggested.

The misdirection did not last long. Someone found the scrapes and dislodged pebbles marking Ourassi's climb out of the basin south. Warriors then tracked him around the basin to the northern side, where Souraka stared narrow-eyed at the hoofprints and horse droppings.

"Someone waited several days for him," a warrior said. "I wonder why they didn't try to rescue him."

"Maybe they did."

Jeneba watched Souraka. What was he thinking? Nothing in his face or eyes told her.

"Shall we follow the riders, majesty?" another warrior asked.

"No. I'll deal with him later. I have the charms he wore around his neck."

Jeneba sucked in her cheeks. She would have to steal those before he used them against Ourassi.

He started to turn back toward camp, then stopped. "What puzzles me is these other charms Tutuo found while we were searching the slope of the basin." He held up a hand. Two objects dropped from it to dangle on leather cords.

The breath stopped in Jeneba's throat.

"One is identical to a charm the slave wore, and this"—he fingered the buffalo talisman—"one of the Nbaba women says is Dasan. Is it, leopard-woman?"

Amazingly, her hand remained steady as she took the talisman and pretended to study it. "It could be."

Souraka took it back. "Interesting. You're Dasa, and sometime after you left my tent, the slave with a charm identical to this other escaped."

Jeneba stood very still, hardly breathing. Fear and leopard strength flowed outward through her, coiling muscles readying for flight.

Souraka smiled at her, a gesture with no trace of humor, baring pointed teeth. "I think I would very much like to see you change back into a leopard."

Except she could not run. They must have that harp. She met his eyes. "This is a bad time to ask, in daylight with a waning moon." She pointed at the crescent of Mala's closing eye high overhead. "How can you doubt me when you've seen me wrestle and race?"

He swung the charm and talisman. "I agree that no one fully human could have done that. Still . . . I want to see you become a leopard again. Warriors, grab her!"

Several of them just gaped in bewilderment. Others, though, leaped to obey. Jeneba tripped the first one to her and knocked a second aside with a hard backhand, but even her strength was no match for sheer numbers. She went down under the weight of them.

"Don't hurt her yet!" Souraka yelled.

With several men hanging on to each of her arms and legs they carried her, writhing furiously, into camp and shoved her into the cage. Souraka slammed the door down. He pushed the pegs in place with a whisper and a touch of gray powder. Jeneba flung back toward the door, but when she reached through the bars for the pegs, her fingers slid past, unable to grasp them.

"I've locked you in," Souraka said. "Don't worry. This is just so I can observe you closely. I'll take good care of you, as I cared for the leopard, and when you've changed into a leopard again, even if just for a brief while, you'll be freed to become my queen."

Spitting in his eye would have felt good. It might also seem to Souraka a gesture of guilt and defiance. So instead, she snarled, "No one orders me when to turn leopard," and retreated to sit at the far end of the cage.

He raised his voice, calling something in his language.

The camp became a bustle of activity. Jeneba watched in horror as camp members untied mats from tent frames and pulled down frames. Moving! When the men came back with the thorn for Souraka, would they be able to find the camp again!

Belatedly, she thought about her original tsara underneath the cage and managed to fish it up between the floor poles. Folding and sitting on the red-ochre cloth not only hit it but made a more comfortable seat of the cage floor.

By midmorning they were on the move, heading south. Everyone carried something: tent frames, rolled grass mats, baskets of personal belongings, all balanced on their heads.

Four warriors carried Jeneba's cage slung on poles between them. Others bore the childrens'.

They set up at the new campsite about sunset, arranging the tents in a circle on a broad hilltop with a spring halfway down one side. The hill and those surrounding it even had some grass. Jeneba waited until the last mat had been tied in place on the frame of Souraka's tent and the awning put in place above her cage, then pushed the red-ochre tsara out of sight beneath the floor bars.

Just in time. Souraka visited the cage, raising the door a crack to push a goat-stomach water bag through.

She snatched it up and drank deeply. No one had offered her a drink all day.

"You're thirsty. Aré you hungry?" he asked.

Starved. No one had thought of her during the hurried breakfast before packing the camp, either. "Yes, I'm hungry."

An answer Jeneba quickly regretted. What the warriors shoved under the door a short time later was not a bowl of food but a screaming boy of four or five.

Souraka bared pointed teeth. "Eat that."

This time she spit at him.

Souraka turned away with mouth clamped tight.

"It's all right," she told the terrified boy. "I'm not going to eat you."

His white-rimmed eyes said he did not believe her. He continued to press against the cage as far from her as possible. But at least he stopped screaming.

No one danced that night. With darkness everyone but the warriors on guard vanished into their tents. That suited Jeneba. She wanted solitude. Once the camp's fires died low enough to make her no more than a shadow to even the guards outside Souraka's tent, she methodically worked her way around the cage, examining it bar by bar, floor, walls, and top, shaking each, testing. When Ngmengo brought the treated thorn, she needed a way to escape and collect it to use on Souraka. Lubeda must have completed the first day of his march toward Yagana.

To her dismay, however, the cage proved strong and solid,

well suited for holding any leopard. Leather bindings lay so
tight in grooves cut for them at the end of each heavy
wooden bar that they must have been wrapped wet and
stretched, then dried with heat to shrink them. She tried the
door again. As before, her fingers skidded off the pegs, even
though Souraka had had no trouble pulling them to shove the
boy in with her. She snarled in frustration.

The boy, who had been skittering out of her way during
the exploration, whimpered.

She sent him a quick smile. "I'm sorry. It's the cage I'm
mad at, not you." It occurred to her that he probably needed
more reassurance than that, but she had no time to spend on
him.

A second examination helped her no more than the first.
None of the bars showed any weakness. Jeneba sighed. Very
well, she would just have to *make* a way out.

The camp sat on rocky ground. Reaching out through the
bars, Jeneba searched around the cage, picking up stone
after stone until she found one with a sharp edge. That in the
cage, she chose a bar at the back end and carefully dribbled
water from the goat-stomach onto the lower bindings, working the moisture in with her fingers. Then she used the stone
to scrape and saw at the softened leather. Between the
toughness of the leather and stopping when one of Souraka's
guards took a turn around the cage, it made slow work.
When the rise of Mala's eye forced her to stop altogether,
the top wrap had been scored but not cut through. Still, it
was progress. She slept the rest of the night.

Restless dreams stalked her: of turning into a leopard and
gnawing the bindings away, of Lubeda's army marching re-
lentlessly toward Yagana. Once a touch interrupted them,
jerking her into wakefulness, but before she struck out, a
whimper identified the source . . . the boy, crawling up beside her, shivering, his fear numbed by cold. Sighing, she
pulled the small body against hers and curled up around him.

It would have been nice to sleep through the day as well,
but hunger slid into the leopard dreams, turning the bindings
she gnawed into the boy's carcass. She woke in revulsion
and after that, the empty snarl of her stomach refused to let
her sleep.

Souraka taunted her each time he passed the cage. "I'll release you the moment you prove you're leopard."

She stared through him, refusing to respond. Until afternoon, when the boy began whimpering in hunger. "He's done nothing to you," she said then. "Take the child back to the slave tent and feed him."

Souraka smirked. "That would be going back on my word to care for you. He's your food and he stays until you eat him. Or he eats you." He bared his pointed teeth. "That's an interesting idea. Perhaps I won't feed any of the slaves for several days, then put them all in with you and see what happens."

She stared at him with loathing. Mala bring Ngmengo and that counter-charm thorn very very soon!

With darkness, Jeneba returned to sawing at the binding. The top wrap parted, then the one under it. The closing eye's late rise gave her plenty of working time. It also marked Lubeda's progress toward Yagana. The Kurasi army had reached Yagana at the dark of the moon. In four more days Mala's eye would be closed again.

As the crescent rose, she saw to her frustration that still a third layer of leather lay under the others, and trying the bar, it felt no looser than before. Wishing wizards and bewitchments on the Chullo who built such a solid cage, she continued to saw at the binding even after moonrise. She must be able to free herself when Ngmengo appeared.

And even after daylight, Jeneba remained by the bar, sometimes just sitting, watching the women prepare food and the herd boys take the cattle and goats out to graze, other times pretending to doze, and when no one watched her, she slipped a swipe or two at the leather. Which meant a few chances, but very few. Souraka held court beside the cage. Or else the boy's whimper, ceaseless now in his hunger, drew attention. Jeneba wondered that they did not hear her stomach, too, it snarled so loud. She felt light-headed.

It was even possible to imagine she heard things above the grunts and yelps of the wrestling warriors... like Ngmengo's voice, calling in Burda.

"Hoooh! Leopard's daughter!"

Jeneba flung up her head. Not imagined. That was a *real* voice, coming from the north! She spun on her knees, heart leaping, and clutched the bars. The bush-man stood on top of the next hill waving his arms. The warriors stopped wrestling to stare. Children quit playing warrior and the village women put down their grinding stones and cooking pots.

Their voices murmured in wonder. "What's that? What's it saying?"

"Leopard's daughter!" Ngmengo shouted. "We come! An army!"

An *army!*

Someone else shouted, too, this time to the south . . . a boy's voice, high and excited. Heads snapped around. One of the herd boys raced across the hilltop toward the tent circle, calling as he ran.

Over the top behind him jogged Nbaba and Tou warriors. An army indeed. There must be over a hundred of them . . . Nbaba in brightly striped hip wraps, white-painted skin, and beaded chestplates of colors matching beads woven into their fringe of hair . . . Tou wearing animal skin hip wraps and red-ochre body paint, feathers woven into their forelock pigtails . . . all carrying spears and long shields decorated with four different zigzag and circle designs. The scents of oils and herbs came before them on the hot wind.

Leading the group between three Nbaba and one Tou with more beads and brighter colors than anyone else trotted Tomo in his drab-dyed Kurasi clothing. The late sun gleamed off his shaved scalp and the heavy scarring of his arms and legs. As one, the warriors stopped well short of the camp and leaned on their spears.

Jeneba recognized one of the Nbaba leaders as Zabama, chief of the camp she had watched Souraka frighten into subjection. Where was Ourassi, though?

"Come out and fight, Souraka, you butchering outlaw!" Tomo shouted.

Souraka's head snapped from the bush-man to the Nbaba to Jeneba. Eyes narrowing, he yelled in his own language.

The warriors whooped and ran for their tents, emerging shortly in war hip wraps and carrying their own spears and shields. Souraka dressed, too. The tail of his leopard-skin rippled behind him.

The Tou marched out to the waiting army. Women and children crowded at the edge of the camp to watch.

Jeneba looked back toward Ngmengo to find the bushman gone. Grabbing her stone, she sawed grimly at the bindings. She must get out of this cage.

War yells signaled the first throw. Cries of pain answered, among them one scream with as much surprise as anguish in it.

The stone was too slow. Jeneba kicked at the bottom of the bar to break it loose. It remained firmly in place. She kicked again and again with all her strength, snarling. It had to give, had to.

The wind carried the smell of fresh blood, and the screams of injured and mortally wounded men.

Jeneba fought a sob of frustration. The bar could not be moved. Now what? Try the door again? She dived for it. As before, though, her fingers skidded past the pegs, no matter how hard she concentrated on grasping them.

Frantically, she struggled to think. There must be something she could do, another way to pull them. Souraka and the warriors had had no problem when they opened the door to put in water and the boy.

The boy!

She spun on her knees. "Boy, if you help me, we can get out of here. We'll find food and no one will ever threaten to feed you to a leopard again."

He frowned uncertainly.

Mala! And there was no time to convince or cajole. Any moment the Tou, discovering that their charm had failed, might retreat. She seized him and held him against the bars. He screamed.

"Boy, reach out and grab that peg. Grab it, or by Ello, I *will* eat you!" she snarled.

Terrified, he grabbed it. At his age he lacked the strength to pull it, though. Jeneba hissed. Then a thought occurred to her. Holding her breath, she reached for his hand and clamped her own fingers over his...and whooped in triumph. Her fingers did not slide away. The peg came loose.

"Now the other one, boy. Quickly!"

With that one out, too, she shoved up the door and scrambled out, across into Souraka's tent, dragging the boy with her. One sweep of her arm tossed the cowhides aside.

Nothing lay beneath.

She stared in disbelief, stomach plunging. No. *No!* The harp had to be here somewhere. In one of the baskets? Or . . . Jeneba pawed through the stack of cowhides. And there it was, tucked between the middle and bottom hide, a curved object folded up in soft-tanned calfhide.

Relief flooded her.

She opened the wrapping at one end just enough to confirm that she did indeed have a bone bowharp and headed for the tent entrance. *Now* she could leave, and as quickly as possible.

Her eyes fell on the boy, squatting in a terrified huddle by the entrance where she had released his hand when they came in. She sucked in her cheeks. No, there was one more thing to be done before going.

Scooping up the boy, she ran for the slave tent.

The wind reeked of blood. Women's wails mixed with the cries of pain and death.

Something moved between two tents. She whirled . . . and gasped in dismay. Ngmengo and Ourassi stood in the space, the Kurasi leaning on a spear. His battered body and face did not shock her but the bush-man did. Ngmengo looked terrible, color leached to gray and branches stripped of thorns.

"I told you she'd free herself when she saw you," Ourassi said.

"I just didn't want to take chances." Ngmengo grinned at her. "Don't look so horrified. I'm feeling much better. You should have seem me the day we—"

She never heard the rest. Behind her came the sound of running feet, and a whiff of familiar scent. Jeneba was already whirling sideways when she heard the singing hiss of a spear in flight.

The blade skimmed by her, so close the trailing end of its shaft brushed her elbow and the boy's buttocks.

She tossed the child to Ourassi and the harp at Ngmengo, then stepped farther into the common area. "You've abandoned your warriors, Souraka?"

"They're all dying anyway. I came to kill the leopard-witch responsible. But I see I've found a thief, too." His lip curled.

Anger flared in her. She watched the second spear he carried. "Your father was the thief. The harp belongs to the Kurasi people."

His eyes narrowed. "That's what all this has been for? Then the harp *will* destroy cities!"

The greed in his face revolted her. So did the sly smile immediately following.

He leaned on his spear. "There's no need for us to fight one another. As allies, with your harp and my invulnerability charms, we'll be invincible. We can conquer the world."

"Which charm?" Ourassi said. "The one you made for your warriors or the better one you use to protect yourself? Jeneba, honor says I should fight him, but I'm not so much a fool I can't see that's impossible. Will you substitute for me?" He tossed his spear to her.

A black thorn gray with ash tipped it.

Souraka's yellow-brown color went muddy.

Jeneba grinned. She was going to enjoy this. "I ought to use just a halter rope or whip. You don't deserve to be fought as an equal. However, I, too, will temper honor with the necessity."

Above his shield, Souraka's eyes went stony. His arm drew back.

Jeneba started to dodge, but he did not throw the spear. Instead, he sidestepped, circling her. Jeneba crouched, watching him intently. He was careless with the shield and did not move it smoothly with him. For a moment, the entire right half of his body stood exposed.

But as she started to throw, she caught a triumphant flash in his eyes and halted her arm. The exposure was not carelessness, she suddenly understood, but an attempt to draw a hasty throw. Unlike other duels where opponents could pick up each other's spears, she had only one chance at defeating him, one throw.

Her grip tightened on the spear. Crouching lower, she circled, too. They eyed each other, feinting to draw the other, dodging. Watching for their chance. But neither threw.

He chuckled. "You call yourself a warrior, leopard-witch, but you hesitate. Can it be you aren't the warrior you claim?"

Taunting an opponent was an old trick. She just smiled back.

"Maybe all you can do is wrestle and run."

Rant on, she thought, and kept circling, silently watching him.

"I think perhaps you don't trust your neutralizing charm." His voice carried a sharp note.

Impatience? She bit back a grin. The leopard blood had thinned indeed. She herself felt no hurry at all. She floated in a calm, timeless pool of leopard patience.

Smiling, she stalked him.

They were collecting onlookers. The common filled with warriors and the women and children of Souraka's camp, and with surviving Tou warriors looking numbed by shock.

"Let me fight him," Tomo's voice called.

At the edge of her vision she saw his head rising above the other onlookers, then movement among them as he pushed through to the front.

Souraka turned toward the movement. In doing so, he failed to bring the shield quite with him, exposing part of his chest. Jeneba hurled her spear.

It flew hard and straight.

Souraka sprang sideways, grinning and swinging his shield. Sick with dismay, she watched the spear deflect harmlessly.

One chance, one throw, and she had missed. Missed for these people, missed for hers. Missed for Yagana. Unless . . .

Jeneba dived for the spear.

Souraka reached it first. His foot pinned the shaft to the dust. He bared pointed teeth and drew back his own spear.

"Jeneba, catch," Tomo shouted.

From the edge of her vision a spear arced toward her. She snatched it from the air.

"We dipped them all in the bone ash!"

Souraka threw.

In one motion Jeneba dived into a somersault sideways to dodge Souraka's weapon, rolled over her shoulders, and coming up on her knees, threw Tomo's spear. The thorn point slipped past the edge of the shield to bury itself in Souraka's throat.

He tumbled over on his back, arms outflung.

Jeneba scrambled on hands and knees over to him.

He was still alive, and conscious. He rolled his head toward her. "The charm. How did . . . you . . . know—" The words faded in a gurgle. A stream of blood ran from the corner of his mouth.

She sat back on her feet. "Ask your father's ghost."

Terror widened his eyes and twisted his face . . . and fixed there. His eyes glazed.

Jeneba jerked out the spear and pulled the leopard talisman from around his neck. He did not deserve such an association. Then she stood and turned away.

The watching Tou and Nbaba stared open-mouthed.

From the direction of the slave tent came Ngmengo and Ourassi, limping, still carrying the child. They nodded approval.

She raised her brows toward the warriors. "When did we decide to recruit an army?"

Behind her Tomo said, "They volunteered."

"They insisted on coming with us when they learned what we wanted to do," Ngmengo said. "They're from the camps where Zabama sent runners looking for a pure black bull. We thought it only just to agree." He unfolded the calfhide. "Shall we make sure we have what we came for?"

Once he unwrapped it, any doubt vanished. Jeneba caught her breath. The men's eyes gleamed, Tomo's with the fervent light of a starving man brought to a feast. The rib gleamed with the patina of ivory, pulling Jeneba's fingers to it, to the carved lines of the snake coiling around it. The harp had the smoothness of ivory, too. Ngmengo plucked the string. It sang with a soft, clear note that reverberated in Jeneba's bones. *Yagana. Yagana.*

Yagana. Their eyes all met. Lubeda would be there in two or three more days, four at the most. They could not hope to reach the city by then. Cold slid down Jeneba's spine. The harp was theirs at last, but . . . what would they be bringing it to?

CHAPTER

FIFTEEN

What would they find at Yagana? Fighting? The Kurasi in Djero servitude? The question haunted Jeneba and the others. None of them said so. No one spoke much at all. Their actions said enough . . . riding and walking with faces set, eyes on the northwest horizon but haunted gazes turned inward. Eating quickly, sleeping restlessly, ever anxious to be on the move again. Pushing themselves and the horses, taking advantage of the animals' few days rest and the grain brought along from Souraka's camp to feed them. As though by single-minded determination the distance would somehow magically shorten and let them arrive before Lubeda.

Nowhere did that hope gleam more fervently than in Tomo, though Jeneba wondered if Yagana's fate concerned him as much as the possiblity of going unrewarded for his efforts. It occurred to her that she ought to watch him, in case he judged their task futile and decided to bolt rather than face Kiba without the glory he had hoped to wear back. If he escaped, she could not go after him until Yagana was recovered, and by that time he might disappear forever.

But there was so much else to worry about. The dark of the moon passed. Four days into the journey, Tomo's horse dropped dead under him. Then two days after that, Ourassi's horse went lame. With only the little bay left, Jeneba felt obligated to offer him to Ourassi. The Kurasi's limp and the lines etching deeper into his face every day betrayed pain he never mentioned. The stain wearing off his skin, too, revealed how pale and gray he had become.

Ourassi tried to refuse. "I think everyone should take turns."

Jeneba wanted to. They were all bone weary, except per-

haps Ngmengo, whose strength, and thorns, returned rapidly, but they dared not risk riding the bay to death, too. If
their legs ached with every step and their bodies groaned
when forced up after resting, at least she and Tomo could
still walk. She refused to ride, and after a long pause, while
Jeneba glared at him, Tomo sullenly echoed her.

The country grew greener each day. Grass and woods covered the hills. Ponds and lakes spread between them. Herds
of game appeared. For all the richness of the land, however,
Jeneba could not forget how close wastelands lay . . . nor
what waited ahead.

One afternoon, with Mala's opening eye climbing the sky,
Jeneba caught a rank scent and remembered something else
she had not seen in Tou and Nbaba territory . . . monsters and
demons. She wheeled, yelling for Ngmengo, just as a nogama charged out of the woods.

The bush-man leaped to intercept the demon. The nogama
slashed its clawed palms at Ngmengo, manlike face twisting
in an animal snarl, but when the bush-man leaped toward it,
it turned and fled. For good measure, Ngmengo followed.

"I'll chase it far enough off that it won't bother us again,"
he called over his shoulder and plunged into the woods.

Between lingering traces of the nogama's smell and looking backward at where Ngmengo had gone, Jeneba did not
catch the man scent until warriors stepped out of the woods
to surround her and the men with spears.

"Who are you?" one of the warriors demanded in Burda.
"Where are you going?"

Jeneba stared in dismay. Not just at being caught by surprise, but at the appearance of the warriors . . . Kurasi,
young men looking like old men, with eyes like bruises and
bones sharp beneath skins leached pale as Ourassi's.

She heard Ourassi's sharp intake of breath. No doubt they
shocked him even more, not having seen himself. "We're
going to Yagana. I'm Biratha's son."

The warriors snorted. Jeneba could understand why. This
gaunt man on a gaunt little horse, wearing no jewelry or
royal ornamentation, only a Burdamu's horsetail hairstyle
and the drawn face of exhaustion and pain, could bear little

resemblance to what they had heard or seen of their king's sons.

"Yagana?" one of them asked. His hand tightened around the shaft of his spear. "How do you plan to reach it?"

"I—" Ourassi began.

"There are only two of Biratha's sons outside of Yagana," another warrior interrupted, "Menekuya and—"

He broke off in turn, staring down the trail past them. Jeneba glanced around. It was only Ngmengo reappearing out of the woods. The warrior, though, suddenly looked the rest of them over again, eyes widening. Now she read recognition in his face, and consternation. Someone had told him about the strange party with Ourassi. He stammered in his own language.

Ourassi leaned on the bay's neck and replied in Burda, "To my everlasting shame, yes, I am Ourassi, he whose greed let King Biratha die and lose Yagana. I will carry the burden of my father's death always, but Yagana can be restored if we play Bisiri's harp where the city stood. May we go on?"

Around them faces twisted in dispair. "You come too late. It's impossible to reach the city. Lubeda Madji's army surrounds the valley. He may even occupy it by this time."

" 'May occupy it.' " Tomo's eyes narrowed. "That means he might not."

Ourassi leaned farther down. "Menekuya has been withstanding him?"

The warrior sighed. "No, only losing ground slowly. The message drums say that Yagana's army intended to remain around the valley until you returned, but on the night of the new moon Menekuya came from prayer and declared that honor required the Kurasi weakened or not to return to Najhadende to meet Lubeda. So he took up the shield and spear of the king and—"

"Took the king's shield and spear!" Ourassi straightened with a jerk, hands going white-knuckled around the bay's reins. The horse tail of his hair lashed. "My brother made *himself*—"

"How long has the fighting lasted?" Jeneba asked quickly. They had no time for rage and indignation.

"Nine days."

Nine days! Even robbed of heart and strength Menekuya kept battling for that long? The Kurasi were people of courage indeed!

"Lubeda tastes victory," another warrior said bitterly. "Djero warriors are visiting Kurasi cities and villages demanding tribute."

Demanding tribute. As Souraka had. Jeneba hissed, anger blazing up in her as she imagined the scene.

"They're also capturing any Kurasi warriors they find on the way to join Yagana's army."

"Menekuya can't have supplies or warriors enough to resist much longer."

Ourassi's face went grim. "Only the hope we'll return with the harp. Warriors, does your village lie close enough to borrow fresh horses?"

The warriors grimaced. "There are Djero there, majesty."

They had no choice but to continue as they were, but faster, while the increased sense of urgency pushed back weariness. Ngmengo led the way, scouting their path to make sure no Djero surprised them as the Kurasi had done.

Tomo bared his teeth. "So this is the reward for your heroism and suffering, your brother stealing the king's spear and shield from you."

The spiral scarring on Ourassi's face twitched, then stiffened into an expressionless mask. "Menekuya is an honorable man. He was right that we must meet Lubeda, and someone had to lead."

His tone ended the subject.

They finally stopped at moonset, camping at the edge of the woods where brush provided cover for them and the bay could graze in a small meadow. With Ngmengo on watch, the rest of them could sleep, but Jeneba found herself at once too tired and too impatient to do so. Her nerves stretched taut, keenly aware of every scent and sound around them. Ourassi remained awake, too. He shifted and sighed, breath hissing through his broken nose, and each time Jeneba glanced at him, he lay with eyes open and staring, like black holes.

At first light they moved on, clinging to woods wherever

possible and hurrying across open valleys. Jeneba watched Ourassi now as well as Tomo. Something in the tense set of the Kurasi's head and shoulders suggested he longed to kick the bay into a gallop and race flat-out for Yagana. From eagerness to carry the harp there, though, or to confront Menekuya?

Just past midmorning Ngmengo came tearing back along the trail. "Djero!"

They dived off the trail into the underbrush. None of it grew quite tall enough to hide a horse but in a hurried debate, they decided that the noise of throwing the bay would be riskier than simply pulling him farther into the woods and trusting to the shadows and the tired hang of his head to keep him from being noticed. Jeneba clamped a hand over his nostrils to prevent a nicker.

The Djero came on foot, a large party of fifteen padding along the trail with spears and shields, peering around them, heads tilting to listen. Shafts of sunlight slanting down through the trees lighted up the red crests of their hair and the bird, lizard, and snake tattoos on yellow-brown arms and chests. In the heat of the day the sheepskins wrapped around them had been dropped to the waist.

Jeneba pressed against the bay, hardly daring to breathe. The Djero walked almost without a sound. Thank Mala for Ngmengo scouting ahead. With so little air moving in here, she might not have caught even their scent in time.

If felt like a lifetime before the Djero passed and they could leave cover to hurry on. But now fear pushed back Jeneba's weariness still more. She ranged along the line from the untiring bush-man up front to the very rear, with her senses spread even wider, testing all sounds and scents around them.

That may have been all that warned them of the second Djero party.

The afternoon air hung motionless. Antelope and bushbuck grazed the meadows. Jeneba caught a glimpse of a little dik-dik browsing on the underbrush. For the most part, though, the land lay hot and still, its silence broken only by droning insects and an occasional birdcall. The humus muffled even the bay's hoofbeats.

Jeneba felt like leopards she had seen sprawled along tree limbs with eyes closed but ears and tail flicking, ready to leap up at any alarm. Her nerves vibrated like a plucked bowstring . . . taut, uneasy.

Then off among the trees to the east movement broke a shaft of sunlight, followed by two more to either side of the first. Red flashed through a sunbeam. She hissed. Djero, and not walking in a group but spread out in a broad line!

She touched the men and pointed.

As Ourassi slid off the bay, though, Tomo muttered, "How can we hide? They'll pass on either side of us. Someone is bound to see the horse."

Jeneba handed him her spear. Maybe not hiding was the way to hide. She took the reins from Ourassi and vaulted on. "You two find cover."

She kneed the bay into a walk straight for the Djero.

They saw her almost immediately. "You! Stay right there!"

One came running to grab the bay's reins. A look at her turned his frown of challenge to a disappointed scowl. "Only a woman."

"She isn't Kurasi," another warrior pointed out. "Who are you, girl? What are you doing here?"

She lifted her chin. "I am Itishana Silla, daughter of Sabulana, sister of Tomo." Tomo's family was as good as any to use. If only her mind were not so empty of excuses for a Dasa to be wandering around Kurasi territory. Forget excuses, then. Fleeing invited pursuit. Attack, however, sometimes startled predators into retreat. She frowned. "What concern is it of yours why I'm here? Why are *you* in Kurasi lands, Djero?"

They bared their teeth. "It's now Djero land. It belongs to King Lubeda Madji."

"Lubeda? You mean he with the snake tattoo on his face? A daring tattoo, so close to his neck. What if a wizard should make the snake real? Ah. I see many of you wear snake tattoos." While she talked, she let her hand creep up to her neck, to the leopard and buffalo talismans and the blood-days charm now hanging on the same cord with the

Kurasi protective charm. "You're all very brave." She dropped her voice and began whispering.

The eyes of the warrior holding the reins went white-rimmed. He jumped back as though stung. "Witch!"

The others scrambled away, too. Several reached for charms around their own necks. "If you harm us, your evil magic will turn back on you!"

For a moment she thought of the witch Souraka killed and shuddered before she could laugh. "I don't fear Djero magic, but . . . I have no quarrel with you just now, not as long as you let me pass."

They moved well out of her path.

Once behind them she stopped and turned to watch their progress through the woods. As she had hoped, they were so busy glancing back at her that while they still probed the underbrush with their spears, they hardly watched what they were doing. They passed unseeing a spear length to either side of the men's hiding place and disappeared among the trees.

The escape brought no relief. If anything, her nerves stretched tighter. Warriors visiting villages to collect tribute did not travel that way. Hunters did.

She urged the bay back to the men. Ngmengo came running from up the trail. The look on their faces told her they were all thinking what she was.

"It might not be Yagana's warriors they're hunting," Tomo said.

Ourassi grimaced. "Who else?" He stroked the wrapped harp under his arm. "Menekuya has lost and Lubeda is tracking down what's left of the army."

"Lubeda could be just hunting warriors cut off from the main army, to make sure they can't rejoin. The valley might not be taken yet."

Jeneba knew none of them believed that.

They traveled all night. After moonset, shortly past midnight, Jeneba and Ngmengo led the way.

In the morning they slid through two more warrior parties using Jeneba's witch trick. After the second time, Ourassi thrust the wrapped harp at Ngmengo. "You better carry this. You're least likely to be caught."

The bush-man hid it among his branches.

Berries and fruit from an orchard in a valley they skirted provided a meal, but Jeneba could not convince her body that food substituted for rest. By midafternoon they were all stumbling with a weariness greater than even the urgency in them. They stopped to sleep and let the bay eat grass Jeneba brought him from a meadow.

It seemed she had barely closed her eyes, however, when Ngmengo shook her. "Djero."

The fiery cold wash of fear brought her scrambling to her feet, testing the air with nose and ears. Mala! She stared in horror at the line of warriors marching through the woods. Moments away from being on top of them. The men were already burrowing into the cover of the brush. She flung herself on the bay.

He moved only steps before they saw her. Two warriors dashed forward to grab her reins.

She smiled down at them. "Ah? You Djero haven't left Kurasi lands yet? You're either very brave or very foolish." One hand closed around the talismans and charms. "There—"

A warrior exclaimed in the Djero language.

Jeneba stiffened. That sounded like excitement, not fear, not the emotion she wanted to generate.

One of the warriors holding her reins peered up at her, eyes suddenly narrowed. "Who are you, Dasa girl?"

"What does *he* say?" She pointed at the warrior who had called out.

"He says you're the warrior woman who fought at Najha-dende." He moved to her leg. "Dismount."

Jeneba brought her knee up under his chin. His head snapped back, teeth cracking together. As he dropped, she rammed both heels into the bay's sides. He plunged forward through the Djero line, dragging the other warrior with him until a hoof caught the man and knocked him loose, too.

Jeneba leaned low over the bay's neck. "Run. I'm sorry, little one. I know you're tired. We have to lead them away from the men and Ngmengo."

A spear hissed past her. She flattened and urged the horse faster.

He tried. His hindquarters gathered and pushed, ears flattening with the effort. Beyond a thicket, a fallen tree appeared across their path. With a grunt, the bay heaved over it.

In midjump he screamed. A hind leg jerked. One quick glance back showed her he had been hit by a spear. They fell, diving head-on into the humus and flipping over.

Jeneba let go. Momentum flung her away from the horse. She landed rolling. Voices shouted in triumph behind her. Another spear skidded into the humus beside her. The bay screamed again, and went on screaming. She scrambled up and plunged into the brush, not daring to look back, not even to see where the horse had been hit this time. His thrashing, though, sounded like an animal struggling in vain to stand.

At least they were chasing her and not stumbling over the men. Now all she had to do was keep them from spearing or catching her. Run, leopard.

Another fallen tree loomed ahead. She vaulted over it, dived through a thicket beyond . . . and skidded to a halt, grabbing a tree for support. The ground opened into a steep ravine. Jeneba grimaced. She could climb down but not up the far side before her pursuers reached here. The bottom afforded little cover for following the stream, either. She ran her gaze thoughtfully up the trunk of the tree to branches growing out across the ravine. If she were truly her father's daughter—no, it was too chancy.

The whoops of the Djero grew louder.

She swarmed up the tree.

A branch sagged under her as she crawled out over the ravine. The drum of blood in her ears almost drowned out the yells of the Djero below. Jeneba glanced back. One of the warriors had started up the tree, too.

She swallowed. "Mala and leopard, help this fool."

Touching the leopard talisman to her heart four times, she leaped.

The spring of the branch helped fling her body into a long arc over the chasm beneath. She whooped in glee. Like the time she brought down that antelope from the rocks, Jeneba

felt as though she floated, as though she could sail on and on
and never land until she chose to.

An illusion which ended abruptly in an inglorious, un-
graceful, and painful landing in a thicket on the far rim. But
the furious howls of the Djero left behind restored all her
satisfaction. She scrambled out of the sharp branches and
jeered at the warriors. Then before they could find a way
across, she slid into the shadows of the woods.

Lesa's eye was disappearing behind the western horizon
before Jeneba found a way back herself. The ravine opened
eventually into a valley, where its stream fed a small lake.
She could have wished, though, that the Djero warriors
camped at the mouth of the ravine had chosen instead a site
on the far shore outside the Kurasi village there, and for
more reason than that it sat sentinel on the path she wanted
to take. Kurasi women stood over the fire, one stirring a pot,
the other turning a spitted pig. The tantalizing smell of the
meat curling out from the camp among the scents of men
and sweat and burning wood set Jeneba's stomach snarling.

For several wistful moments she debated hiding until dark
and sneaking down to steal some of the food. The moment
faded. It presented too much risk. Besides, she needed to
find the others. They would be worried that she had been
captured.

Sighing, Jeneba crouched and slipped from bush to tree to
bush down the side of the valley behind the camp. If only
the wind would change and drive the cooking aromas
away—

The thought chopped off in a chill down her spine. Something in that camp besides the food smelled familiar. She
pressed against the bottom of a tree, sniffing. Mala, no!
Among the human scents lay Tomo's and Ourassi's.

Peering around the tree, she searched the faces in the
camp. There, near the fire . . . arms around the outside of
updrawn knees, wrists tied to bound ankles. Blood crusted
Tomo's right shoulder and the left side of Ourassi's face.
They had not been taken easily, then. Good. Yet the wounds
meant that trying to rescue them would be difficult. Even if
they walked on their own they could not move fast enough

to escape pursuit. They might ride, of course, but if she approached the horses hobbled and grazing on the far side of the camp, her leopard smell would only send them into a panic.

Could she use *that?* She crouched behind the tree, thinking hard.

"Jeneba."

The whisper came so softly human ears could not have heard it. She whirled. "Ngmengo?"

Up the slope south a hand beckoned to her from a thicket.

Jeneba checked the camp. No one was looking in her direction. She sprinted from her tree to another, to a bush and up to join the bush-man.

"What happened?"

Ngmengo bared his teeth. "Not all of them chased you. The rest stayed behind, searching the area until they found the men. They know about Yagana, and they knew you'd gone with Ourassi and another man to find a way of recovering the city. They'd heard about our escape from that lake village, too. They asked Ourassi where I was. I don't know if they believed him when he said I'd abandoned the rest of you, but they didn't go on looking for me." He paused. "The horse caught a spear in his side, but he didn't suffer. One of the warriors cut his throat. The last I saw a leopard and her cubs had found the carcass."

Her vision suddenly blurred. Even in death the bay served a leopard. Did horses leave a ghost? If so she hoped it haunted those Djero. She wiped her eyes. "Do you think stampeding the horses will be diversion enough for us to rescue the men?"

Ngmengo shook his head in a sharp rattle of branches. "From the way they talked, they have strict orders about keeping the men guarded. I heard them say that tomorrow they're taking them to Lubeda to tell him how to recover Yagana."

Jeneba sucked in her cheeks. Maybe there would be a chance at them on the trail.

There was not. If anything, the Djero became more careful, more watchful . . . tying their prisoners on horses tied to warrior-ridden horses on each side and surrounding everyone with other riders and warriors on foot. During rests the men remained on their horses. Guards handed up food and water. Jeneba and Ngmengo followed all day without finding a single opportunity for a rescue.

Lubeda's camp offered even less chance. With sinking heart Jeneba saw he did indeed hold Yagana's valley. She and Ngmengo hid among the trees where they had sat a lifetime ago while he sang for her and ate the food she brought up from the city. Below them now, Djero warriors patrolled the sides of the valley and a huge camp spread over the meadows where she had practiced spearwork with the Kurasi army. Lubeda's open-sided tent stood in the center of the barren red earth that had been Yagana. Warriors hauled Ourassi and Tomo to a place near it and tied them with arms stretched sideways to stakes on either side.

She frowned at the camp. Lubeda had not brought this many warriors to Najhadende. Did they come from other cities, from armies of other kings he promised to divide Kurasi lands with?

"We can probably sneak in toward morning and play the harp," Ngmengo murmured. "The moon will be down and they won't be able to see us."

Jeneba glanced sideways at him. "And bring Yagana back to servitude?" She shook her head. "It's better lost."

"I don't know. If Menekuya surrendered, why aren't more prisoners down there, and if they quit and ran, why does Lubeda have so many warriors busy hunting them?"

She whipped around to stare at him. Lubeda might just want Menekuya, but . . . if the warriors hunted because Lubeda still feared the Kurasi, then: "Bringing back Yagana will restore their heart and strength."

Ngmengo grinned.

Mala's eye opened wider each night. Moonset did not come until after midnight. Jeneba waited for it in the fork of a tree, dozing fitfully despite her weariness, roused by every new sound and scent. Ngmengo blended with the brush beneath. Once she thought she smelled men—not the Djero warrior patrolling this edge of the valley—but the few crackles and leaf whispers that might be footsteps receded before she could see who made them and the scent dissipated, carried away by the night breeze.

With relief she watched Mala's eye drop over the horizon. "Let's go, bush-man."

The valley spread in shimmering, ghostly grays beneath the fiery glitter of the sky. The crocodiles lay silent at this time of night but a horse nickered now and then, answered from the lake by the bellow of a hippo. Whispers carried to Jeneba, too, as she and Ngmengo crept soundlessly down the valley side, warriors exchanging words to reassure themselves they had company in the darkness.

Poor men. She almost pitied them, blinded by night, so limited in other senses, too. She also rejoiced in those limitations. If they saw and heard as well as she did, it would have been much more difficult slipping past them.

Still, the closer they came to the valley floor, the deeper among the Djero, the more cautiously Jeneba moved, watching everything around her, tasting the scents in the air, testing each step.

Where the path entered a fruit grove, her care rewarded her. The ground felt . . . wrong. It gave slightly beneath her weight, loose and yielding where it should have been hard-packed. She knelt to explore the dust with her fingers.

Someone had dug here. Digging, too, she discovered why. Branches covered with leaves lay a finger-length beneath the surface, across the full width of the path and beyond. *Pitfall,* she mouthed up at Ngmengo.

He nodded to show his understanding.

On her feet again, Jeneba used her toes to trace the edge of the trap and work her way around. With the end almost under the thorny brush planted around the grove to fence out wild grazers, circling became a tight squeeze. Thorns gouged one thigh and kept a piece of her tsara.

"Ngmengo," she whispered, "maybe you should—"

But he followed almost on her heels and was already caught, his branches tangled in the bushes. He pulled but did not come loose. She leaned across the bush to help work him free, losing more skin, on both the bush and Ngmengo, until she bled from countless sticks. Each time a branch came loose one place, it caught somewhere else. Yet slowly they made progress until a single branch remained snagged.

Ngmengo pulled that loose with a final jerk. Too much jerk. He overbalanced. While Jeneba stared in horror he teetered on the edge of the pitfall, arms flailing desperately in an attempt to regain his balance.

She grabbed for him . . . missed his arm. Thorns bit into her hand. Yelping, she jumped back.

The bush-man lost his fight for balance. He tumbled backward into the middle of the pitfall and fell through it in a splintering crack of wood.

Jeneba flung herself on her belly at the edge of the pit. "Ngmengo, are you all right?" she hissed. He lay sprawled on his back at the bottom, groaning. "Can you reach my hand?" She stretched her arm down toward him.

He opened his eyes but made no move to sit up.

"Ngmengo!"

Mala! Had he broken his back? She looked around desperately for something that would let her jump down and climb out again with him. Nothing seemed likely to work. The branches covering the pit were all too short.

Then the air carried a sudden increase in human scent. Footsteps padded behind her.

Jeneba rolled. Too late. A club flashed through the air above her and smashed into the side of her head. She plunged headlong into a dark, bottomless, silent pit of her own.

CHAPTER

SIXTEEN

Light and sound returned slowly. Her head throbbed with a force that threatened to knock it off her shoulders. Jeneba tried to touch the sore place but could not. Opening her eyes, she discovered why. She sat on the ground with arms stretched to stakes on either side. Like Ourassi and Tomo near her, and like Ngmengo.

"Finally," a voice said.

She looked up into a face lighted by a nearby fire. A snake tattoo curled from one cheek across the forehead to the other cheek. Lubeda gloated. "This is one time I don't mind being wakened in the middle of the night. Now I have all of you."

Keeping her eyes open hurt too much. Holding her head up hurt too much. It weighed as much as an elephant calf. Jeneba closed her eyes and let her head drop forward.

Something struck her arm a stinging blow. "Don't pass out!"

She jerked upright again to find Lubeda waving a spear shaft in her face.

"Answer my questions, warrior woman, if you want to avoid more pain. What will bring back the city? You might as well tell. You've already failed at the only hope of rescue. King Menekuya won't try; he's fled."

Ourassi flung up his head. "I told you, my brother would never run!"

Jeneba, too, could not believe that Menekuya would run away from a battle, particularly the defense of his city. There was no disputing that Lubeda held control of the valley, though.

The snake writhed on Lubeda's forehead. "And I've told

you, he has." He glanced around at Jeneba. "Once we forced his army back to this valley, the army lost courage." Disgust twisted his mouth. "The bush became too small for them, as my people say. They fled. Now, I order you again to tell me what the seer told you to do to regain Yagana or I'll torture it out of you."

Ourassi's mouth clamped into a stubborn line. He said nothing when Lubeda swept a brand out of the fire and passed it close around the Kurasi's head, even when strands of the horse tail withered in a stench of seared hair.

Lubeda spat. "Hopeless. You'd be foolish enough to die before you'd reveal anything, wouldn't you? Now the Male-kuro isn't of the same blood at all though he's refused to talk to me, too. He stinks of fear. When I start inflicting real pain and threatening your life, I wonder what you'll do then, Tshemba Diasi?"

Tomo's gaze jumped toward Jeneba and away, terror and shame in it.

Lubeda turned away from him to smile at Jeneba. "Our newcomers are daring, trying to rescue two cripples from the middle of an army. What else are you?"

He passed the brand by Jeneba. Biting her lip held back sound but she could not help flinching as a flame licked her ear.

"I suppose you think you're brave, warrior woman. You aren't. You're just stubborn, and a fool. All you'll earn for your silence is pain. But . . . what about you, bush-man? Would you like to avoid becoming a bonfire?"

Ngmengo began wailing long before the brand even came close, however. "No, please! Keep it away." He sobbed, tears rolling down his face.

Jeneba stared in disbelief, then remembered that he had cried that way the first night she met him.

"I'll tell you anything you want to know!"

"Ngmengo, no!" she yelped.

"I don't want to burn up! It's in my branches. If you'll untie one of my hands I can bring it out so you won't hurt yourself."

Suddenly Jeneba understood his behavior. What did it

matter who played the harp as long as it brought back Ya-gana?

Tomo snarled curses.

"Be quiet. He knows what he's doing," Jeneba snapped in Dase. From Ourassi's sudden quiet, he realized that, too.

Lubeda untied one of the bush-man's wrists. Ngmengo reached in among his branches and pulled out the calfskin. "We were told to play it here on the city site."

While a guard retied Ngmengo's wrist, Lubeda peered into the wrapping. "What a beautiful instrument. Bone, isn't it?"

Jeneba held her breath.

The Djero did not unwrap the harp, though. Instead, he raised a knee and in a sudden savage movement brought the package down across it. Their horrified cries echoed the sharp crack of bone.

Lubeda straightened, smiling. "So much for Yagana. I wish you kind dreams." And tossing the calfskin in the fire, he strode back to his tent.

The earth swam around Jeneba. She stared at the fire, pain settling in her throat and chest, pain so great that she no longer noticed the throb in her head. The harp destroyed! And Yagana . . . lost forever. She stared at the fire in despair.

Tears glistened on Ngmengo's cheeks. "I thought he would play it. If he had I would have given—"

"You stupid fool," Tomo spat.

"It isn't his fault," Ourassi said wearily. "I thought Lubeda would play it, too." His voice rasped with pain and bitterness. "We're all fools. The gods must hate Yagana to send Jhirazi visions that would make her think *we* could restore the city."

Hopelessness washed through Jeneba. Her chest felt so tight she could hardly breathe. Why had this happened? If the gods wanted to punish her and the men for their pride and greed and cowardice, she could understand that. However little she liked it. She could even accept that the gods would do it by making them go through so much to find and bring back the harp, then fail on the point of success, but . . . why inflict the punishment on Yagana and all the Kurasi people as well?

By first light Jeneba ached all over . . . her head, her arms from having them held sideways, her legs from sitting in almost the same position all night.

Their guard changed. She hated him on sight. He kept grinning.

"Uncomfortable? Don't worry. We'll let you up in a while, just before you mount."

Ourassi lifted his head to focus dull eyes on the Djero. "Mount?"

The grin broadened. "We're sending you on to Murijenaja to be palace slaves, except the bush-man. He'll be on exhibit for the city. Maybe we'll let him fight lions or leopards. And when we catch King Menekuya, he'll join you."

Ngmengo shuddered. "Fight lions and leopards! I'm a praise-singer, not a warrior."

The guard snickered.

"I'll show you. Untie me so I can play something for you."

"A praise-singer sings. You don't need to be untied for that. What would you play anyway?"

"The instrument is in my branches. Bend down here and you can pull it out. No, lower. Careful of the thorns."

Jeneba frowned at the bush-man. What was he doing now?

The guard reached in among the branches. As his hand came out Jeneba bit her lip hard to keep from crying out. Bisiri's harp! The brightening light gleamed soft and yellow off the bone curve in his hand.

The guard straightened, running his hands along the carved rib. Jeneba stared. How was this possible? She had seen Lubeda break the harp, had *heard* it. Then understanding came. The bone flute. Sometime while he carried the harp, Ngmengo had switched the two instruments. Lubeda destroyed the flute. That's what Ngmengo's tears were for.

"Isn't it beautiful?" Ngmengo said. "It has a lovely tone, too. Pluck the string and see."

The guard reached for the string.

Jeneba held her breath.

He stopped with his finger on the string. After a moment, he pulled his hand back, stared at the harp a moment longer, than turned to look around. For what? A commanding officer? Lubeda?

Her gut knotted. Hurriedly, she said, "Do it."

He glanced down at her with a frown.

"Call your superiors or the king and let them have that thing."

"Jeneba," Ngmengo hissed.

The men turned quick, angry glances on her, too. The guard did not miss them, she was glad to notice. He eyed each man in turn, then the harp again, frown deepening. "What do you mean, girl?"

"You don't want to be responsible for that much power."

"Power?" He snorted. "It's a harp."

"Of course it is," Ngmengo snapped.

The guard frowned at him, eyes narrowed. After several moments the guard turned to Jeneba. "What is it, girl?"

In Dase in a threatening tone, Ngmengo said, "I think I see what you're trying to do. I hope it works."

Jeneba stared at Ngmengo as though frightened. "It's a . . . a harp, as he says."

The guard's spear moved in a blur. Jeneba found the blade at her throat. "You're lying. I don't know what he threatened you with, but if you don't tell me the truth I'll run this blade through you."

It needed little effort to pretend fear. Jeneba strained back from the point. "It's a weapon," she whispered. "The bush-man says the name of someone he wants dead, pulls the string, and the person dies. Please, it's dangerous. It'll kill anyone anywhere. Give it to the king."

The guard pulled the spear away, snorting again. "Magic bow."

"If you don't believe me you could say the king's name and pull the string," she said. "But don't. It's too much power for you."

"Is it?" He grinned. "I know a good test. The bush-man called you Jeneba, didn't he?"

She widened her eyes. "Oh, no, please don't. Not me!"

"Jeneba," the guard said. He plucked the string.

It vibrated with the same soft, clear note Jeneba heard when Ngmengo plucked the string in Souraka's camp, but

this time it did not stop reverberating in her bones. The
sound swelled, spreading outward, simultaneously joyous
and sad, until Jeneba's flesh and the very air resonated.

Come again, it sang.

The guard dropped the harp as though the snake had become real. "You tricked me!" he screamed, and lunged for
Jeneba with his spear.

Come again, my city.

The ground trembled. The guard stumbled. His spear slid
past Jeneba, just catching her tsara.

Soul of the Kurasi.

Soul of men.

The ground trembled harder. As though spit by something
which found them distasteful, the stakes holding the prisoners shot up out of the ground. Jeneba jumped to her feet.
The guard scrambled up, too, white-eyed. From his tent
stumbled Lubeda, blinking in alarmed, sleepy incomprehension.

Come again, shadow in the mind,
Longing of my children.
You are the strength of my heart.

The air shimmered and rang.

Come again, come again, Yagana.

Like heat waves rising from the plains at midday, the air
rippled. Yagana appeared out of it to rise above them . . .
carved copper-red walls overhead, grass of the four commons underfoot. Scents. Sound. Sound thundered around
them, animal cries and voices, people yelling in joy and
anger. People poured out of the three markets toward them,
converging on Lubeda's tent.

Jeneba snatched up the harp before someone stepped on
it.

Lubeda shrieked, a cry of pain and horror cut off sharply.

The Kurasi whirled and charged back up the commons out
of the city. Jeneba stared at Lubeda's tent, ground into the
turf along with scattered pieces of the king's body.

"Even Kurasi can be brutal in vengeance."

She turned to find herself looking into Jhirazi's eyes.

The priestess held out a hand. "I'll take the harp." She
hugged it to her, smiling at Jeneba, and past Jeneba at Our-

assi. "We knew what was happening. We were here and yet not here, and we saw everything. Menekuya has been watching, too. Listen."

Beyond the noise of the city came whoops. War yells.

Ourassi ran down the empty west common to the steps up to the city wall. Jeneba followed with Tomo, Ngmengo, and Jhirazi. Ourassi's color changed at every step, brightening back to glowing copper.

Then she forgot everything but the sight beyond the city wall. Down the valley sides poured yelling Kurasi warriors, converging on Djero who gaped groggily from the warriors to the city walls and the gates disgorging screaming, club-and-spear-wielding citizens.

Some of the Djero realized what was happening. Those dived for spears and shields. But there were not enough, and not soon enough. The Djero lost almost before they were awake.

Menekuya came marching in from victory through the west gate. Ourassi met him.

For a long while, neither man spoke. Jeneba held her breath. Finally Ourassi broke the silence. He used his own language, but Jhirazi translated for Jeneba and the others. "I knew you wouldn't run away."

Menekuya shook his head. "I realized we couldn't withstand Lubeda. It would only lose more lives. So I let him have the valley and waited for you and for Yagana. I knew its reappearance would restore our strength."

Ourassi bit his lip. "What if I hadn't come back?"

Menekuya smiled. "I knew you would. None of your faults is lack of determination or courage."

Ourassi stared hard at him. "If I were king, I would have fought to the death for the valley."

If I were king. The words lingered in the air.

Jeneba sucked in her cheeks. Menekuya stared at Ourassi, saying nothing. The silence stretched out for a lifetime. What could be going through the mind of each? Mental preparation for Ourassi to challenge Menekuya for the sword and shield that should have been his?

Again it was Ourassi speaking first, softly. "I would have lost Yagana a second time. You are a man of wisdom, courage, and honor, my brother." He dropped to his knees and fell on his face at Menekuya's feet. "Majesty, my king, I pledge to serve your sword and shield to the end of my life."

Menekuya lifted Ourassi to his feet and threw his arms around him.

Air came back into Jeneba's lungs. She heard Jhirazi sigh in relief, too.

Jeneba grinned at Ngmengo.

Jhirazi nodded. "It is good. Menekuya will make a good king."

Menekuya turned. Eyes older than Jeneba remembered traveled over her, Tomo, and Ngmengo. "We owe you a great deal."

Jeneba shrugged. "Honor required it."

"Nevertheless, I would repay you somehow. Ngmengo, I think we can find a way to remove your bewitchment and make you a man again."

For a moment the bush-man stared at him in disbelief and hope, and a touch of lust as his eyes wandered down Jeneba's and Jhirazi's bodies. Then with a rueful smile, he shook his head. "I'd only get myself in trouble again. I don't know that I want to give up the advantages of being a monster, either . . . as long as I don't have to be alone again."

"You can always travel with me," Jeneba said.

He grinned. "Done. Besides, I've promised Bujhada to sing praise-songs of his from one end of the world to the other. That's going to take more than a mortal lifetime."

"What about you, Tshemba?"

Tomo's face twisted sourly. "There's nothing you can do for me but kill me."

Jeneba frowned. "Why? You fought well and faithfully. You told Lubeda nothing. And we've saved Yagana."

"That changes nothing," he said bitterly. "If Lubeda had really tortured me I would have told him anything he wanted. I worked all my life to be a great warrior, a noble of courage and honor. And in one craven, cowardly moment, I destroyed it all. I'm not the man I thought. I'll never be the man I want to be, not if I save a hundred cities. I was a fool to think I could." He sighed. "Maybe the gods will smile on me in Kiba and I'll be sentenced to death."

Kiba. Jeneba stared at him. She had looked forward all these days to returning him home. Now how far away and petty Kiba suddenly seemed from this place and moment. What would actually be served by taking him back? Not the honor of his family. Punishment for him? He inflicted far greater on himself than Mseluku would. Her vindication? It occurred to her that she no longer cared what Kiba thought. Her mother was right. Dasa were not the only people in the world, and what they scorned, other people accepted, or even admired.

"When do you want to start back?" Tomo asked.

"Who would I take back?" she replied. "I think Tomo Silla died the night the half-men took our warriors. All that's left is Tshemba Diasi. No one in Kiba knows him."

"But," he began, and stopped.

"Tomo, none of us—" Jeneba began, but he was turning away, not listening. She sighed.

Jhirazi shook her head. "A very sad man. I hope he finds peace somewhere."

Menekuya raised a brow at Jeneba. "Is there anything you want, warrior woman?"

For a moment she could think of nothing, then memory of the bay crept forward. Her eyes prickled. "I could use a new horse, and a bed, somewhere I can sleep undisturbed for a month!"

The king chuckled. "You may have your pick of my herd after you're rested. Jhirazi, will you please take her to the guest court?"

Jeneba followed the priestess. Up the common she saw Tomo again, trudging alone through the celebration and the beauty of Yagana, a darkness amid light. She sighed. Poor Tomo, so lost in his own despair he could not see that everyone in the group sent after the harp was less than he wanted to be. That did not have to destroy any of them, though.

And it had not, she realized in a sudden burst of understanding that sent quiet exhilaration spreading through her. Quite the opposite. Being less than they wanted made them *more* than they thought . . . happy with the benefits of a bewitchment, contented in freedom from the greed for power, proud of leopard breeding. Jeneba would have leaped into the air and shouted praise-songs if exhaustion had not given her trouble just walking. But she decided that when she had rested and enjoyed Yagana and its warriors for a while, she would go back to Kiba to visit. She would tell her mother everything. Sia Nyiba could appreciate it.